The Gardener's Wife

JANE ALLISON

Cahill Davis Publishing Limited

To my dear husband who has worked
with me throughout the process!

First published in Great Britain in 2021 by Cahill Davis
Publishing Limited.

First published in paperback in Great Britain in 2021 by
Cahill Davis Publishing Limited.

ISBN 978-1-8381820-3-8 (eBook)
ISBN 978-1-8381820-2-1 (Paperback)

Cahill Davis Publishing Limited
www.cahilldavispublishing.co.uk

THE GARDENER'S WIFE

Chapter 1

Philip Manners leaned on his walking stick as he stood by the fingerpost, looking down the hill towards Low Shadworth. The evening sun was dipping behind the ridge, and the village below him seemed to glow a deep, satisfying red. *The colour of poppies*, he thought.

He made a tall and handsome figure as he stood, supported by his stick. An observer might note his studious face, firm chin, and blue eyes. The stick suggested, perhaps, an accident of youth and caused his shoulders to stoop as he leaned on it. His hair, greying at the temples, gave him an older, distinguished air though he was still in his forties. His brow was inscribed with lines etched by the huge responsibility he felt towards his position as head of the school opposite him. The tenderness of his blue eyes and mouth that seemed as if it would often be smiling gave balance to his careworn face.

His school stood four-square beside the main highway, proclaiming itself an imposing establishment, a renowned Quaker school for the children of those whose beliefs drew them to its title and who were pleased to give their offspring the benefits of its excellent reputation.

The school lay in the village of Shadworth, which was divided into two quite distinctive halves. The one, High Shadworth, stretched uphill in a rambling fashion until it reached a summit of scattered stone houses, a public house, and a Methodist chapel. Low Shadworth, on the other hand, which Philip was admiring from his vantage point, began right by the ancient fingerpost. From there, the traveller may gently amble down a leafy lane to a collection of brick-built terraced dwellings. Opposite them, the visitor would find an old school made of grey stone proclaiming itself Infant and Junior Village School, which served the children of Shadworth who came here from the terraces and outlying farms to learn their letters and their times tables.

Behind Philip lay his office, his responsibilities, his staff of highly intelligent teachers, many of whom he had himself appointed. And in his home within the school grounds was Harriet, his wife, to whom he had been married for a number of years. The war, which they'd said would be over by Christmas, was still raging across the English Channel, and boys he had himself educated and shown a better way, the Quaker way, had nevertheless left early to throw themselves into battle, glorying in the challenge to their manhood. He regretted this deeply, for it denied everything he had tried to teach them about the paths of peace.

His thoughts turned unasked, as they often did, to Emma Holt, the wife of his school's gardener. He knew she had sons who had already joined up, and Philip wondered how she was feeling. Harriet could have no concept of what it would be like to be a mother in that situation—childless Mrs Manners. He knew what people said: *"What a shame she hasn't given the head his own children."*

No, Harriet would never feel that heart-rending agony of fearing for one's own child. Yet, childless as Philip was, he himself felt a fatherly fear for every one of his students that had left for the front.

He couldn't remember now a time when he hadn't admired Emma Holt and her fortitude against all the odds. Her indomitable energy in answering the practical needs of his school had drawn his attention to her soon after his arrival in Shadworth, back in 1904. He smiled as he remembered the many times he had remonstrated with her for taking too much on:

"Mrs Holt, you surely can't be carrying such a load of washing back to Holt House?"

"Mrs Holt, have you spent all day helping Cook out with the catering for the staff party?"

Of course, it never made any difference. She never took a scrap of notice.

And now, with the passage of years, he found himself thinking of her every day. She had been so resolute in ensuring her sons and her youngest child, Florence, had an education and she had confided in him how important it was for them to rise above the mere rote learning offered by the local school.

Philip's first acquaintance with Emma had come when he'd found her in his school library, searching for a book on the rudiments of the English language, whereby she could teach her children herself how to write correctly and convincingly. He had been struck by her beautiful, shy, wide-eyed glance at him as she'd apologised for her presence. He had assured her she might use the library any time she needed in between all her other commitments. Her astonishment that he had bothered himself to speak to her had been written all over her face. Nevertheless, he hadn't been able to help enjoying her embarrassment as the flush had risen up in her cheeks when she'd thanked him and hurried away. The many more times they'd met in the library had soon convinced him she was a woman of indomitable spirit, courage, and bright intelligence.

Now, standing by the fingerpost, he thought with pleasure of the bond between them, forged first in those library visits and strengthened through the many occasions in which she came to discuss the needs of his staff. A bond that, even with the passing of the years, would not be denied. He was convinced she felt it too, though nothing had ever passed their lips to confirm it. However, he also felt a profound sense of the danger of their situation. He felt proud he had helped her to recognise her value and her capacity for scholarship outside the daily routines she had to fulfil. But he knew he must repress all the other emotions he felt for her—she, a wife and mother; he, a married man in a position of trust.

But, oh, *how different it could have been if we were both free.*

He thought back to all the times he had discovered her in the library after she had delivered the washing she had just laundered, and to all the cakes his staff had enjoyed, freshly baked in her kitchen. He often heard her pushing her bicycle with its huge panniers full of her wares past his study window as she sang. Emma and her husband, Jack, were Methodists, and he knew she knew all the old hymns.

Will your anchor hold in the storms of life?

Philip could always reckon on her sneaking into the library afterwards and there he would find her. He introduced her to books he thought she should read, knowing she had a voracious appetite for literature, for he himself taught English Literature to the boys in his school. He loved the works of George Eliot and Dickens, Hardy and Austen and he spread them before her with pleasure. She read them avidly and then shared with him, in those moments before leaving for home, which ones she had enjoyed the most. He admired her immense enthusiasm for these classic texts. He'd smiled to himself as she'd devoured *Adam Bede,* for, in the character of Dinah, the fervent Methodist preacher, he couldn't help but see Emma herself. Though she was not young, having raised four children, she had never, in all the ten years of their encounters, lost her early wonder and pleasure in the books he introduced her to. And the speed with which she returned them never failed to amaze him. She had read them and taken them to herself like a bee at the nectar of a flower. He smiled as he stood remembering.

"I don't like Hardy's way of treating Tess," she would say. Or, "I love the way Silas Marner changes as he starts to love little Eppie. 'Eppie in de toal-hole'. What a gorgeous story! I do think George Eliot is my favourite, sir."

"I've never had a student quite like you, Mrs Holt."

Then she would blush, and before he could say any more, she would leave. Of late, she had stayed beside him just a little longer and with a new confidence, to share the pleasure of the books with him.

He leaned on his stick and shook his head with a sigh. This wouldn't do. There was a kind of disloyalty in such thoughts. High tea would be being served in the schoolhouses, and he had to return to his vocation; a vocation that he had loved for many years. He limped back through the imposing school gates slowly and thoughtfully, passing the windows of the different houses—Applegarth House, Ayton House, Fox House after that great Quaker founder himself. As he passed, the figures of the heads of the houses presiding at their tables nodded acknowledgement of their very much respected head. Peering into each dining room, he reassured himself that all was in order, going along in the quietly settled routines he had set in motion when he had arrived those ten or so years ago.

Harriet was standing, watching him as he slowly mounted the stairs to the door of his own quarters.

"Philip! Why can you never be found when I need you? My father has written to remind you of the charity concert in a week's time. He and Mother plan to come and let his curate take the Minster Sunday services. You have so much to arrange. Have you contacted that woman about the cakes we want for the evening reception yet?"

"I take it you mean Mrs Holt, Harriet? She has a name. Jack is out in the kitchen garden; he's spent all day digging and planting. I'll have a word with him. How many people are we expected to feed?"

"At least seventy-five are expected to attend; we've sold that number of tickets. That son of hers and her daughter can bring them up when she returns the staff laundry."

"Harriet, you have a very patronising attitude to those who serve this school. I don't appreciate it, my dear. You may be a bishop's daughter but that doesn't give you licence to look down on any other human being. Now, I'm going to the study before it's time for lights out in the dormitories."

"Philip, that is most unfair. I'm merely thinking the woman has a routine which will be helpful on the day." Harriet turned on her heel and returned to her sewing.

As he limped back towards the boys' dormitories, Philip shuddered, not from the pain of his wretched leg, but from frustration and a sense of the coldness that, through the course of their fourteen-year marriage, had iced up his and Harriet's sterile union.

And once the bishop arrives, he thought, *I shall be back in my role as the unfit son-in-law.*

Philip sought out Jack Holt, his school gardener, to put in the request for fancy cakes, and that good man, with sleeves rolled up and spade in hand, smiled cheerily as was his wont and promised to give Harriet's requirements to Emma.

"She won't flinch at it, sir. I believe she would cater for the army out in the trenches if you asked her." Jack was always ready to sing the praises of his wife of whom he was inordinately proud. The fact that Philip shared Jack's adoration of Emma made him especially sensitive to Jack's feelings. Yet, as he left Jack, he couldn't help but relish the thought of her. That bond, forged between them over the years, prevailed over the radical difference in their backgrounds. From that first long-ago time in the library, he had recognised increasingly how much she cared for others and how willing she was to serve whoever needed her. They met only within the confines of the school, but he knew, whatever he asked, she would willingly undertake.

He increasingly had to remind himself that he really had no business to be thinking of her at all.

Chapter 2

Emma wiped the sweat from her brow and with it, the tendril of hair that had fallen on her forehead. She made for a congenial sight as she worked in her echoing kitchen, hair pinned into a coil around her forehead, revealing a smooth, broad brow from which, underneath, her hazel eyes shone with life and warmth. Her waist, despite her having borne four children, remained as slim as in her youth. It was infinitely appealing to Philip Manners who, in his weaker moments, longed to be able to hold her against him and feel her slender body next to his heart.

She had baked throughout the afternoon to produce the assortment of little cakes she knew his lady staff admired, with enough to cater for the charity concertgoers as well. Now they rested on the huge wooden table in the middle of her kitchen, an array of delicately decorated fancies of various colours and toppings. Her skills in icing had been fully applied.

And this was not all for she'd spent the morning boiling the water for the suds in the washtub and peggy-sticking the ladies' blouses with all her energy till they emerged fresh and steaming from the pot. She'd then put them into the wringer before hanging them out to dry on her long clothesline in the garden. There, as the hens clucked and pecked, they dried in the sun, ready for the smoothing iron Emma was heating on the hot coals. As she worked, Jack watched her from the old stool on which he often perched to sit awhile with his pipe in the sun.

"Why not stop a minute, lass? You've been at it all day without a second to yourself. Come and sit by me and tell me what you've been reading." And with that, he grabbed her by the waist and pulled her onto his lap as she went to walk by him.

"Jack, give over. Behave yourself." She smiled. "I've got a hot iron waiting for me in the kitchen."

"What about a husband who wants some attention?" came the joking response.

She jumped up and dropped a passing kiss on his forehead. "You old rascal. You're getting too old for this."

Jack threw his head back and laughed as she went into the kitchen.

She thanked God for the garden she and Jack had managed to plant around the house they had worked so long and hard to purchase. There, she had brought up three boys and her only girl, Florence, her youngest, who was now growing into a lovely young woman. But, oh, her boys. Her grand stalwart sons. Could she be prouder? No. But could she bear that each one had had his heart set on joining up to follow the flag? She hated the propaganda—the posters showing mothers proudly waving their boys off to fight. And how the propaganda had worked on Will and George already. They had taken up the call to volunteer early and were now out there. Goodness only knew what their surroundings were.

She was torn in one sense: she would have hated to see them accused of cowardice. People dreaded the giving of white feathers.

And so do I, she thought. Yet she knew that Mr Manners taught his pupils the Quaker belief in non-violence at the school and that he did not approve of the war at all. His opinions meant a great deal to her. Neither could she bear the tension of dreading news from the front every day. Her sons' letters gave nothing away but she scoured the news for information about the trenches. Rumours of rats and lice put the fear of God into Emma's maternal heart. She would at all costs try to prevent her youngest son, Harry, from going. At least his love affair with young Maggie Granger was keeping him from rushing to join up, but the pressure was on for every young man who dreamed of glory to go.

She called to Florence to find Harry so that between them they might get the cakes up to High Shadworth in time for the concert set to start at half past seven. She knew Mrs Manners, in her usual superior way, would demand the laundry, but it was impossible to get it ready and aired in time, as well as addressing the pressing demands of the school kitchen. Between them, she, Florence and a very unwilling Harry got out the large bikes with the panniers attached and loaded the trays into them.

"Eh, Mother, why do you say you can do it all when you know you're hard-pressed?" muttered Harry.

"Don't talk nonsense, Harry. You know we all must play our part, and you benefit from the money it brings in. Stop your grumbling."

They went in through the back of the school to the large, well-equipped kitchen, and she wondered, for the hundredth time, why on earth these people wanted *her* fancies. Connie, the cook, greeted her between deep breaths as she ran the back of her hand across her damp forehead. Time was running out, and she had to put all the refreshments out in the dining hall before the peripatetic musicians arrived to set up for the concert.

At that moment Connie was surprised to see the head limping down the path to her domain.

The head stepped into the kitchen. "Mrs Holt, you have done the job just as Jack said you would. We can only thank you yet again."

As Emma's heart leaped against her will at the sight of him, she lowered her eyes lest Cook should see the pleasure in them. "Why, sir, it's nothing, just a few cakes. But I have to apologise that I could not manage to finish the laundry tonight. I'll send it up in the morning."

"Do no such thing, Mrs Holt, it's all too much. Surely Monday will suffice."

"No, sir. I must keep my promise for the ladies' sake. Come, Florence, we must stop Harry from dawdling and drag him homewards. Sir, excuse us now."

Philip stood silently as she turned away through the kitchen door, and Cook looked on with mild surprise at his expression. He walked slowly back towards his own quarters, knowing Harriet's parents would have arrived and would now be ensconced in the lounge, wondering where their host had vanished to.

Harriet greeted him shrilly. "Where have you been? Father and Mother are here and getting ready for the concert. People are already beginning to arrive."

Philip had no time to answer her, as her father, the bishop, dressed in his formidable gaiters and high collar, was extending his hand to him. "What are you serving up tonight, Manners? I am hoping your welcome to the concert will not be advocating the pacifist cause you Quakers espouse."

"I think you'll find it's all a simple offering from some of our talented musicians under their peripatetic music teachers. The money for tickets, I grant you, will be sent to the charity supporting our boys out in France, but Harriet will assure you my views about that horrific enterprise will remain undisclosed. Nevertheless, sir, can you ever visualise a situation in which Jesus Christ might be willing to plunge a bayonet into another human being?"

His father-in-law turned away from him with a look of absolute disdain to face his more than sympathetic daughter. Harriet, ever ready to agree with her father, merely shrugged. Philip thought how tragic it was that the beautiful and charming girl he had married as a very young man had become the sulky and petulant woman who now stood before him.

"Well, Harriet, we should head for the hall and leave this husband of yours to take his place as headmaster. Come, my dear, let us take our seats at the front. I hope you've reserved them for us, Manners."

Philip took a patient breath and made his way through the groups of waiting musicians with words and smiles of encouragement as he passed on his way to the front of the school hall stage.

"Friends, we welcome you here tonight to this feast of music our boys have prepared for you. We are so grateful to you all, not least to those who have travelled for some way to get here. Welcome. There are refreshments provided in the dining room at the close of the performance. Enjoy them but be mindful that the money we take tonight will go to bless and help the young men, no longer boys indeed, who are serving at this very moment in the hellholes of Northern France."

There was a hush from his audience as he bowed his head for a short moment and then they applauded him as he limped down to his seat beside Harriet. Her father was already frowning at his words but Philip no longer cared. He saw at the edge of the stage the banks of blossoms that Jack Holt had planted in boxes, and he sighed with the effort of subduing his thoughts of Emma.

Chapter 3

As dawn broke the next day over Low Shadworth, the rooks in the elms were making a huge fussy cawing so high up in the treetops that they seemed almost to be touching the sky. The dusty lane, the cottage terraces, the tranquillity of it all untouched by progress and the safety of its fellowship painted a picture of great beauty. Holt House was very much part of that picture, standing four-square on its own as the cottage row ended, opposite the little junior school in its weathered grey stone. Above the gate and the path to the front door was an archway of climbing roses, planted by Jack in earlier years, and the whole house had an air of solidity and comfort.

The door opened onto the kitchen where a large cooking range dominated the space. In the corner was an old grey armchair and a somewhat less comfortable horsehair sofa beside a fire ready for lighting. A huge stone bread bin stood on the floor opposite and an airer on a pulley reached up to the ceiling, almost always full of the clothes dried in the sun the previous day, ironed and now airing. Beside the neatly folded family clothes were the pristine white blouses that belonged to the more exalted owners up at the Quaker school. The aroma of homemade bread pervaded the atmosphere and Emma's kitchen pronounced itself to be a most hospitable place for anyone who might care to cross its threshold.

Yet the lady of the house, much like the head at the Quaker school, was unquiet in her soul. She had hardly slept as Jack, beside her, dreamed his deep rhythmic slumber, untroubled by fear or the business of his day. His philosophy was always to take one day at a time, for he sincerely believed what he often quoted when she was obviously fretting about the future: "'*Sufficient unto the day is the evil thereof.' Don't forget the good Lord's words, Emma.*"

His contentment was evident to all those who knew and loved him. Last night, he had kissed her and pulled her down beside him on their bed with all his old passion, sighing as he felt the release of his desire. He had fallen sound asleep afterwards. She had lain wide awake and anxious for her beloved sons out there in constant danger, hardly daring to contemplate what could happen to them. Every night in her prayers, she pleaded with the Almighty for their safe keeping. But the tears she shed came unwanted, for they sprang from her thoughts about someone else entirely.

What were those tears about? she asked herself, though she knew the answer. They were tears of sadness for something that could never be and for someone whom she could not even call by his proper name. Oh, the tender gentleness of him as he'd stood in that echoing school kitchen.

How different he is from Jack.

She sensed his tiredness and something of his sadness but knew his set jaw revealed his strong determination to maintain the high standards of the Quaker ideals he cared so deeply about.

She had admired him for so many years ever since he had shown her such consideration as she'd scoured the shelves of the school library, feeling guilty for being there at all. She had been determined, however, to find books to help her educate her children. Though she felt unworthy of the attention of such a great man who was so admired by the community, he had never treated her with anything but concern and reverence, lifting her out of her lowly background to a sense of being his equal. Thanks to him, she had acquired a liberating sense of her own intellect that could meet his on its own terms, despite their different worlds. He had guided her as to what to read on these occasions, and she had thrived under those years of his tutelage. She relished the books he gave her and indeed, she had felt, even then, a bond with him that was completely inexplicable to her; a bond which had grown stronger and stronger with the years, despite the fact that their only opportunity to meet and talk had been in the school grounds.

So there were tears but tears that she knew must be wiped away resolutely. She loved her husband dearly and their life together was satisfying and companionable, though she sometimes feigned sleep when he returned from The White Swan a little worse for wear, expecting a loving embrace. He was a man whom the whole village regarded with enormous respect for his innate wisdom and steady, unruffled approach to all the troubles that spoiled the tranquillity of their lives under the duress of war. Jack Holt, a man who could be relied on. Of course he helped many of the villagers out with extra vegetables he had grown and eggs from the Holts' chickens to eke out their meagre wartime provisions. And Emma had leaned on his strength throughout their marriage as she'd raised her boys and their younger sister through the thick and thin of poverty and hard work, saving and striving with Jack to achieve the very best they could for their family.

No wonder then that she knew she could not afford to allow another man into her heart. But she also knew, as she had lain awake tearful, that it was already too late.

How much I love simply to see him or to stand talking about his beloved books. Thank goodness for the school library. Yet I don't know how I find myself thinking such disloyal thoughts. Oh God, forgive me! I must be careful.

As she rose with the early spring sunshine, she determined to work even harder at those tasks which were her daily bread, for she knew that in working, she could try to dispel this unasked for emotion which had awoken in her long ago. So to the staff blouses with their precise and numerous pintucks requiring a very careful hand with the iron. The school governors had demanded that the lady staff should wear pure white, pintucked blouses, so Emma's laundering of them had to be absolutely faultless.

Those mighty men behind the scenes have no concept of what it's like to keep to their rules. More's the pity, she thought to herself. But she smiled as she worked for this service rendered to the school, she believed, was a kind of service to the man who presided at the school. She would take the blouses up to the back kitchen that very morning while trying to avoid all encounters if she could.

Soon, Jack was at work in the vast and beautiful school garden, planting the perennials with which he would present a glow of rich and variegated colours to surprise and feast the eyes. He hoped the boys would take pleasure in what lay around them as they studied, though he knew their minds were on higher and nobler things. And he also knew what was in the hearts of the sixth form lads all hankering after glory in France.

Though he was not himself a pacifist, Jack understood the views of the head in this matter and shook his head at the gut-wrenching knowledge that Will and George, his own boys, were at that very moment in the trenches of Northern France.

As he worked, he heard a stifled cry. He stood up from his kneeling pad and walked slowly towards the quiet sound of sobbing. Why, it was little Charlie Hopton whose acquaintance he had made only last week when he'd presented a bunch of flowers to Edna Wright, head of Applegarth House, in her house dining room. Jack knew Edna loved the spring primroses.

"Whatever's the matter, Charlie? You should be in class now I believe. Don't cry; tell me what it is."

"I want to go home, Mr Holt, but I know I can't. Mother and Father really want me to get an education here and so whatever can I do?" And his sobs only got louder as Jack leaned down to his small blonde head and touched it gently.

"Charlie, you must come with me and tell Mr Manners all about it. He'll know what to do to cheer you up, and I've got an idea. It's those Cheviot Hills and the animals you're missing, isn't it?" Jack smiled and reached out his hand.

Kath Hanson, school secretary now for many years, was typing away at her desk as Jack approached, holding young Charlie's hand. She was in her pristine office outside the head's room, surrounded by lists and official-looking forms. Everything was organised to the most minute detail, as was her custom.

Kath looked up. "Whatever is it, Mr Holt? The head's very busy this morning and Charles should be in class. You can't interrupt him." As she spoke, the head's study door opened, and Jack gave a sigh of relief at the sight of him.

"Sir, I wouldn't bother you for the world but we have a very sad youngster here who's suffering a touch of homesickness for his Northumbrian roots." Charlie was clinging to Jack as Philip bent to take his hand.

Philip's heart melted at the sight of the small first-year struggling to regain his composure. "Mr Holt, come into my office, and let's see what we can do."

"Mr Manners, I think I have a solution. The child is missing the farm and the animals he's so fond of. The weekend's coming and, if you'll allow it, I could take him home with me for a bit of mother love from Emma and a chance to help me feed the chickens. Then I could walk him to Tempest's farm up the lane where we can visit the cattle and the sheep. There may be newborn lambs to see there, and maybe it'll be a comfort."

Kath Hanson looked up from her typewriter to listen to the head's response, though she already knew with a certainty that this somewhat unusual suggestion would be affirmed. The head relaxed rules when he saw a child in distress and Kath knew for a fact that Mrs Manners would frown upon it. She merely smiled quietly to herself and watched on unsurprised as Philip invited Jack to sit in the chair on one side of his capacious desk and patted Charlie's head as he stood by nervously. He smiled across at them both, thought for a minute, then got up to shake Jack's hand.

"It seems to me a very good idea. What do you think, Charlie?"

Charlie's smile said it all.

"I will come down myself on Sunday morning to walk you back to school, young Charles. Now, you must return immediately to class. Miss Fairclough will be wondering what has happened to you." And with that, he ushered Jack and the boy out, nodded at his secretary and closed his door.

The firmness of his early resolve had slipped somewhat, and Philip sat upright in his chair behind his desk, randomly fiddling with the papers there. He had allowed himself the luxury of a visit to Low Shadworth and had found a perfectly sensible reason for such a visit. Little Charlie would gain so much from the arrangement and it was all very worthy. And yet, had Philip not the previous night determined to maintain a strict distance from the woman happily married to his friend and groundsman?

Chapter 4

Sunday dawned; spring was flourishing in Shadworth. Cherry blossoms were beginning to burst out of buds into flouncing pink effulgence. Buds less garish were extending themselves towards the warming spring sunshine, while the incipient horse chestnut candles were starting to announce themselves up in the branches. A thrush was singing vociferously in the elms, and the church bells were ringing in the morning service up in High Shadworth.

Harriet Manners, the bishop's daughter, was heading up to the Anglican church conforming to her upbringing, despite her status as the wife of a Quaker head. Indeed, she was furious with her wayward husband who had announced his plan to walk down to Low Shadworth to pick up young Hopton and return him to school later that day. There was no need for him to mix himself down there with the villagers, the *hoi polloi*. No need at all. And yet, in fourteen years of marriage, she had never been able to persuade him to acknowledge his status and she knew she never could. She had not been able even to persuade him to employ a maidservant for their home, which she felt was her due as the head's wife. No, he would not countenance it, asserting his belief in equality within his staff. She had no idea what the villagers themselves thought of her, though she didn't particularly care.

Always giving herself airs without warmth or interest in us or even the boys of her own husband's school. Not like Mr Manners at all. He's always got a smile and a word when he's in the village. How did he get himself hitched to such a one? went the gossip in the local shop where she always felt uncomfortable. She at least felt at home in the environs of the Anglican church up in High Shadworth. There, she had a cluster of friends with whom she enjoyed socialising, insulated from the working village culture.

In the school Meeting House, Philip kept a Quaker silence, and boys brought up in the tradition sat with heads lowered as they allowed the quiet to inspire them as they had been taught to in their homes. His own thoughts were less than holy; more troubled and contrary. Yet he slowed them and controlled them into a prayer for the boys in his care, for his staff, for his wife so full of anger, for the conflict raging over the channel. His head was well down as he sat, but he rose to his feet to speak quietly of the need for peace and for the safekeeping of the troops out in the trenches, naming those boys of his own school who had gone to fight: Daniel Latimer—one of his brightest sixth-formers, Christopher Elliott, Richard Holmes, Graham O'Connor.

Spirit of God, hold them safe!

At Holt House, Emma cooked the Sunday roast for her family and for the child who had been restored by fresh air, the loving warmth of her home and a visit to Tempest's farm where he had bottle fed one of the new lambs with Jack. She thrust the unruly wisps of hair back from her hot forehead as she served up the Yorkshire puddings. If only Will and George were there to enjoy them too. She couldn't help but wonder what Philip Manners' mean-spirited wife would be serving him for his lunch. She failed to restrain a leap in her heart at the thought that he himself was coming to pick Charles up. She had baked her special meringues and filled them with cream for tea, and maybe, just maybe, he would have time to eat one.

Unbeknown to her, Philip had actually eaten in George Fox House quarters with the staff and boys there. It was good fare, albeit plain and canteen kitchen cooked. But Cook took pride in providing nourishing meals for the pupils and staff. Harriet had refused to join him and was eating instead with her intimate women friends from the staff in the private school dining room. There was an air of martyrdom about her which the staff did not fully comprehend. Only that she preferred their select company to that of the boys, a sentiment which those who joined her shared as they partook of their meal, resplendent in their beautifully Emma-ironed, pintucked blouses.

Lunch over, Philip took hold of his walking stick and, with a jaunty step, set out for the fingerpost and the quiet lane down to Low Shadworth. The spring sun was warming the afternoon, but as he walked, a sudden weariness came over him.

It must be a combination of the heat and this confounded leg of mine, he thought. He slowed his pace though his heart was beating hard at the prospect of his albeit brief visit to the Holt House.

Nearing Low Shadworth, the beads of sweat gathered on his brow and he knew he must get there and stop awhile. He pushed Emma's gate open and, leaning hard on his stick, drew close to the front door. Just as he was about to lift the knocker, it sprang open and there she was, greeting him with that warmth he knew to expect from her.

"Mr Manners, come and sit for you look almost done up. Sit. Forgive the kitchen chair. There. Let me get you a glass of lemonade and one of my meringues. I made them this very morning. We'll let them revive you while I fetch Charlie and Jack in from the chickens." She looked anxiously at his pale brow and worn face with a pang of longing she hardly dared to acknowledge. She contented herself instead with a gentle touch of his shoulder.

"I'm so sorry, Mrs Holt. I don't know what came over me as I walked down. I think it's the heat. It is passing already, and I really must not take up any more of your time. Thank you so much for caring for young Hopton. I knew he would benefit from a visit to you and Jack." Inwardly, he thought about how he must repress his sense of joy of her company, relief, and the pleasure at that tender touch. Her meringue tasted like some kind of heavenly angel's breakfast.

Philip, what on earth is the matter with you? he told himself sternly. *It cannot be.*

Sipping the lemonade, he watched sadly as she left him to call the others in from the garden. And there were Charles and Jack, both beaming.

"Mr Manners, sir, I've had such a fine time. I fed a baby lamb up at the farm, and I'm so full of lunch, just like at home. Please, sir, can I come again?"

Jack was laughing with pleasure at the boy's enthusiasm, and Emma was smiling beside him as she tucked the boy's jacket round him. She gave the boy a hug and assured him he could come again, looking at Philip's face hopefully as she spoke.

"Charlie, we'll have to see. There are other boys back at school who will be jealous of you. Come, we must get back." Taking the boy's hand, he turned to both Jack and Emma. He felt an almost physical pain at the sight of them standing together with arms interlocked in the unity of their home. The prospect of the walk back up the hill awaited him, and he uttered a silent prayer that his leg would be up to it.

It was as if Emma read his mind for, turning to her husband, she gestured to him to accompany them as far as the fingerpost. "You mustn't overdo it, sir. Jack will go with you, and you can take the walk steadily. Charlie, behave now for Mr Manners."

One last look at her beautiful face and Philip set off through the gate with Jack beside him, hoping that his countenance would reveal nothing of his inward thoughts.

Chapter 5

The weeks following were ones of hard and conscientious work, made more intense by Philip's determination to repress thoughts of Emma Holt which nagged uncomfortably at his Quaker conscience. Harriet was busy with her church women and her favourite ladies of the staff, working on knitting socks for France and organising parcels to be sent out to the trenches. It gave her a sense of satisfaction and indeed pride which pleased Philip to recognise.

At least she cares something for the poor boys out there.

She enjoyed playing hostess in these meetings and had gathered a small band of loyal followers who enjoyed the favours of the head's wife. They nodded their agreement with her attitude to his pacifist position, and she was careless in allowing them to see her discontent. Of course, all this made her no less cold in her treatment of Philip himself, though she allowed herself the occasional luxury of a visit to his study to chat with Miss Hanson and pretend to have interest in his work.

Miss Hanson noticed that his study door was increasingly closed and his temper a little frayed by the constant stream of staff needing attention and boys brought to him for his advice and sometimes discipline. One of the teachers, Miss Kenning, was a constant visitor. She was a frail little thing.

She obviously has no control in the classroom. Will he lose his temper with this girl? she wondered, but at every turn, despite his frown and his terse command —"Come in."—she left smiling and reassured. He had actually taken her class of fourteen-year-old villains and warned them of the consequences in his study if they did not cease their evil tricks in her lessons.

He occasionally limped into the kitchen garden where Jack was busy planting seeds in readiness for a summer crop of vegetables. Emma never appeared for which half of himself was thankful. His resolve would not weaken that way. But one morning, he found Jack—on his knees as usual— distressed, shaking his head, surrounded by young, unplanted lettuce plants. Philip knew instantly something was wrong, and his heart lurched.

"What is it, Jack?"

"Oh, Mr Manners, sir, our young hothead Harry has enlisted and is due to leave in two weeks for his regiment. What's worse is he's gone and married young

Maggie Granger on the quiet. We had no idea he was serious about her, and he's set up a rented cottage for the two of them. He's barely got tuppence to rub together, so we'll end up financing it, I expect. His mother is beside herself now there's another mouth to feed, no decent wedding, and Harry's going to war. She has dreaded this moment for months since Will and George left thinking themselves proper heroes. Oh, Mr Manners, what's the world coming to?"

"I don't know, Jack. I am so sorry this trouble has come to you both. All these boys are taken in by the propaganda. Please give my best wishes to Mrs Holt. Our thoughts in the Meeting House are for all the families suffering this same loss and fear." As he spoke, he knew his own prayers would be especially for her.

He spent another night sleepless, and the knock on his study door the next morning merely added to his sense of huge foreboding. It was Miss Hanson bearing the news that two of his sixth form literature class had been into town to enlist for themselves. He sent for them angrily, demanding to know why they dared go against all he had tried to teach them, but his heart melted at their faces.

"But, sir," they argued, "You wouldn't want us to be branded as cowards. They are giving out white feathers to boys who refuse to join up. Think of all the posters everywhere."

He sent them to their house rooms, acknowledging that there was no use in trying to prevent them, and slammed his study door shut so vehemently that Kath Hanson jumped at her desk.

Oh God. How can I deny them what they feel so strongly about? And after I've just taught them Henry the Fifth.

He knew that all the propaganda had indeed made it almost impossible to stay at home despite all the potential for higher education he longed to offer them. He particularly detested the posters of triumphant mothers waving farewell to the marching troops, fondly and proudly clutching their little ones to their hearts.

"Ugh!" he pronounced out loud. "How I loathe all this." And from the next room, Kath heard him and sighed. Patriotism surely need not demand the death of a generation of young men. Kitchener's pointed finger offering them glory paid no attention to the horrific consequences of brutal warfare in a cause that had simply grown out of a domino effect of treaties.

What had driven Harry Holt to join his brothers? Philip knew the answer. It was the same answer as from his own students. And of course, Harry had no Quaker upbringing to strengthen him against the peer pressure. Methodists had no mandatory doctrine of pacifism in the way that Philip's Quaker faith demanded. They could choose to fight for a just cause or not. That Kitchener was deceiving them all, he felt keenly. This was no just cause. How he wished he could visit Low Shadworth and share something of this with the woman he could not dismiss from his mind. He knew she, like her husband, would be suffering at forfeiting yet another son. That he did not go was solely due to his tenacity and strength of will; his sense that it would be wrong to do so.

Meanwhile, Emma, having tried all in her power to maintain her dignity in front of Maggie and Harry and indeed Jack himself, spent the next precious two weeks sewing warm undergarments for her son whilst making curtains for the cottage he had acquired. Maggie was a sweet girl, shy and obliging, with brown hair in curly ringlets, and blue eyes as bright as cornflowers.

No wonder Harry fell for her, thought Emma. She was not at all worldly and somehow seemed not to realise what was about to happen to her. But the day dawned all too quickly and the four of them set out to Shadworth Station, main line to Sheffield, thence to the southern camp where the regiment was gathering.

It was a bright May day and skylarks were rocketing up from the fields, singing their hearts out above them, as they arrived. Bright yellow buttercups were filling the meadows, and the station platform was garlanded with triumphal banners wishing the boys farewell. Emma was surprised how many villagers were in the same position as herself, solemn-faced and tearful. Yet there was pride in their eyes.

Oh God, thought Emma, *He is here with his boys too. The boarders have no parents on hand to wave them off, and of course he has felt it his duty to take their place. How grey he looks; how sad. I know he hates these awful farewells glorifying this ghastly parade of patriotic fervour.*

Mrs Manners had clearly agreed to accompany him with a few of the other ladies of his staff. He was surrounded by them all in the melee of hugs and well wishes and there was his wife, standing on ceremony, half enjoying the status of her position. Jack and she had no part in it—their business was all with Harry and his little wife—but Philip's eyes met hers as she patted Harry's shoulder, and she managed a nod in his direction as her soul leaned towards his like it was the most natural thing in the world.

"Goodbye, my dear son. We shall look after Maggie. Try to write to us if you can, my dearest."

Harry smiled weakly, nodded, and stepped into the carriage.

The young men were on the train, leaning far out of the windows as the engine slowly puffed out of the station. Maggie was crying into her handkerchief. What had they done? What had their countrymen done to embark on this death-seeking adventure? Jack put his arm round Emma, knowing how fearful she was feeling at parting with the last of her sons.

"Come on, lass. Bear up. You can't let Maggie see you upset."

A tearful Maggie linked arms with Emma, and somehow it jolted her into the courage that was never far from the surface.

"Maggie, let's be brave together. That's the best way to help Harry. We've got to keep strong, sweetheart."

"I know, Mrs Holt, I know," whispered Maggie, and Jack smiled to himself. *Trust Emma to find a way of holding the world up!*

Harriet, meanwhile, drew her arm through Philip's as they left as if to claim her possession of him. Barely acknowledging Jack Holt and even less so his wife, she turned to the other ladies of her entourage, dabbing her eyes with her lacy handkerchief. Philip leaned heavily on his stick and walked away with her.

"She doesn't deserve the head, and I bet I'm not the only one to think so. What a cold-hearted fish she is," said Jack as the three of them turned for home. "Dry your tears now, you two."

"Would you take it hard, Mrs Holt, if I go home to Mother tonight? I know she misses me. We've been very close, especially since Father died down the pit. And I feel a bit homesick myself at parting with my dear Harry."

"Oh, Maggie, of course you must go," said Emma and Jack almost in unison. And they hugged her lovingly.

What were the thoughts of them all on that doom-laden afternoon? Leaden thoughts. Leaden thoughts indeed.

Chapter 6

The news from the front as May 1915 neared its end was almost too much to comprehend. The second battle for Ypres had seen the Germans counterattack and retake the ground they called The Hill on the fifth of May. There were rumours of the Germans using a deadly gas which rendered the recipients unable to breathe and choked them in a long and suppurating gurgle of foam and phlegm. Deadly it was and most effectual, as the German hosts were able to advance using its malignant cloud and so retake Ypres itself. It was reported, though in general terms, that thousands of men had died in that manoeuvre.

It was at this point that Emma and Jack received a letter from Will.

Dear Mother and Father,

I write to let you know I'm managing out here. I like to think you're not too far away from me in your thoughts, and I like to think they are happy thoughts and that home is just the same. I wish I could come and have Sunday dinner like old times, but I know I can't.

Mother, I'm worried about George. He's awful gloomy all the time and I can't snap him out of it. I think the dugout gets him down—he hates the rats and they seem to be everywhere. I can't stand them either, but the lice are worse, Mother. They get inside our uniforms and there's no getting rid of them.

George's mate, Billy, was taken to the camp hospital, but George could see he was dying on the stretcher. A sniper got him as he went up over the top. This has hit George hard. He's had to go over the top four or five times since that happened, and I know it's all getting too much for him. It seems so unfair that someone like young Billy should have copped it and George keeps on and on about it. But he knows it's no use. We just have to obey orders no matter what. And you know what they do to deserters, Father? They put them up against the wall and a firing squad shoots them. I wish you would write to George, Mother. At least he's not been split up from me and I pray to God he won't be.

I'm sorry this note is a bit too full of woe. I shouldn't be worrying you with all this. We'll come through somehow. I do keep my spirits up most of the time, but when we have to go over the top, it takes all your grit to do it, knowing full well the enemy will attack and we only gain a yard or two for all that.

Closing down now with all my love, Will.

This epistle—sent so much from Will's heart, containing the first amount of truth they'd received from any of their sons - sent Emma into a spiral of utter distress. Jack could not console her for some time, and she paced the kitchen floor as the bitter knowledge sank into her. She made a pot of tea, then promptly forgot she had made it, so by the time she remembered it, it had changed into a hideously dark brown brew.

"My boys, Jack. How can I stand this? How can any of us stand this? I must send George a letter straightaway." And sure enough, she sat with her writing pad and wrote a message of assurance to her beloved George, then ran up the lane to post it.

Jack, steady as ever, had his own way of dealing with his fears for his sons. He set off up the lane to do some more digging in the school gardens, encountering Mr Manners by the hall door. There, he unburdened something of it with him. In status, Philip may have seemed so much above him, and yet, was so understanding and so dismissive of the gap that yawned between them in the eyes of the world. In their common humanity, Jack was at ease and knew he could count on the head as his friend.

"I'm so sorry for you, old friend. How is your wife taking it? I'm sure she'll busy herself again soon."

"Aye, sir. Doing the laundry and smoothing the ladies' blouses with the hot iron is a kind of soother for her, though I don't know how that can be."

Philip smiled despite the sadness in his own heart; despite wishing he could see her for himself and bring her comfort.

She is Jack's wife, you fool, he reminded himself and turned to Jack.

"I'll make sure to get the staff to gather up their laundry then. We must bring her this odd comfort if we can."

Sure enough, the next morning, the pile of washing appeared as promised, brought down by the school porter, and Emma was left with little time to fret. The washing must be done. She had endured a sleepless night and felt unutterably weary, but once more steadfast, she turned to the task which the two men had mutually decided was the best idea to keep her from her fears.

She had a new challenge that morning coming in the form of Shadworth's own stationmaster who rode up the path on his bike and knocked on the door heartily.

Emma, with arms covered in suds and surrounded by wet washing, hurried to open the door.

"Mrs Holt, I'm here with a favour to ask of you. It's about a job."

"Mr Firbank, to what do we owe the pleasure of this visit?"

"Truth is, Mrs Holt, all my men have vanished to the front, and I am very short of help at the station. Would you consider filling the post of assistant station master for a while till I can restore my numbers? As you know, our station here is on the main line to Sheffield and thence to London, and it is vital work to keep it running smoothly. You, of all the people I can summon to mind, are the one I could trust to help me out. What do you say? It would bring you a little bit of earnings a week towards your living expenses."

Emma paused, standing open-mouthed for a moment. "But... surely you need a man for that sort of job, Mr Firbank? Though far be it for me to denigrate the role of a woman." But as she spoke, despite her initial apprehension, she felt the stirrings of the possibility and of a role that she knew she could fulfil. It would mean putting more household duties onto Florence when she had to be at the station but she was very proud of the growing girl and knew she would take it on willingly.

The lead weight in her heart lifted momentarily. There was nothing more she could do for her boys at this present time. Perhaps serving in this way, enabling the trains to run and carry folk to their destinations, could be her small contribution towards the war effort. She knew Jack would say she must do it. His gardening work—producing food and service to the school and other folks in the village—kept him from taking such a task on himself. She could wash and iron the ladies' clothes just as efficiently even if she took less time to rest. She could agree and then that bit of money would help Maggie in her new cottage while some could be saved for the return of her boys, God willing.

To Mr Firbank's delight and relief, she accepted. He shook her hand warmly and suggested she come to the station as soon as convenient for he could see the pile of laundry from which she had emerged. He thanked God quietly to himself that such a woman as Emma Holt lived in Shadworth.

Concern for her boys was never far from her thoughts but there was a brighter spring in Emma's step as she ironed the blouses that afternoon. Once she'd completed her job, she rode up the hill with the huge pannier of laundry to the school kitchen, glancing only momentarily Mr Manners' study window as she passed.

If only . . . she thought but shrugged the fancy away with a sigh.

Chapter 7

Philip had no idea of all that had happened to Emma as May turned to June. Still the war went on with no sign of an end, and more and more young lives were lost in the futile bombardment of enemy lines that gained only yards, not miles, of territory. He loathed this stalemate with all his being and its consequences for the young men out there in Europe. He was not unaware of the nationalistic fervour which gripped the country, yet felt a desperate need to keep the pacifist ideal alive for the boys in his care. He had seen still more sixth-formers enlist, against all his protests. Moreover, his father-in-law was constantly haranguing him about his views, and Harriet's enduring support for her father stirred up a constant source of conflict between them.

On the morning of June 20, a shock cut him to the quick. Miss Hanson appeared at his door bearing a printed telegram with the news of Daniel Latimer's death in action—Daniel, his best student Daniel, for whom he had hoped a place at Oxford would be forth-coming once the war ended. He put his head in his hands and then down on his desk. Miss Hanson hastened to him, enquiring as to what had happened.

"Oh God. Not Daniel! *'Oh, my son, Absalom. Absalom, my son. Absalom,'*" he muttered, resorting to the ancient biblical text and King David's words to express his grief. Those words from the second book of Samuel were, for him, a way of articulating the agony of loss.

Kath Hanson looked on, astonished at his strange words. He could barely speak but proffered the telegram to her with a shaking hand.

Our son killed in action. Can we meet up as soon as possible? Address to follow. David Latimer.

"Miss Hanson, can you reply to this and assure them I can come to London as soon as it can be arranged? That would be a help, Kath. I must tell Harriet and check the train timetable."

"Of course, sir. You must go home now. Leave me to arrange everything."

As he limped away, he felt weighed down by the huge pain of this news even though Daniel was not his own flesh and blood. And then he thought of Emma Holt so bravely carrying not one but three boys inside her heart and found himself astonished at the force of his desire to share this grief with and be comforted by her. She was Jack's wife and yet, like a magnet, she drew him to her. All that lay between them made him certain that she felt the same for him.

How can I know that? And yet I do. Nonetheless, he must instead face Harriet and tell her about this trip to London. He would have to endure her objections and her wrath.

God help me. He sighed.

He was right. She fought him all the way, denying him any sympathy for this loss and accusing him of neglecting the school by hurrying off.

Harriet, in marrying Philip, had assumed she would be first in his priorities and was, and had been for a long time, resentful of the commitment he made to the school and to his pupils. She could not fully comprehend the depth of his feelings for the well-being of the boys and the maintenance of the Quaker values he held so dear. She had been very spoiled by her over-indulgent parents and had assumed life would always give her everything she desired. So, Harriet was hurt by Philip's different priorities and turned to resentment instead. She never quite managed to revive the warmth of their earlier affection which he continually tried to keep alive.

"Come and walk with me down to the river, will you, Harriet? You can pretend it's Christchurch Meadows if you like?"

"Whatever for, Philip? It's getting late. And anyway, your leg won't stand up to it anymore."

That had been tough to take. That she resented him for the brakes on his bicycle failing on the fateful day of his accident in Salisbury was incredible to him. He had lain in the emergency ward at Salisbury Hospital for several weeks, at first unconscious and then awake to the fact that his knee would make him permanently crippled.

How could she be so callous and unforgiving?

The damage done to his knee so long ago sometimes felt challenging to bear, not only in the awful pain it caused him, but in all the emotional repercussions on his marriage.

She keeps on paying me back for something I could not help.

"Should we book a table at The White Swan this evening? Alan Lorimer could take prayers instead of me."

"Don't bother, Philip. You know you always prefer to be in chapel rather than out with me."

And thus, degree by degree, love grew scarcer and scarcer as she reduced his attempts to please her with little more than reproachful sneers. And so the downward spiral whirled irrevocably on. The support she, by this stage, gave him was only to satisfy her own interests, and just as he expected, she resisted his impulse of kindness towards the Latimers in their grief.

Nevertheless, despite Harriet's objections, by 22 June, Philip was on his way to Shadworth Station with the well-wishes of his staff and reassurances from his deputy that the school could manage for two days without him. So it was with great surprise that as he stood waiting for his train, leaning heavily on his stick, he looked into the eyes of Emma herself in some kind of official uniform. There she stood in a dark blue, double-breasted jacket buttoned to the chin with some kind of peaked cap perched on her head, her lovely hair tucked inside it. Even so, to his eyes, and in spite of it, she still made a beautiful picture.

"My dear Mrs Holt, this is a pleasant surprise. What on earth are you doing here in that strange garb?"

"Mr Manners, I am the assistant stationmaster for the interim. Kindly show a little respect for my uniform." She laughed. "And anyway, what are you doing heading for London in the middle of term?" Her laughter faded as she looked at his face comprehensively, seeing in his eyes all the anguish of the past two days.

"I'm on my way to visit the parents of one of my finest students. He came all the way from London to be educated at my school. He's been killed at the front, and all his promise has been lost with him. God, I'm so tired of this wretched war." He sighed. "When will it end? Why can we not learn the lessons of love rather than the lessons of hate?"

He looked at her and she looked back. All that she felt for him was in that look, and he allowed himself the luxury of believing she cared for him. He, denied any loving kindness from Harriet, now let hers wash over him. She took his arm and led him into the empty waiting room. His train was not due for at least ten minutes, and this moment belonged to them. He followed her. All he could manage was her name.

"Emma..."

Then, in the silent waiting room, he resisted no longer. He pulled her into his arms and kissed her. It was an ardent kiss, full of a tenderness so long repressed. She returned his kiss with a passion long locked away as what had remained unspoken for so long was released in a flood of mutual recognition. Then he held her close, gently pushing back a lock of hair from her forehead. They both knew that they had at last acknowledged something that should have stayed hidden.

But the train was indeed now due, and Emma had to be on the platform to receive it.

"Oh, Mr Manners. You must go, and I must be back to my duty. We will meet on your return. Have you got your return times? I am on duty for Mr Firbank again tomorrow if you're back then. We need to talk."

He nodded in acquiescence and turned away from her to go stand once again on the empty platform, this time with a throbbing heart.

"Goodbye, my dear," he said as he stepped slowly onto the train. He made his way to the window and stood there looking at her as he steamed off to London and all the affairs of the day.

What have we done? was the question in both their hearts. *What have we done?*

Chapter 8

As the train slowly drew into Shadworth Station the next day, Philip's eyes searched the platform for Emma. He knew she would be there watching out for him.

He had hardly slept at all in the Latimers' spare room, having spent the evening comforting them as best he could. He smiled a weary smile, aware of how futile his efforts had been. Their utter grief had been a palpable presence in the room, and nothing he could have said would have even approached it. He had found, finally, it best merely to sit beside them in a Quaker silence.

Nevertheless, he'd had to discuss with Mr Latimer what they wished to do in school for their dead son. It had become clearer as the evening wore on that they wanted some kind of memorial service for Daniel in Shadworth for all who had known him there. They had sent him to Philip's particular school, many miles away from London for it had a prestigious reputation in the Quaker community and beyond.

Thoughts of Emma and their plight had to give way to the business in hand. *And a very good thing too*, he thought sadly. *But now I must enlist her help to implement their wishes. Perhaps that too is a good thing.*

From the platform, Emma saw the train approaching, and she told herself very sternly she must still her beating heart. There must be no weakness today.

She too had slept fitfully, dreaming wild dreams of what could be; dreams she knew to be pure fantasy, doomed to evaporate with the morning light. And as she had lain next to Jack where he slept untroubled, she had been horrified to think of how the knowledge of what had been admitted that day would cause him immense pain and outrage. She could not betray him in such a way, yet would not and could not deny what she felt for the man she had kissed just yesterday.

And now Philip was here.

He stepped carefully out of the carriage, leaning hard on his stick.

He looks worn out, she thought as she hurried to greet him. Other passengers were leaving the train too, and they glanced at the woman in the station uniform attending to the gentleman so earnestly. In passing, they noticed that she was not very interested in assisting them.

"You must join me in the waiting room if it's empty," she whispered. "I still have to signal to the guard that it is all clear to go."

"I had forgotten that you were a very important worker on the line, Mrs Holt," he said, unable to resist the impulse to tease her just a little. "I'll follow you. I have to ask you a huge favour for the Latimers though, as if you haven't already got quite enough work to keep you occupied."

"You must not tease me, sir," she retorted. "And anyway, you know I'll do whatever you need for them."

It made him wince to hear her response.

"Emma, you must never call me 'sir' again. We've gone beyond that. My name is Philip." And having reached the safety of the waiting room, much to his relief now empty of passengers, he took both her hands in his and looked very solemnly into her eyes.

"My dear Emma," he whispered with terrible sadness. "We cannot do this."

"I know," was all she could say. For they both knew they must once more repress what they felt with all the implications of what had happened. And as she nodded in response, they covered their pain in practicalities as he told her of the Latimers' request and what that meant for her. The catering for the memorial would demand her spending hours preparing and icing the fancies for which she was renowned. Sausage rolls and meringues and all the delicacies that the school cook could never manage alone.

"The date is set for the memorial in the Meeting House followed by the afternoon tea in the school hall. It will be the twentieth of August as they have requested, Emma. Can you do it? I know it's so much work."

"Florence will help me, as will Harry's lovely young wife. And, Mr Manners—I mean, Philip—it will be salutary for me to be busy. Nay, it may save me from myself. We must try to forget what happened between us yesterday. We owe it to others."

He knew by 'others' she meant Mr Holt and Harriet. He felt the keen bitterness of the truth of what she was saying, and he dropped her hands and shook his head. "May God help us, my dear." And with that, he made his way out and headed for the station cab to take him home to his wife.

Emma stood on the empty platform, watching his receding back as she ached for him. She looked around at the old station buildings with their dark blue paint peeling, the cheerless waiting room with its grimy windows and no fire in an empty grate. But at least it had protected them from the view of other passengers. Mr Firbank had planted a few boxes of geranium plants which sported their bright scarlet blooms along the edges of the station offices, belying the sense of human neglect. Emma shook her head at the large poster on the wall, however, for there was Kitchener's finger pointing at any young man who might be tempted by it.

Oh no you don't! she thought and sighed as if the world was on her shoulders, which was how she had often thought of it in relation to her children.

I do try to hold the world up for them.

There ensued a time of awful anguish for these two who had fallen in love so, so unexpectedly; so unintentionally. Their sense of the betrayal of others was acute.

How has this happened to me? thought Philip. *How have I allowed this to capture my soul?*

He spent more and more time in the Meeting House praying for the strength to withstand the powerful impulse to resign his position in the school and take Emma away with him, despite the values of his deeply felt faith. And he prayed to love Harriet better as he prepared the memorial for the Latimers, asking God for some kind of sign to help him.

Strangely, it was the season that brought some comfort. At Tempest's farm, the fields were golden. It was haymaking time, and the Shadworth air was redolent with the scent of the newly mown grass. He often walked down towards the farm at dusk, and the sight of the farmer's pristine, neatly built haystacks reclining on the stubble as the summer sun filtered down gave him a kind of benediction. A skylark, who must have a nest nearby, often soared into the air from the ground as he stood and would hover over the field, giving her song full throttle, its sweet melody like a hymn of praise. Somehow, he felt then that God was not far from him in his effort to hold fast to his intention.

Yet Harriet's father's regular visits made it harder to hold that faith. While her mother sat serenely in the sitting room and caused no waves of fury in him, her father constantly harangued him about the war and showed not a modicum of regret at the terrible losses being incurred and reported from France. The bishop's attitude was that, at all costs, Britain and the empire must triumph.

He is certainly Kitchener's man, thought Philip. *Nothing less will suffice, no matter how many English corpses are littering the fields of Ypres.* The bishop might have been a man of God but Philip could not discern in him the compassion of a disciple of Christ. If only Harriet had just once shown an ounce of support for her husband in the constant arguments over the supper table but she was her father's daughter at every point.

Strangely and ironically, it was Jack Holt whom he found the most companionable and who shared his horror at the news updates. He was always busy in the school gardens, creating a chaos of colour amongst the flower beds by his careful stewardship. But Jack was never too busy to stop work and share the latest news from the front with him.

Kath Hanson smiled to herself as she watched Philip limping down towards the garden in a break from the constant stream of staff and students demanding his attention at every turn. She knew it was a consolation for him to take those moments when he could, but she had no idea of the struggle within Philip as his respect for Jack grew. Jack's wisdom and steadiness were renowned by all who knew him, and Philip felt the shame of his own hidden desire. Indeed, they were friends and that friendship meant a great deal.

Emma, meanwhile, was questioning over and over where it had all begun. What had set them on such a road that seemed like perdition?

Yet, deep down, she knew the answer. It was his tenderness that had taken her heart, his understanding of his boys, his respectful treatment of her and of Jack as his equals.

I know I was shy of him at first and it felt like I was trespassing in his library, but when he found me in the corner there and showed me the books he loved that I could borrow and read, how much I loved sharing what I had learned with him in those snatched times. And I just knew his wife was ice-cold and denying him affection. I just knew.

It was indeed the talk of the village how Mrs Manners spoke to him in public with disdain. *How could she?* thought Emma. *I would know how to make him feel young again. I would know how to ease his weary look, if only I could.*

She knew he could, with one smile, make her feel young again. A princess from a fairy tale, not the careworn, overworked woman she really was. She, Emma Holt, forty-seven years old. She, born and bred to work in Shadworth with the ordinary folk. How could she even think of such a man, such a scholar, such a well-loved head of such a prestigious school?

But now, to her wonder, they had at last shared the passion that had grown between them. He returned her love. That moment in the station waiting room became very precious—a kind of talisman to keep hope alive despite everything—a moment of acknowledgement she felt God would not condemn for it was very pure. Equally, however, she knew it could not be any more than a talisman. It must go no further. It was totally illegitimate.

Her love for her children saved Emma, at this time, from falling into total misery. Jack, in ignorance of its hidden cause, nevertheless helped keep her strong for them all, never allowing her to indulge in too many tears, always encouraging her to look on the bright side and keep on hoping. She knew he was right and that she had to keep up her courage for their sakes. It was her old maxim of holding the world up for them all.

Indeed, she was ruthless for her family. Florence had gone to stay with young Maggie Holt, Harry's bride, and was flourishing in the happy fellowship of sisters-in-law. But as for her boys, she maintained a steady flow of letters to the front, especially to George who never wrote in reply but of whom Will kept her informed. Harry was in a quite separate outfit, serving near a French town whose name he was not allowed to impart, but with French troops, acting as soldier-servant to one of the officers there. She believed he was in a more secure environment back with the officers at a distance from the trenches. But though the truth of the situation came through every line of Will's correspondence, Emma knew he was holding a great deal back from them, acutely aware of the censors at the front, but also trying to protect them from the ugliness they faced every day. What he did write told Emma they were clearly overwhelmed with the tortuous forays over the top, dreading the snipers' bullets, watching their fellows fall to the ground like the seeds Farmer Tempest sowed at Low Lane Farm. And their dugouts stank of rum and urine. Will told her that much. Poor Will desperately wanted to reassure his mother, but in every sentence, he let out the truth of the horrors he saw.

And so she busied herself cooking the delicacies that the ladies at the school ordered from her whilst laundering their blouses to immaculate condition and sending them all up to the school with Florence and Maggie's help, avoiding Philip's study whilst yearning for even just a glimpse of him.

And Philip kept his study door firmly closed except for students and staff in need, venturing out to talk with Jack only when he was sure she would be down in Low Shadworth on her station duties. He continued trying to give Harriet more attention, though it was constantly thrown back at him and reinforced by her father's enjoyment of his discomfort when the war was discussed.

It was a time of stalemate, of strict repression, and of much silent pondering. And then, with only two weeks to the date set for Daniel Latimer's memorial service which he had prepared conscientiously and only needed the catering to complete the plans, there came a blow which shook it all asunder.

Chapter 9

The boy on the bicycle was unaware, whistling as he approached the Holts' gate that morning, and Emma was completely unconscious of him as he parked the bike outside. He knocked and she answered, her hair wet with the effort of peggy-sticking the hot tub of washing. She wiped it out of her eyes and then froze, mouth dropping as she saw the young visitor proffering the telegram.

"This came for you, ma'am. You *are* Mrs Holt, right? No reply expected."

She could hardly speak in answer but held out her hand for the offering, trembling. The boy, innocent yet conscious of the blow he had just delivered, turned wordlessly back down the path. Her legs buckled and she sat, there, on the doorstep for her head was reeling almost to fainting. Slowly, she opened the telegram and read in silence:

Deeply regret to inform you that Private George Holt, King's Own Yorkshire Light Infantry, was executed for cowardice on August 6, 1915 after Court Martial. Lord Kitchener expresses sympathy.

Secretary, War Office.

She let out one long, loud scream which penetrated to the nearby cottages. "Oh God, my George. My son. My son, George! God help us."

After hearing the scream, Florence came running with Maggie to see what the matter was and found her there on the step, head in hands.

"Florence, you must get Father." Emma must have dropped the telegram for it was there on the ground at her feet.

Florence picked it up and read its contents. Horrified, not only at the news but also the sight of her strong mother sitting on the doorstep motionless as if all life had drained out of her, Florence turned to Maggie. "Get her indoors, will you, while I fetch Father?"

And with a last look at her mother, Florence ran for all she was worth up the lane, past the fingerpost, through the school gates, until she reached Kath Hanson. She knew the head's secretary from her times bringing back the laundry, and at sight of Kath, she stopped for breath, spilling out the news that so broke her heart to repeat.

"Come with me," said Kath, taking Florence by the hand. She led her down to the kitchen garden where she knew Jack Holt was working.

Even in his study, Philip could hear Florence's searing sobs, and opening his door, he could see Kath disappearing down the path with her. Something told him that he must follow. Something had happened. Something bad. *Please, God, don't let it be one of the Holt boys.*

Turning the bend in the path, there was Jack clutching what could only be a telegram in one hand and holding onto his daughter with the other. She was weeping on his shoulder as Miss Hanson stood aghast beside them.

"Mr Manners, it's George Holt," Kath said. Almost under her breath, she added, "Executed for cowardice in France." Kath Hanson was appalled that the boy had died in such a shameful way.

Jack, standing there, could sense her shock and air of condemnation. He returned her gaze, daring her to comment. He, himself, was cringing inwardly at the disgrace of it, but overriding everything was an image of his son facing a merciless firing squad, alone.

"Jack, Florence, come to my study. Miss Hanson, bestir yourself and bring sweet tea as fast as you know how. Jack... Jack, steady yourself. You have to be strong now."

Soon after they reached Philip's study, Miss Hanson brought the cups of scalding tea. He urged Jack to drink and Florence to stop her tears. He knew who would be in terrible need at that moment and wished he himself could hurry down to her, but he restrained his own feelings as he knew he must.

"Mr Manners, sir, George ran away. My son ran away. My God, how could he? How could Will have allowed it to happen? And now he's dead!" As Jack spoke, his face grew red with a kind of rage he had never felt before. "They've taken a boy's life; my own son's life. How could any man send a boy to be shot for being afraid? How, sir? *How*? Florence, it just can't be true."

Jack stopped and shook his head as if he might drown in a sea of troubles, and Florence reached up to kiss his cheek. Both Philip and Kath could have wept at the sight of them in such distress.

"George wasn't a coward—I'd swear my life on it. But, oh God, I can't believe he's dead. He's dead! He'll never come home to us again. Oh God. My own son labelled a coward, dying a coward's death. I don't know what this will do to his mother."

At the mention of Emma, it was as if he suddenly realised he'd forgotten all about the one waiting at home. "Mr Manners, I must go home. My poor Emma."

"Go, my friend. Florence, look after your father. Hurry now."

Miss Hanson helped him urge them out the door, and he watched them following the path back to the gates with a rising sense of fury in his own breast. He limped to his desk and sat heavily; his own face ashen.

"We are losing a generation of our sons and, good God, we ourselves are killing them, Miss Hanson. This war is a God-forsaken thing." Silence filled the study as he sat, lost in thought.

Kath poured some more tea out for him in a gesture of comfort. The secretary felt for her employer keenly, knowing his feelings about the war, knowing he cared for the Holts. Kath Hanson also knew his powerful feelings against the use of violence of any kind. His Quaker principles lay at the very foundations of his school.

She shook her head at the huge implication of what he was saying and clearly feeling. She found herself unable to resist the thought that George's desertion had somehow brought disgrace on the family. Surely it was a shameful thing to run away from duty. But she pushed the thought aside.

Jack Holt must never catch me thinking such things.

It was past lunch time and school was quiet, as most of the boys were home for the summer vacation. The house heads had all left for their own holidays, and she, Kath, was only doing mornings to catch up with all the correspondence before retiring to her own small cottage in High Shadworth. She knew Mrs Manners would be expecting her husband.

"Sir, your lunch will be spoiling. You should perhaps return home and tell Mrs Manners what has happened," she hesitantly suggested.

He sighed at these words and looked up. "Thank you, Miss Hanson. You are indeed, as always, absolutely right. Let's shut up shop for today. There will be much to do tomorrow as we prepare for the memorial service. Best to stop for now. You, too, must go home."

He left her to lock his door and very slowly walked down towards his house. His confounded leg throbbed as he walked, and he was almost glad of the pain. It was nothing to the pain of the household in Low Shadworth, but the awful truth was, he could do nothing about that.

Harriet was waiting. He apologised for his lateness, only to receive a tirade of abuse in response.

"Can you never keep time, Philip? I have cooked lunch. You could at least have had the courtesy to arrive punctually."

As he told her wearily what had happened to George Holt, he watched her face and saw in it not a scrap of compassion or of real sympathy. In his heart, he had known that she would not care at all for those she deemed less than herself. But he found it hard to reconcile that his own wife could be so unmoved.

"That's bad news. They will have sent a firing squad to execute him. I am sorry for Jack. But are you surprised? These village folk have no sense of honour, you know, no backbone. They know no better."

Philip had endured Harriet's insensitive snobbery many times before but something in this comment touched him on the raw. Before he could stop himself, his hand went out and gave her a resounding slap on her face; a slap he regretted immediately. But he knew it was far too late as the slap resounded and her cheek grew red with the sting of it. How could he have allowed his rage to surface so violently? How could he have done such a thing?

She was in fact devastated that her principled, pacifist husband could actually have hit her, and she stepped back, astonished and furious. Though Harriet kicked against his pacifist beliefs, she had always relied on his patience and gentleness. Her shock was intense. Harriet held her fiery cheek in dismay, and Philip was mortified.

"How dare you! What is it about you and those Holts? That wife of his gives herself too many airs. Just because she's a good cook and half the village hold her in some kind of awe doesn't give them the right to expect *our* attention. They are nobodies, Philip. Nobodies. And you dare to slap me? Were it not for the Latimers' ceremony, I would go home straightaway. You're supposed to be a man of God." She turned on her heel and swept up the stairs, her face white against her reddened cheek.

He was truly appalled that he had used such violence on her. He had not resisted the impulse to hurt her at her malicious comment. Then she had made it far worse by condemning Emma for something of which she was entirely innocent. How dare she speak like that of someone who served the school with such unselfishness?

If you only knew, Harriet, how deeply I care about "that woman" as you call her.

Yet, he knew he should have had more sense and held back. He could not allow his inner feelings to show. He deeply regretted what he knew only too well—that Harriet had little tender-heartedness in her soul, brought up as she had been with over-indulgent parents and with no love, or very little, left for him.

He followed her upstairs where she lay out on her solitary bed. It had been months now since she had slept with him.

"Harriet, I am deeply sorry. Try to understand that your comments about the Holts were absolutely spiteful, and that's why I reacted as I did. They are good people, Harriet, and just as brave and educated as you, though you may not believe it. Do you remember those words of John Donne in his sermon at St. Paul's? *'No man is an island. All are part of the continent. Therefore, do not send to ask for whom the bell tolls. It tolls for thee.'* Harriet, we have no child, but can't you understand how it might feel to lose a child and in such a way?"

Harriet turned her head away and muttered into her pillow, "Indeed, we do not have a child—did you think I had forgotten that? And do not quote John Donne at me. After the Latimers' service, I shall return home with Father, and you may see how it feels to be alone in school without a supporting wife for a while. You may manage on your own."

With those words ringing in his ears, he turned on his heel and limped slowly down the stairs. He felt even worse when he realised he had reminded Harriet of their childlessness. He knew it was still a very raw hurt which she had no choice but to accept, and he also knew he had been unable to help her deal with it, for in her pride she had turned in on herself and had not let him get near her. Nevertheless, partly in anger as well as regret, he took up his stick and set off for the fingerpost and the walk down to Low Shadworth determinedly, knowing only that he would see Emma and offer his sympathy and his love.

He was sure of one thing: his anger at the treatment of those troops in their suffering, shot for being afraid in the face of evil, was not to be abated. He intended to write in protest to those in higher places responsible for such colossal misjudgement. And he would tell Emma and Jack. That was at least something he could do.

Chapter 10

As Jack and Florence arrived home, Maggie was waiting there almost beside herself with anxiety for Emma had retreated to her bed, fully clothed. She just lay there on top of the eiderdown, facing the ceiling, silent and without tears. The sun was pouring in through the windows and lighting up the photographs that Emma had arranged so carefully on the dressing table, each son smiling back at her. It was afternoon now and the light was the golden light of a sun that was low in the sky. But it was as though it could no longer delight her.

Will anything be able to delight me ever again? she thought.

Jack pleaded with her to speak to him; it was to no avail. Florence brought her neat egg sandwiches, crusts removed, the eggs from her own hens. It did not move her, and she would not eat. The others ate the sandwiches, and Maggie tried her best for her best friend's sake to cheer them along. But Florence was finding it difficult not to think of her big brother of whom she had been very fond, and Jack was drawing very close to his wits' end as they watched the sun going down. He slammed the cups of tea down on the wooden table and slopped the milk as he poured it with a shaking hand. So, Philip's gentle knock on the door made them all jump, and Jack let him in, astonished that the head should have taken the trouble to come down. Yet Philip was determined enough not to care that Jack was surprised and proffered his hand to him as if to share in his grief. Maggie was overwhelmed to see the Quaker head in the very kitchen of her mother-in-law's home, but Florence somehow sensed it was important that he had come.

"Would you come up and see Mother, Mr Manners? She might just rouse herself for you. Goodness knows, it might be a comfort."

Jack nodded in agreement with Florence, and they all went up together to where Emma still lay absolutely prone.

Philip softly touched her shoulder. "Emma, Mrs Holt, we are all so sorry for this news, and we just want you to be comforted by everyone's sympathy and care now. There is nothing for you to be ashamed of in George's death. He was just a frightened boy in a situation that was all too much for him. Try to believe that and trust God to have him in His care."

Emma made no movement as if something in her had paralysed her. Jack looked away at Philip's words, fighting with his own inner turmoil. But Philip persisted, promising that he would write to their MP and all those in power to put the record straight about what constituted cowardice and what did not. It was certainly not the action of a young man hardly out of school, placed in a situation of abject violence and terror repeated over and over every day and far from home. Nor was it cowardice in those who were conscientious objectors and steadfast in refusing to take arms. Indeed, in his heart, Philip felt the generals were closer to being labelled cowards themselves as, from the safety of their comfortable quarters, they commanded men to go out and die for a cause that, to him, seemed out of all proportion.

He looked down at Emma lying prostrate and unresponsive and longed to be able to take her in his arms and reassure her. He wished she would only show some sign of awareness of his presence, but it was not forthcoming. His heart bled at the sight of her so desperate and so isolated in her grief.

Not to mention how Jack's feeling, he thought. And he found himself equally desperate for he could not reach her and Jack, in his own grief, could do no better.

Unfortunately, Philip's presence and touch could not get past the cocoon of grief with which she had wrapped herself. She could not move for anguish. So, the three went down to Maggie, and he shook hands with them all.

"Mr Manners, thank you for your trouble," said Jack. "The sun is going down. Will you allow the girls to accompany you up the hill?"

"No need, Jack, I shall manage fine. Can we spend a moment of quiet together? It may just help." The circumstances had moved him to suggest it, and as they all stood in the scullery of Emma's hospitable home, the silence allowed a sense of God's peace to come down and bless them.

It was hard walking back with his leg throbbing, but he limped slowly, glad that he had at least been able to show his care for her and for the family. And that evening, he felt not a shadow of remorse that he had done so.

How ironic it was, he thought, that the two women in his life should that night be lying on their separate beds, one unwilling, the other too devastated to speak. And yet he himself slept soundly despite his sadness.

But that night, once Florence and Maggie had gone, Jack Holt drank his way through the remains of the bottle of Scotch he had been saving for their Christmas and fell asleep on the old horsehair sofa in the kitchen.

The morning came and went at Holt House. Jack himself had a huge headache, thanks to the whisky he had consumed. He stumbled up to the bedroom he and Emma shared, hardly able to articulate all that lay on his heart. He could think of nothing he could do to alter the situation or to cheer his wife, and he stood and looked at her, still silent and tearless, still as she'd been the night before.

"Emma, lass, can you come downstairs and eat a little? This isn't going to change things. We must go on living, and George would want it so. Emma, I can't stand it either."

A knock on the door alerted him, and leaving her there still prone, he went down to answer it. It was the telegraph boy again. He opened the telegram and read the first bit of good news they'd had in the past couple of days. He ran back up to Emma, waving it hopefully.

"Emma, Will has got forty-eight hours' leave at home. He'll be arriving at the station at six o'clock. Emma, rouse yourself, please. Please, love."

There was the sound of another knock on the door, and to Jack's astonishment when he opened it, there stood a group of the villagers all holding posies of flowers. Maggie and Florence were with them, and they pushed him to one side and welcomed them in. Each neighbour had come to show their concern for a family and a mother for whom they held the greatest respect.

Florence ran upstairs to her mother and begged her to come down, to try to withstand her grief in this moment. She herself was full of sadness and could not bear for her mother not to be the strong lady she relied upon. She went over to her and hugged her. This was no longer something Emma could resist. Her daughter needed her. She sat up and returned the hug silently.

"I will come, my Florence. I must try." And with those words, she descended to the good people of Shadworth who had defended her from the gossips in the village shop who were all very quick to judge George of cowardice. The group had made their way to Holt House, outraged at their less than kindly neighbours, determined to show their moral support. Emma thanked them in amazement as she took the posies they had brought her.

"Don't you fret any more, Mrs Holt. Never you mind what some folks will say. We all know that George was the bravest little lad growing up. There must have been something awful happen to make him do what he did. Have no fear. We understand. Let folks think what they like."

Jack was standing, lost for words, as one by one, they left the little family in the quiet of the kitchen. She went and put her head on his shoulder, and together they sat at the wooden kitchen table while Florence and Maggie busied themselves making lunch. Jack kissed her very gently as she sat there silently, relieved that she had at last emerged.

Something of Emma's resilience returned to her then. There were things to be done if Will was coming home, and the thought of Mr Firbank at the station made her square her shoulders. She would not let the scorn of the gossips get her down. She could hold her own with any of them.

Just let them try. I'm in charge at Shadworth Station, and they can't go far without encountering me. So, Emma began at last to face up to the horrible reality that had struck them all down. And knowing that Philip had been there brought her comfort as she wondered yet again how such a man could care for her. But her children needed her, and the thought of Will's advent acted like a tonic to her will.

Jack allowed his relief that she was returning to herself to revitalise him, and he took this opportunity to go out into his own garden and begin work on his potato patch. He breathed in the scent of the good soil as he dug, listened to the sounds of the chickens clucking round the seed he threw them, and allowed the beauty of the afternoon to soothe his pain. He rammed the spade into the soil perhaps a little more brutally than usual. When Maggie appeared beside him, he barely noticed that she was wanting to speak to him. She touched his jacket and he turned.

"Mr Holt, I don't know how to tell you this at this time, but I'm bursting to tell and to tell Harry's mother. Mr Holt, I'm expecting. I'm having a baby." Young Maggie burst into tears.

Jack thought, as he often had, how remarkable God's timing seemed to be. A baby coming just as he had heard of his beloved George dead never to come home again. How could he possibly come to terms with the enormity of it? What a terrible irony." He stood speechless there in his beloved garden and swept his hand across his forehead as if in astonished denial.

What were the classic words of the quote Emma had talked of?

Thou met'st with things dying, I with things newborn.

Though he was no Shakespearean devotee like his wife, he always listened when she spoke about what she was studying. The quote came irresistibly into his head at that shattering moment, and he gently took Maggie by the shoulders and marched her into the kitchen.

"This child has something to tell you, and this time it's good news and we can't but celebrate it even on such a day as this." Maggie looked at Emma and Florence but could not speak.

"Nay, lass, spit it out." Jack smiled. "This brave lass has just told me she is going to have Harry's child, Emma. It's strange timing but I can't help but be pleased for all that." Jack watched as the truth of it dawned on them and lightened up their sorrowful faces.

Emma flew to the weeping Maggie and embraced her with a look of such tenderness that would have broken Philip's heart if he had seen her then. But Emma's mind was hurrying on as always. She was immediately anxious for Maggie's mother.

"Maggie, have you told your mother? It will mean so much to her." As she spoke, she thought of her own pregnancies, though she could not bring herself to think particularly of George's birth which had been so easy and quick. It had been in her own bed at home with just Mrs Townsend, the doctor's midwife, beside her. The advent of Will, her firstborn, had been a different matter. She had been in labour for hours to no avail until, at last, Dr Thomson had been called and had used forceps to bring Will out.

What things I have gone through in this life, she thought. *And when Harry and Florence arrived, I never got a night's sleep for months.* She had to smile to herself then despite the agony in her soul.

I remember crawling to do the middle of the night feed and shouting at Jack that there is no God. Oh, Maggie, you've got it all before you, child. But there IS a God, and I pray he's listening to us now.

Florence, regarding her mother who had gone into some kind of reverie of her own, found herself moved beyond tears and hardly knew how to deal with either her mother's profound grief or her own. The two pieces of news that had come on the heels of each other had to be assimilated somehow. Jack was already feeling the terrible gap yawning open in his life for lack of his beloved son.

At last, the time came for them to walk down to the station to watch for Will. There, they waited together with full hearts.

As Will descended the steep steps from the carriage, his mother ran to him and flung her arms round him. His father looked on while Florence and Maggie pushed for their chance. The tears fell then, long checked and now released in a flood. Will's face was grey with the stress of the task of bearing home the details of George's death as well as the hasty journey under strict orders to return promptly after the time allotted to him.

As they walked home with arms around each other, he told them of George's increasing terror in the trench and at the destruction all around him, of the sight of his friends extinguished by bullets and mortar, of the dread of another gas attack like the one to which they had been subjected the day before he ran away.

"I can't write it all down in my letters, Mother. They get checked by the officers in case we give something important away. Words can't really describe it anyway if I'm honest. The dugouts are like hellholes. The vermin and the stench of sweat make me feel quite sick, and there's always the dread of the order to go up into the trench and take our turn on duty up there.

You never know who'll be next in line for a bullet and whether it'll maybe have your name on it."

As Will talked nineteen to the dozen, unloading all he had long been repressing inside, he sat closer and closer to his mother where she listened aghast at his story while Jack banged the cooking pots Emma had set on the stove and needlessly stirred the contents over and over.

"Sit down, Father," begged Florence, herself ashen as she took it all in.

But worse was yet to come as Will began to recount the events surrounding George. He shuddered at the memory of the two military police who'd marched George back from his flight between them, passing him as they'd marched without a backward glance, grim-faced and determined to punish a branded coward. He leaned his head on his mother's shoulder as he spoke, and all the bitter memories of it brought Will himself to tears. She stroked his head and bit her lip.

How helpless we are in all this, she thought. *So unable to do anything, so inarticulate, so much at the mercy of powerful people who have no idea of the suffering we must endure.* Emma's eyes blazed with anger.

"George was not a coward, Dad," reiterated Will. "He was just a frightened boy, and surely no one should have the right to take a life just because someone is afraid. I know he refused to be blindfolded at the last to show his courage. Mother, you do understand, don't you?"

Emma hugged him closer to her and promised him that they all did indeed understand. She told him of Mr Manner's promise to write and protest the evil of the situation and felt, growing inside herself, a huge and bitter hatred for those who perpetrated it. It propelled her into renewed action, and she stood, at last, and took the old spoon out of Jack's hands to drain the potatoes for mashing and rescue the roasting beef from the stove—a joint she had been saving for Sunday before the devastating news had hit them. Maggie, meanwhile, who had stood quietly in the background, now at last told Will *her* good news and begged him for any news of Harry. To the relief of them all, Will was able to report that all reports he had heard of Harry told him he was very safe with the French, acting as head cook in the mess kitchen.

As she watched Will hungrily attacking his plate, an enormous weariness descended on Emma. Her head began to droop, and she felt sleep overcoming her for sleep had evaded her completely the previous night. She was appalled at her weakness.

"Forgive me, my dears. I can't seem to keep my eyes open. I know it's still quite early but I'm done up. Will, it's so wonderful to have you here."

Jack smiled at her concern, knowing she'd hate sleeping while she had her son close by and for so short a time, but he reassured her by pulling Will to his feet and ushering him to the door. "Emma, I'm taking the lad to The White Swan for a drink. That'll put us both right and you can rest. I promise we'll stay sober, or as sober as needs be to get home. Will and I can ignore any comments. I'll happily punch anyone who dares. Is that fine with you?"

"Go, the pair of you, but keep out of trouble. Maggie and Florence, you two should get some sleep now. We have a lot to do tomorrow. Life doesn't stand still no matter what, and it's the Latimer memorial in less than a week now."

She mounted the stairs, put on her nightgown, and fell fast asleep. A benediction indeed to that tired soul.

Chapter 11

This short but precious time with Will was speeding by all too quickly, though it had acted as a kind of ease to the wound that had been so deeply inflicted on them all. That and the news of the baby to be born took something of the agonising edge off their thoughts of their dead and disgraced son whose grave would be unmarked, without ceremony, so far away.

But it could not staunch the bitterness Emma, in particular, felt against those in their seats of power who could play with the lives of youth so peremptorily. Nor did she suffer lightly the whispering behind her back in the village shop. At the word 'coward', she turned around and faced the woman who had uttered it.

"You should think before you speak of others, my friend. You never know what awaits you around the next corner." She strode out of the shop furiously whilst the other women looked askance.

And alongside all this was the knowledge that Will would soon have to go back to the horrors that awaited him. And how could she rest at all knowing the chances of his staying safe and alive were so low?

Yet she turned back to her tasks determined to stay strong for them all. Her weakness had been betrayed with the advent of the fateful telegram but now she would brace herself to face whatever came. No one would see the frantic din of her thoughts and prayers that she knew would torment her through every waking moment. Nor would they ever see the deep love she carried inside for Philip Manners. Yet her love for Jack never faltered, and she thanked God for him and the strength he imparted to her every day.

Mr Firbank was very relieved to see her standing bravely on the station platform as the family waved Will off with many tears and many hugs and assurances of love.

"Mrs Holt, I cannot say how sorry I am you have had such dreadful news. How are you? And do you feel, when you are ready, you could recommence your duties here on the station? I myself have been shouldering that task in the meantime but, my word, Mrs Holt, I'll be glad to have you back."

Emma, through her tears, smiled at the kindly old man and reassured him she would fulfil her tasks again.

Recently, a desperate need to see Philip had started simmering within her again, and she knew she had the opportunity freely to do so with the memorial catering now so pressing. It was August 17 already and the ceremony was set for August 20.

Meanwhile, Philip had had to put a strict curb on himself. He couldn't forget the sight of Emma prone on her bed like a flower knocked down by the wind, its stem broken. The desire to be beside her in her grief was powerful but had to be repressed with all the willpower he could muster.

He had to attend to the minute details of the service he had planned for Daniel and that helped him in his turn to straighten his shoulders to the task. He had a great love for his boys, and Daniel had been one of his finest students. He knew Daniel must be honoured fittingly. Miss Hanson, despite the fact that it was officially holidays, had much to sort out for the printers. Meanwhile, the bishop was proving difficult to manage, insisting on a role in the gathering, against Philip's better judgement. He felt it obligatory to allow it, as he was attempting to placate the still furious Harriet. He knew he must try to keep his promise to himself that he would do all in his power to love the woman to whom he had been married for fourteen years. This was the way forward he and Emma had sworn to follow that day on the station platform, though in truth, in this matter, he was doing no more than humouring her.

There was a knock on his door and Kath announced the arrival of the very one who filled his thoughts despite himself. He resisted the impulse to rise and embrace her and had to smile wryly at the effect that would have had on his secretary. He could see Emma was absolutely in control of her emotions.

"Mr Manners, I've come to see what you need for the afternoon tea. It's getting so close now, and I have much baking to do. We are expecting many guests, I imagine. I've also got to be on station duty earlier that day, so I must be in advance with the preparations."

Conscious of Miss Hanson's presence, he replied in kind. "Thank you for coming, Mrs Holt. I believe my wife has given Cook her requirements, so a visit to the kitchens might be salutary. Let me accompany you down there. Miss Hanson, can you continue with all the correspondence for the service in the meantime?"

"Of course, sir," she replied, somewhat surprised that he should be prepared to go in the middle of so much work. But she assented gladly to his obvious desire to be of comfort to Emma, though she herself was over-pressed with the paperwork the memorial had thrown up.

So it was that Philip and Emma found themselves together at last for a few brief and very precious moments. He looked down at her as they walked and gently took her by the elbow. He could see on her face the newly wrought lines on her forehead and the tightness around her drawn lips revealing so much of the pain they were silently containing. She looked older and very, very tired, and he longed to take her in his arms and console her.

"My dear, I am so sorry for what has happened and feel so useless in the face of it. My brave, sweet Emma, can you manage all this? It's come at such a time and yet we cannot cancel it. The Latimers have their own agony. Yet, I promise you, I will write to Military Headquarters and to the local MP to show my abhorrence at their unpardonable way of dealing with George and other deserters."

She simply shook her head and sighed as she looked back up at him, enjoying, despite herself, the pleasure of seeing him in all his gentleness. But the kitchens loomed in front of them, and once again, there was the need to hide their feelings and straighten their shoulders to the task. Bitter tears started down her cheeks, but she knew she must brush them away.

"You mustn't say any more, Philip. You are making me shed tears all over again and I can't give in to it. I must recover my willpower again. There is work to be done."

At that, Cook appeared in the doorway and welcomed them in. She produced the list of extras she knew Emma would make so magnificently for the gathering: the fancies, the meringues, the cream horns, the tiny pork pies for which she was famed in Shadworth. She felt remorse at the same time as she noticed Emma's weary look and remembered the grief that had so violently come upon the Holt household. She herself had seen Jack in the garden and had told him of her sadness and anger that such a thing had happened to his son.

She was a little surprised at the look on the head's face as he stood beside them, but she shrugged and put the stray suspicion away, knowing his care for every minute detail of the Latimer memorial. He would want everything in place for the event.

"Cook, thank you. We know it's a challenge for Mrs Holt at such a time, but we know she can do it."

Emma smiled at that. Taking the list, she nodded at them both and made her farewells, promising them it would be done. Truth was, she could no longer bear to stay beside him and appear unmoved. She knew she must flee and get home to banish all emotion.

He watched her hurry back down the school drive towards the gate, reminding himself of the requirement of his position. Kath would still be in her room working and Harriet would be champing at the bit to know that he had made all the arrangements for the service, including the part for her father. He suspected that the part he had outlined for the bishop would not satisfy him sufficiently, but he had no intention of kowtowing to that man's ego. This service was his and his alone to lead.

Chapter 12

The Quaker School,
Shadworth,
Cranston,
Yorkshire

August 17th, 1915

To Military Headquarter,
Aldershot.

To whom it may concern,
I write as the headmaster of the Shadworth Quaker School for boys who come to me at eleven until the age of eighteen. I have a particular concern at this time about the news from the front. As a Quaker, my attitude to war in general and to the war being waged in France must be obvious. Violence should never be the answer in an international dispute.

I abhor the huge loss of life being reported for it seems to me to gain very little end result. Your policies do not appear to take into consideration the innumerable casualties it is creating without an end in sight.

My particular reason for writing, however, is to beg that there be an end to the policy towards deserters. We have an example of it in our village here. My gardener's son has been court martialled and shot for running away from the front in a state of abject terror. This seems to me not only merciless but totally unjust.

What can it gain to take the life of a boy whose energy and potential has been wasted by your action? He was a frightened boy who could take no more of the vileness of the trenches and of the daily command to go over the top into the face of the enemy. Surely that does not deserve capital punishment? Boys are never to be treated as mere cannon fodder. They need care and counselling before all else. I say this as headmaster of an institution that deals with the nurture and education of boys, some of whom are much the same age as the troops in your care.

What is more, I know our young man in question was not alone in his terror. Of that, we have been daily informed. How many more lives must be taken by those who are on the same side, let alone by the enemy?

I write with all courtesy but that does not belie my anger at your actions. If this is really a Christian coun-

try, how can we continue to fly in the face of the Christ who taught a better way—the way of love and peace?

I remain, sirs, your humble servant,

Philip Manners,
Headmaster.

August 18th, 1915

My dearest Maggie,

I am writing to tell you I'm alright and still alive and kicking. I hope you'll let Mother and Father see this letter too. I am so thrilled at the news, Maggie. I'm going to be a dad! Oh my. I do hope you're looking after yourself. Trust Mother to be in charge and Florence will be right by you too.

I can't bear to think of our George. It's like him to have been frightened by all that's going on. He never did like fighting and such, even when he was little. I can't believe he's gone, Maggie. If it's a boy, we'll call him George, shall we?

I'm liking cooking for the officers. Most of them are Frenchies, but not so bad for all that.

Well, my duck, I'm closing now with all my love,

Your Harry.

The Quaker School,
Shadworth,
Cranston,
Yorkshire

August 18th, 1915

To Mr Frank Jacques,
MP for Castleford,
c/o The House of Westminster,
London

Dear Sir,

As you are the MP for the constituency of Cranston and its surrounds, I am writing to ask for a meeting with you to discuss the progress of the war and its repercussions on the life of the village and of my school, the Shadworth Quaker School, which, as you are aware, is within the boundaries of your constituency.

As headmaster at the school, I am deeply disturbed by the reports of the treatment of deserters at the front. Shooting frightened young men is, it seems to me, absolutely inexcusable.

I would like your views on the matter and look forward to your reply.

Yours faithfully,

Philip Manners, Headmaster.

To this letter, so carefully worded, there was no immediate reply. However, Philip did receive a missive from Military Headquarters.

Military Headquarters,
Aldershot

August 19th, 1915

Mr Philip Manners,
Headmaster,
Shadworth Quaker School,
Shadworth,
Yorkshire

Dear Sir,
Thank you for your letter of concern on the subject of our treatment of deserters. We have taken note of your comments.

There is, in fact, no possibility of changing the rules that have been clearly outlined in these circumstances. They are carefully considered and in fact most necessary. To allow a soldier to behave in this cowardly manner would be to open the floodgates for all other men in the same state of mind. Our army would be quickly decimated, as many of our troops suffer the same fears and might see the opportunity to desert as an easy option.

As a result, sir, I hope that you will be able to see the rationale behind the court martial procedures and, though we regret the loss of life this involves, we see no other solution at present.

Yours faithfully,
W.H. Graham (Brigadier)

On receiving this cursory reply, Philip despaired at the deep inadequacy of their response.

Chapter 13

The weeks had scurried by since his visit to London, and now, at last, the day was dawning for the special memorial he had so diligently ordered. The Latimers were due to arrive on the ten to three into Shadworth; the bishop was already ensconced in Philip's sitting room with Harriet and his wife. As expected, his father-in-law looked clearly angry at the small part he had been asked to fulfil. Philip noticed the pronounced redness around his collar and felt his father-in-law's irritability had grown more marked than ever. Indeed, Philip wondered if he should enquire after his health or at the very least mention his concern to Harriet. But he knew she would not countenance any reference to her father's appearance even if it came from concern for him. Harriet was busily reinforcing her father's annoyance at Philip's order of service and was fussing round him. But she was certainly not going to miss out on the welcome party at the station for she enjoyed her status in such situations. She liked to play the Lady of the Manor.

Meanwhile, Emma, Florence, and Jack, with Maggie beside them, had wheeled the bicycles laden with the afternoon tea requisites and delivered them to Cook. Philip had studiously kept his door shut on those proceedings, acutely aware that they were going on but so busy putting the final touches to the service that he had no spare minute to leave his desk. Besides, he knew Harriet would be checking on the contents of the trays with her usual air of superiority. That, he could not bear to behold.

By lunch time, with that part of her job done, Emma had hastily donned her station uniform and cycled to the station. She was on duty on the platform for the arrival of the afternoon trains and for this one very important train. She had slaved over her hot oven to complete the orders and now regretted her promise to Mr Firbank that she could manage the afternoon rota despite having to return to the school to help serve the tea afterwards.

She watched as Philip and his wife arrived on the platform, noting her hand on his arm in that possessive way she always did when in public. Philip looked anxious and tense as they waited and barely glanced along the platform as if he knew it was important to maintain the part he had to play. Once again, Emma felt the familiar pang of anguish at the impossibility of their situation and the almost uncontrollable urge to run to him.

But the train was pulling in and out stepped the Latimers with several other members of their family to be greeted effusively by Mrs Manners as Philip stood aside. He took Daniel's mother by the arm and led her gently towards the waiting cab.

She looks so drawn and hopeless, thought Emma, and recognised the same emotion as she herself was suffering—the longing for a son that would never come back. She stifled a cry and squared her shoulders. She must fulfil her duty here, then hasten back to school to don her waitress apron.

I am one uniform and then another, she thought. *But I will not allow myself to succumb to this sense that I have no worth in all the parts I play. I'm not giving in to all this agony. I refuse to go under like Hardy's Tess. My anchor will hold.*

In the school hall, Miss Hanson felt immensely proud of her head that evening. He led the memorial with such dignity, speaking eloquently about the character of Daniel and then kept the silence—a silence pregnant with the spirit of God. Finally, as if recalling the image of Daniel to everyone's mind, he read the words of John's gospel which left not one eye dry:

"*In my Father's house are many mansions. I am going to prepare a place for you—if it were not so, I would have told you.*"

Then he stopped and looked around the huge gathering of those who had come especially for Daniel's sake and said almost in a whisper, "These are the words of promise for you, Daniel. We can be at peace now for you are at peace."

Next up was the bishop who made his speech about honour and the empire. Kath saw Jack Holt take a grip of his wife's hand and shake his head.

Yes, thought Kath. *The bishop's idea of honour and the head's are two quite different things. And Jack's son, George, had his own honour in refusing to be blindfolded to face the firing squad. Jack told me that, and I know he could do without having to listen to the bishop glorifying the violence.*

Indeed, her headmaster, true to his beliefs, came to the rescue and led the company in the Lord's Prayer as the final act of the ceremony.

As they left the hall, Philip stood at the door with the Latimers by his side, thanking all the guests for coming. At this point Harriet and her parents stood back for the Latimers, then they all filed into the school dining room where the feast had been spread by Emma and the others enlisted to be helpers. And what a feast it was. The company were amazed at what lay before them, and even Harriet had to grudgingly admit that that Holt woman had done them proud.

"Will you come and meet Cook and the lady who provided the delicacies for today, Mr Latimer? She and her husband lost their son at the front too," said Philip, steering them towards where Emma and Jack were serving the tea with Cook.

"Come, Philip," protested Harriet. "The Holts have a son who was shot for desertion in very different circumstances from Daniel. Surely the Latimers will not wish to meet them. Daniel could never be accused of cowardice."

The words were meant for Philip alone, but Emma overheard, and her cheeks, crimson already from the effort of the mammoth day, turned burningly scarlet. Philip's heart turned over with that piteous look, and his fury at Harriet was barely controllable. The Latimers saw his lips pursed in anger and turned away embarrassed without a backward glance at the Holts while Philip wrenched Harriet's elbow and drew her aside.

"You do not speak to anyone with such contempt in my hearing," he said, the rage still boiling inside. "You have lessened all that we prayed for in the memorial, and it is unforgivable."

"You talk of unforgivable? You who dared to slap my face? Leave me alone." Harriet hurried to her father's side who, fortunately, had missed the encounter.

Emma, standing behind the serving table, watched as she stormed away. She felt the unutterable shame and sadness of it all over again, standing there silently whilst wishing the ground might swallow her up. Philip knew it and frowned with frustration.

The moment was saved in the end by the parents of young Charlie Hopton, come down from Northumberland to support the Latimers.

"Is this the lady and gentleman to whom we owe so much for cheering up our Charlie?" came a soft Northumbrian burr beside Philip. He jumped and quickly pulled himself together. There stood a round, rosy-cheeked woman and a burly man smiling at him and looking towards the serving table.

He led them thankfully to the Holts where Emma was standing, still in some kind of reverie.

"Mrs Holt, can I interrupt your thoughts to introduce you to Charlie Hopton's parents?" he asked, hoping to move her thoughts back to the moment. The kindly couple grasped Emma's hands and thanked her so kindly for what she had done for their young son. Philip watched as she straightened her shoulders and acknowledged them, back to her indomitable self and the mask of assurance.

"It was Jack's idea really," said Emma. "But he did love my Yorkshire puddings. He was a pleasure to entertain and must come again if Mr Manners will let him?" she said, looking at last at the man who stood beside them. She managed a smile again, and he saw it with much relief.

"We shall have to see. What do you say, Jack?" said Philip. But Jack only grinned his agreement.

"We have heard about your son, Mrs Holt," said Charlie's father. "We are so deeply sorry to hear of it. We wonder what the world is coming to when our own soldiers kill each other."

"You are absolutely right," responded Philip. "There is everything to understand about running away from sheer terror. When will humanity comprehend that?"

"God knows, and only He can bring us all back to sweet reason, Mr Manners. You must believe that or all hope dies," said the good old farmer.

"Thank you for your kind words," said Emma. "But, Mr Manners, you must look after your other guests now. I can see that the Latimers are preparing to leave for their lodgings for the night. As for us, we must begin to clear up now. Mrs Hopton, if you will forgive us."

With one last glance at Philip, she and Cook began the huge task before them. He'd returned her look with such sadness in his eyes that she'd felt the pain of it like a physical wound. He limped slowly back to where the Latimers were standing, now with Harriet and her father. She allowed herself one more look and saw once again his gentle dignity, that quiet strength that had won her love despite herself. She watched as he took Mrs Latimer, weeping now, by both hands, talking softly to her with words of comfort. The bishop was looking on with a look somewhat resembling disdain, but Harriet was busily negotiating the couple to the hall door, back in the part of headmaster's wife, though she kept her eyes averted from her husband while she made much of bustling around them.

To work now, thought Emma, and picked back up the remnants of the day.

Philip knew the ice in his relationship with Harriet had hardened even further during the course of his protest, but he hid his feelings successfully in order to give the proper attention to the bereaved and grieving couple. As they left, they were profuse in their thanks for his service of them and for Daniel. He felt very humble in the face of such praise, but he sensed the bishop's cynical eyes on him as they departed.

"Well, Philip. They certainly appreciated your efforts, though I thought you could have done so much more to project the needs of the war effort this evening," said his father-in-law. "And Harriet tells me she is ready for a break from the business of your school. She is going to come home with Mother and me for a rest. I trust you have no objections?"

"Of course not," he replied. "We will manage the beginning of the new school year until she feels able to return." Harriet gave him then a look of such venom that he felt the poison of it seeping into his bones. Remorse, yes, but he could not help sensing a relief at the thought of her absence, though he recognised it as a dangerous thought.

Thus, the evening sank into night as all returned to their places of rest. Emma and Jack were very late back to Holt House, having helped with the clearing up. They retrieved their trays and slogged their way back with them on the panniers of their bicycles. Emma felt such weariness as she crawled into bed next to Jack that she could hardly speak. She was glad of his nearness. Through all the years of their marriage, she had loved him, and knowing his love for her, she determined to remain faithful to him from here forward.

"Jack, thank you for tonight. I couldn't have done it alone. But, Jack, what a vile woman Mr Manners is married to. She humiliated me in front of the Latimers, insinuating George was a coward. How could the head have got such a wife?"

She slept soundly as soon as her head touched the pillow. Jack smiled to himself, thankful that she could show such resilience despite all that had happened and all the issues they were facing. And, fortunately, he was completely secure in his ignorance of what lay in Emma's innermost heart.

Chapter 14

Harriet and her family had left for Worcester the day after the memorial service when the Latimers and all the other guests had departed. It had become suddenly very silent in the school and its beautiful grounds, though it was merely the lull before the storm. Philip Manners allowed the quiet to sink deep into his soul. He knew he had honoured Daniel Latimer to his own satisfaction, and though he did not even admit it to himself, the absence of his accusatory wife was liberating. There was time to get ready for the onset of the hordes of boys who would be descending soon enough.

He limped slowly to the fingerpost and stood lost in thought for a while, wishing things could be different, picturing Emma Holt in his imagination as his own, then subduing the dream before it took any real shape. He looked down towards Low Shadworth but did not venture there, submitting himself to his own discipline.

Thus, the days sped to the beginning of September and the new term at the Quaker School. The three heads of the school houses arrived the day before the onslaught, and he held a staff meeting with them, reviewing the needs that would occur and the list of the new boys who would be allotted to them. Each house would receive twenty new first-year boys to make up their full quota of one hundred and forty boys each. Among the names they reviewed that day, they saw several boys whose brothers were in school already or who had left to take up university places. To their great sadness, they each remembered that many of those who had left would now be not at university as they had hoped but in France, serving in the trenches.

As Alan Lorimer, Head of Ayton House, commented that day, "God forbid that any more should be dying out there like young Latimer." Jim Fletcher nodded in agreement and sat quietly in deep sorrow.

"I did not teach my students how to kill when I took them through the methods of calculus," remarked Edna Wright.

"My friends," said Philip, "Despite these grim reminders, we must look forward in hope. We will teach them how to be courageous in whatever they have to face, please, God."

His colleagues smiled at his steady reassurances, and they all worked hard to feel prepared for the next day. In the adjoining room, Kath Hanson listened as she typed and once again thanked her good fortune to work with such a headmaster. She was anxious that he was alone in his house at the start of such a notoriously busy period and wondered, not for the first time, how he had managed to be married to Mrs Harriet Manners. Kath sometimes wished she was ten years younger for she felt sure she would have known how to make him happier. She herself had never married and had been content to remain a spinster, dedicated to her work at her beloved school.

The boys arrived, and the autumn term began. Philip and his staff barely had time to breathe on those first weeks of settling back down to work. The routine of the houses was re-established, the boys were allotted to their dormitories, and classes began in earnest very quickly. Philip visited each house at lights-out time to help his colleagues establish the pattern of the school day and found himself eating in the different house dining rooms nearly every evening. He thought to himself that at least this way he need not cook when he finally retired for the night. That was perhaps the loneliest moment—when he thought of how Jack Holt would be sitting at the table with Emma. He had chatted with Jack as he'd walked through the gardens one morning. Jack had been on his knees, planting spring bulbs well in advance of himself as usual.

"How are you, Mr Manners? I hear you are on your own at the moment. But these young scoundrels will be keeping you busy, I'm sure. Have you had any more news of your boys out there?"

"No, nothing from the boys as yet, Jack, but I'm praying we hear nothing but good news. There seems to be a bit of a lull out there at the moment, according to reports. They are gaining very little territory and the enemy is still holding on to Ypres despite all our troops' efforts. I dread to think how many lives are being wasted just to get a few yards nearer the enemy trenches, and they are using gas when they retaliate, we are told. It's difficult to bear."

"It drives Emma nearly wild to think of Will in the middle of it all, but thankfully, he is staying safe. I pray to God he stays that way, sir."

"I share your prayers, Jack. Please pass on my good wishes to Mrs Holt. She may be getting a request to do the staff laundry soon, I suspect. I heard them muttering to that effect last evening."

"Just let her know, sir. She'll gladly do it for them."

Philip just nodded in assent and headed slowly back up to his study, feeling that old sense of incredulity that such a love had grown between Emma and himself, unasked and now irrevocable. What on earth could he do about it? Maybe if she brought the laundry back, he might get a word with her.

But it was not to be, as commitments to staff with discipline troubles and constant meetings piled on top of him, giving him no leeway or rest. His main and only pleasure during these weeks was his new class of sixth-formers who were studying for their Highers in English Literature with a syllabus of Shakespeare and the Metaphysical poets. He had studied John Donne while at Oxford and had a lifelong admiration for his poetry which he delighted in passing on to his class. The eight boys studying with him soaked up every moment of his wise teaching and adored his lessons. Alan Lorimer's history students were envious of them, and they loved the rivalry between the groups.

And Emma, toiling over the steaming hot, soapy water, peggy-sticking the washing and ironing it all with careful precision over the tucks and bows, thought wistfully once again, *Is this what I amount to? Is this all I am allowed of him? If only I could stand beside him and let the world think what it pleases.*

No, you stupid woman! Have a little sense. How have you embarked on this hopeless relationship? What an utter fool you are to dream such dreams.

If she could have only sat at his feet and shared those lessons of his, she would have gloried in the opportunity, for though she never paraded it, she lacked no intellectual acumen. Of course, his love for her had recognised this truth in its inception. Some deep instinct in them both had propelled them towards each other.

The weeks rolled by, and October came in on a rush of heavy gales and with them, the return of Harriet. She made her presence felt very quickly in her usual regal manner, checking on the heads of houses and the new first-year boys as if she had never been away. Edna Wright was heard to remark to Jim Fletcher that she never could feel any warmth emanating from her towards the boys and what a pity that was.

"There's no hope of that." Jim had laughed. "You know that ice runs through her veins, Edna."

It was certainly true that Harriet was so completely unlike her husband whose affection for every boy was obvious to all his staff. Yet she was very friendly with some of the younger women staff and set up her little cosy group of them again, meeting at her house to drink tea and sew garments to send out to France. Kath Hanson was never invited to join them, and though it made her feel her age in being excluded, she was glad not to be favoured by such a woman. Kath's loyalty was all for her headmaster. She knew his main pleasure lay in his teaching, and she noticed his reluctance to leave for home each evening and grieved for him. She had been his secretary for all ten years of his headship, and she sensed the restraint in his relationship with Harriet who consistently demonstrated a complete lack of warmth towards him.

Why is she so merciless towards him? she asked herself.

As half-term approached, however, a surprise visitor arrived at Philip's study, no less a person than Mr Tempest of Tempest Farm—that farm young Charlie Hopton had visited many months back. His request was quite simple. Would Mr Manners allow some of his students to use the half-term holiday to come down to Low Shadworth and help him with his potato picking? It was a tradition well-known to the local folk and, indeed, well-loved by all. Ronald Tempest was very short of labourers thanks to the war taking some of his village lads.

"They'll have a jolly time of it if you'll let them come, Mr Manners, and it would surely benefit them. Get some colour in their pale cheeks. Ask Jack Holt—his sons used to come and share in it in their time. And my wife will put on a spread for them all at the end of the day. What do you say?"

Kath was listening to this hearty invitation, and she smiled to herself as Philip stammered a reply.

"Why, Mr Tempest, I shall have to ask my heads of house if they are willing to agree to this, but I must say, the idea seems to have a lot of merit. Can I let you know my answer tomorrow when I have had a chance to ask them all?"

"Aye, sir. I look forward to your agreeing to it. I could certainly do with a bit of help, as there are fields of potatoes awaiting digging and sending out." Farmer Tempest shook Philip's hand and strode out of the study.

Philip turned to Kath. "Well, well, Miss Hanson. Shall I say yes? Do you think the others will agree? It seems a lovely idea."

As Kath nodded, he left with a positive energy she had not seen from him in some time. After speaking to his colleagues, they all gave their agreement enthusiastically. Jim Fletcher was especially pleased. He had spent his boyhood on a farm and still persisted in taking long country walks every weekend around the country lanes outlying Shadworth. Everyone he met recognised him as one of the heads of year at the school, but Jim had no airs and always had a cheery smile and time for a chat as he passed by. The boys had a great fondness for Mr Fletcher, and Philip knew he would join in the potato picking with gusto. He also knew for certain Charlie Hopton would be pleased and could not help the thought that Emma might be part of the scheme. At the prospect, he felt a lifting of the sadness he was carrying in his own situation.

Chapter 15

With the ready agreement of his colleagues, Philip was able to promise Mr Tempest that some of his boys would help him out, and it was arranged that the farmer would send his largest cart to pick the volunteers up early on the morning of October twenty-second. He had begged Harriet to join them, but she had scorned his request.

"I am certainly not coming down to shiver all day with your students. I'm amazed that you've agreed to the whole enterprise. I shall entertain some of the church people with lunch at home. You can please yourself."

"So be it, my dear," he had answered regretfully wondering what he could possibly do to win back the old friendship they had enjoyed long ago.

The day dawned cold and clear. Autumn had certainly arrived, and the elms along the lanes had turned a magnificent golden-amber hue, though their leaves were falling fast in the freezing wind. Tempest's potato fields with their long furrows were well-frosted and lay open and pristine in their white icing blanket, ready for the fork. The rooks were cawing loudly overhead.

The boys were thrilled to be out in the open, and their heads of houses had ensured they were fitted out with scarves and gloves. Miss Wright had opted out of venturing down but the heads of Ayton and Fox houses and some of the younger staff had accompanied Philip and now stood on the edge of the field watching. Indeed, as Philip had predicted, Jim led some of them to join in the job alongside the boys, leaving their older colleagues behind. Alan Lorimer kept Philip company as he leaned heavily on his stick. His leg was throbbing painfully as if the cold had penetrated right through to the bone, but he would not flinch at it. No one must know he was struggling. Yet he was thankful for a coffee break when Mrs Tempest invited him into the warm farmhouse kitchen where he sipped the hot coffee thankfully.

Cook sent picnic parcels for everyone at lunch time, so it was a very happy gathering of all those who had worked hard all morning as they ate their lunches in the open air.

"It feels like holidays," said Jim Fletcher. "My mother used to pack up a picnic basket for the two of us on a sunny day after school to take down to the beach near our home. By, Philip, those were good days. I'd have them back in a shot." He stretched out his long legs on the grass and laughed. As it was, not one boy complained at the heavy work of heaving out the potatoes from the frost-laden furrows.

As the day wore on to dusk and the boys were gathering in the big barn for their well-earned supper, Philip looked up from Mrs Tempest's table with a jolt of his heart. There stood the Holts come to help with the festivities.

"Jack, Mrs Holt, this is a pleasant surprise. I didn't expect to see you here."

"Mr Manners, you must know you can't keep Emma away from a spot of cooking," said Jack, smiling. "Mary Tempest needed some help. It's a brave supper she's put on for your lads."

Emma barely looked at him as she donned her large white apron, for, indeed, she could hardly bear to see him again after the long weeks of absence. She thought she had managed to control her emotions but there he was, and she was once more trembling inwardly at the sight of him.

"I've just come to help out this time. Mary has plenty of food for you all. I'm just her slave for the evening," she told him as Mary Tempest scurried up to her, wiping her hot brow as she went. As she spoke, she could not prevent a blush of pleasure from appearing on her cheeks. She was hurried away to the farm kitchen from where the scent of a hearty stew was emanating.

"Come, come, Mr Manners and Mr Lorimer. And you, Mr Fletcher, let's go to the barn. The tables are set out for you all, and it's a veritable feast there." Jack smiled. Jim rubbed his hands together in anticipation. Jack led the way and the others followed, Philip slowly, wincing a little from his troublesome leg but with a kind of relief inside that this evening he would at least be in Emma's company.

The boys were already gathered around the long trestle tables, and there she was standing behind the serving table with Mrs Tempest, doling out huge bowlfuls of beef and parsnip stew. As he took the bowl offered to him, he looked straight at her, and she looked back, no longer able to resist. They exchanged a moment of understanding, unspoken and mutual, reminding each other without words that this inexplicable love they had had not gone away. After that, he was much cheered and was able to share with the boys and his colleagues with a lighter heart, joining in the merriment around the table with an abandon he rarely showed. She noticed it and rejoiced to see him happier. If he could bear it, so could she, though, in truth, it felt like a forlorn kind of hope.

"What a good idea this was," said Alan Lorimer. "It will have done the boys so much good." He hooted with laughter as young Charlie Hopton ran up to Mrs Holt and hugged her in a spontaneous act of appreciation. "Our gardener's wife must have some fans." He laughed.

"Didn't you know, Alan?" said Jim. "We're all her fans, I reckon. It's her baking that's so good."

"Yes, I believe so," answered Philip. "She does seem to be some kind of mother figure to Charlie." As he spoke, he wondered if he could possibly stand to be so close to her and yet so distant.

The evening came to a close with much applause for the cook and her helpers. The head stood up to give the vote of thanks, and in response, Ron Tempest got to his feet to give a toast to the boys of Shadworth School and their teachers. His gratitude for all their hard work knew no bounds. His potatoes were all gathered in, ready for sending out, and he was much relieved.

The farm cart drew up outside the barn and they all piled in. Last came Philip, and Ron Tempest shook him warmly by the hand.

"You'll come again, I hope, sir," he said, and Philip smiled in response. Out of the corner of his eye, he saw Jack Holt linking arms with Emma for their walk up the lane to their home.

Oh God, was all he could think as they pulled out of the yard. *Harriet will be wondering why we have been gone so long.*

Chapter 16

Winter descended on Shadworth and a quiet seemed to blanket the school and its inhabitants. Jack Holt maintained his garden there but there was little to do amongst the dead rose beds and mulching vegetation. The only sign that spring might not be far behind was the small buds on the camellia bushes surrounding the kitchen garden. Within the kitchen, Cook was serving up hot steaming stews to warm the boys' hearts. At Holt House, Emma busied herself with the laundry but allowed Florence to take it to the school without her so as to prevent any temptation which might conflict with her faithfulness to Jack.

On the Western front, there was something of a lull, disturbed by regular smatterings of mortar bombs and shelling from both sides. The trenches were riddled with mud, rats, and lice, and the young men within dreaded every new day as to what each might bring. Yet, despite all that, they managed to cheer their evenings with the grog supplied by the officers and with card games around the makeshift tables. Will, alone now without George and still grieving in his heart of hearts, had made friends with a young private from Cranston, Albert Jones, and the two shared talk of their families back home, remarking on how close Shadworth and Cranston were geographically.

"Did you ever go and play football in the Valley Gardens on Saturdays, Will? Me and my brothers used to join up with a few lads there and kick the ball around."

"Why, of course. Me, Harry, and George used to get the bus to Cranston with a picnic and get buns from Hagenbachs for afters. Do you remember Hagenbachs, Albert? Best cakes ever except for my mother's."

Laughing, the two of them would forget for a while their situation and take great delight in these memories.

Will was also very pleased when he was called in to his captain's inner sanctum to be told he was to be awarded a stripe, making him a lance corporal and thereby taking more responsibility for the others. He hadn't believed that possible after his brother's disgrace and felt a qualm of guilt that he could be pleased to be awarded by those same superiors who had treated George so cruelly. But he wrote home with this information to Emma and Jack, and it eased, for a little while, the tight band of anxiety and pain that Emma carried within. It also healed something of Jack's wounded pride after what he still felt, certainly in the eyes of the world, was George's disgrace.

In school, Philip found himself teaching English to lower school classes. His young recruit to the department, Miss Kenning, had never quite mastered the use of effective discipline and was still having some difficulties. More than a few of Miss Kenning's reprobates had found themselves sitting outside Philip's study, anxiously awaiting his ticking off, though it was nearly always gentler than they'd expected and they often found themselves promising to be better in spite of themselves.

As well as that, his sixth form literature groups, lower and upper, needed much preparation time, so in the evenings he often had to study which gave Harriet yet another excuse to accuse him of neglect. He often felt overwhelmed by the stress of all the work, yet doing it was a salve to his inner torment.

Not only was his teaching making heavy demands on him but also the pastoral needs of the boys. Miss Wright summoned him late one night to her house block where Matron was desperately trying to wake up and bring back to reality a young first-year in the deep throes of a nightmare. The other boys in his dormitory were fast asleep, but he was crying out so loudly that it astonished Philip that they had not woken. He sat at the child's bedside and gently stroked his small clenched fist until it gradually unfurled. He spoke very quietly and soothingly as he sat until the cries faded and the little one opened his eyes. Then Philip took him into his arms and cuddled him in silence while the sobs subsided. The two women stood by watching, much relieved that the head had managed what they could not.

"Jacob, can you tell me all about it?" he asked once he could see the child was recovering, having withdrawn him to Edna's own suite of rooms.

Slowly, Jacob told him how he had heard from home that day that his big brother in France had died from a wound on the Front. He had been dreaming about it in terror. And yet, waking, again there was nothing to alleviate the hard and awful fact of the death. Matron brought him hot chocolate, and as he sipped, the three looked at each other, shaking their heads at the unspeakable horror of war and the human waste of it. But young Jacob's head was by now drooping against Philip's shoulder and so he carried him back to the dormitory and laid him back down on his bed, tucking him in lovingly. As Edna Wright watched and then shook his hand gratefully, she thanked her lucky stars that this man was more than adequate to his role. But little did she realise how much pain he was enduring in his leg as he carried Jacob without the support of his stick.

Returning to his own house, he was greeted by Harriet with something of her old affection for him as she brought him his own hot drink and sympathised with the story he told her. It was reassuring that her affection had not completely died. When his leg was first damaged by the cycling accident in Salisbury, she had played the part of a warm and loving wife for a while, and that memory was cheering. He could never betray her again—a thought that gave him no pleasure.

In Low Shadworth, Emma too had to comfort one in distress. Mr Firbank called on her one morning near to tears with the news that his only grandson had enlisted, lying about his age to do so.

"He's only a boy, Mrs Holt. Sixteen years old and they took him at his word he was eighteen. My wife and his mother are beside themselves. And here am I supposed to run a railway station."

Emma put on her winter coat and made up a basket of cakes she had baked half an hour earlier before taking his arm and ushering him out of the house. She walked him back to the station master's house and hurried to Mrs Firbank and her daughter. She put on the kettle herself and made a huge pot of scalding hot tea which she forced into each of their hands.

"Drink this and take courage, my dears." She smiled meekly. "We must all keep up our brave faces for the sake of the lads. Believe me, I know it's not easy." After offering her words of encouragement, she simply sat beside them and stayed with them till they had recovered themselves.

Jack couldn't help but smile when she later told him what she had done. "You think your cakes are the answers to the world's ills, my Emma. Will you never stop trying to hold the world up for everyone? Never mind, lass, you seem to work some magic with them."

"Oh Jack! You hold too much store by me." To which Jack grinned in his old homely way.

As winter proceeded, it cast its white mantle over the village. It had a strange beauty of its own. The high elms with the rooks' nests topping them in assorted twiggy patterns against the skyline; the barren hedgerows save for the occasional drooping heads of a few late haws, their red darkening to black; the cattle in Tempest's fields snorting their white breath out into the icy air, huddled beneath the bare trees; the mist of the frosted air hovering above the lanes all contributed to the sense of stillness that was replicated in the lives of Emma and Jack, of Philip and his school.

The term passed into December with the weight of work unremitting. Philip was, however, suffering increasingly from his crippled leg which he had taxed too hard in carrying young Jacob. An infection had set into the troubled knee and walking became increasingly difficult. The cold had somehow bitten deep into the kneecap and chilled the whole leg. Harriet—in a shrill, unsympathetic mood—forced him to go to Doctor Thomson, afraid that she might find herself coping with an invalid.

"Go, for goodness' sake, will you? What am I to do if you collapse? You are so stubborn and so self-willed, Philip. You think of nothing but your job and the boys. You neglect yourself and have no concern for my feelings."

"Harriet, you know that to be untrue. But I must keep up till at least the end of term. I am needed in every area of school, as you well know." He sighed and found himself yet again wondering how his wife could have lost all sense of the old, easy relationship they'd once had. Indeed, he could not help but think how unfair her accusation of him was in light of his attempts to mend things between them and her complete refusal to acquiesce. He shrugged the thought off quickly as unworthy, but he had to admit that he did indeed need a doctor.

"Very well, I will go and see Leonard Thomson and see if he can give me anything for the pain."

He retreated to his study to find the kinder ministrations of Kath Hanson there who took one look at him and rang the doctor herself straight away. She confided to Jack Holt that the head was going to kill himself if he did not rest—a fact that reached Emma as Jack sat down to his supper.

"What do you mean, Jack? Has he seen Dr Thomson? Can you speak to him and remind him no one is indispensable? That wife of his should be insisting he rest."

Jack looked at her oddly at this outburst and promised he would do his best, though he felt it wasn't perhaps his place to advise the head. Nevertheless, he knew Philip thought of him as a friend.

The next day, Kath Hanson found herself answering the door to him. Philip was at his desk, pale as a shadow and clearly in pain. He assured Jack he had aspirin to dull the pain and he would be back to normal soon, but Kath, listening from her desk, shook her head as Jack looked back at her. That one look prompted Jack into action.

"Mr Manners, sir. I'm going to accompany you home to rest. I've heard these things don't work unless a person rests. Let me help you." Without waiting for a reply, he and Kath helped Philip to his feet as he winced with pain and protested. Giving him his stick, Jack helped him to the door and half carried him along the path to his own front door. There, he paused, and as Harriet appeared, Jack took his courage in both hands as he spoke.

"Mrs Manners, Miss Hanson and I feel the head needs to stay in bed till he recovers from this attack. Forgive me for delivering him home." Jack fled, hoping against hope she would rise to the occasion.

I know damn well what she thinks of us villagers and of what happened to our George. But she can think what

*she likes of me. I don't give a tinker's cuss. Just so long
as she looks after the head.*

Harriet, appalled that this mere gardener was inter-
fering in her family business, pulled Philip into the
house and slammed the door.

"I told you this would happen. How demeaning that
you let yourself be helped home by that man." As she
spoke, she saw that her husband was close to fainting
and at last rose to the occasion. She laid him on his bed
and rustled around the room in a quandary as to what
to do. He watched her with a half-smile on his face
but could not speak. As she administered the doctor's
prescription, he nodded his thanks and fell asleep. She
hastily left his room and ran back to her sitting room
thankfully. She knew she was guilty, over the twenty
years of their marriage, of losing much of the love she
once had for him, and she felt a huge antipathy to the
thought that she must play the part of a compassionate wife, at least till he recovered.

There was a knock on the door. Miss Hanson had
called the doctor again, and he hurried past her into
the hallway. A swift examination of the leg and Dr
Thomson wasted no more time.

"Mrs Manners, if we do not make Mr Manners rest
his leg, he will lose it. I think he should be in hospital,
and I've called for an ambulance to come from
Cranston. I'm so sorry, but a quiet stay will allow the

correct medication to do its work. Do you under-stand?" he asked as she stood dumbly before him.

Pulling herself together, she nodded and followed his instructions to pack a small suitcase for her husband to take with him to Cranston Infirmary. And so, with that, Philip was forced to admit defeat and allow them to take him. He resisted weakly but had no energy to do more. He was relieved to see Alan Lorimer and Jim Fletcher, two of his stalwart heads of house, called in something of a panic by Kath, watching as they loaded the stretcher into the ambulance.

"Philip, have no worries about school or your classes. It's nearly the end of term anyway. We will take charge till you are better, and we shall manage very well with a little adapting of the timetable," said Jim.

"We'll have you back to normal in no time, sir," added Alan. "Your sixth-formers can work on their own at revision; it will do them no harm. Get well, sir."

Jack was watching from a distance as they drove off and could not help feeling a little surprised that Mrs Manners had not offered to go in the ambulance with him but rather had shaken the doctor's hand and retreated into the house as they all left.

"Emma will be up in arms when I tell her," he thought, knowing that had it been him in that situation, she would have cosseted him and cared for him without stint.

That evening, Jack shocked Emma with his news; news she had awaited anxiously throughout the day for about the man with whom she had so carelessly and irresistibly allowed herself to fall in love. But now she knew it, she was horrified and consumed with fears for him. Moreover, she was careless in her way of responding to this news.

"Jack, do you think I might take some of my baking to the infirmary? Oh, Jack, how could his wife not accompany him? Will you come with me tomorrow? We could take the two o'clock bus and be there for a little time during visiting hours? What do you say?"

Jack looked back at her, half-comprehending something of what she was feeling but resisting its implications. He tried to clear his head to rid himself of such an unwanted thought. And he felt indulgent, especially in the light of Harriet Manners' complete lack of warmth, compared to which his Emma was like a flaming and dynamic force for good.

"Very well, Emma. But if he has other visitors, we must hold back."

Had Jack known what was in Philip's heart as he lay there with his knee swathed in antiseptic-soaked bandages, allowing the nurses to dress his leg at carefully timed intervals, he would have been much more unwilling to let her have her way. For Philip, in a steady state of drug-induced relaxation, was dreaming of

Jack's wife as if she were next to him and belonged to him. It was a fantasy he denied himself every day in his rightful state, but his present condition had allowed him to throw discipline to the wind for this brief time.

The next day, as the worst of the pain was easing, he had a stream of visitors from the staff at school. Edna Wright had appeared with a bunch of grapes and an assurance that all was well in Applegarth house, including young Jacob, of whom he enquired anxiously. Kath Hanson arrived with a handful of notes penned by a few organised sixth-formers wishing him well and promising him they were revising. When he laughed at one of the messages, she could tell he was gradually returning to his old self, and her heart lifted. Harriet had appeared early but left, making the excuse she had a meeting with her staff seamstresses.

So, he was at last alone in his private room when Jack and Emma walked in. Emma had a firm grip on herself as she approached the bed, but her heart melted as he looked up at her and she saw the heavily bandaged knee.

"Oh God, Mr Manners, what have you been doing? Jack has told me all about it. I've brought you some little cakes to cheer you up. What have the doctors said? Does it pain you very much?" All this spilled out of her as she looked at him, and he could not resist taking her hand for a second. Then he remembered Jack watching them and turned away to him.

"Jack, had it not been for you and Kath, it might have been too late to remedy this leg of mine. But the doctors say the antiseptics are beginning to conquer the infection and they will not need to keep me too much longer. Thank you, Jack. I'll always be in your debt. And it's kind of you both to come."

Her heart was pounding, as was his, as they looked at each other, and the pain of their hidden understanding struck them both forcibly at that moment—the man whom she so admired and loved, the woman he held in the highest esteem and wanted for his own. And there between them, a lifetime of a marriage and a man they both in their own way cared for and respected standing beside them.

Jack said rather gruffly, "Well, Mr Manners, get well soon. The school cannot go on for long without you. Term will soon be over, and Christmas is coming. Emma, we must go if we are to catch the bus home. Are you ready?"

There were tears in her eyes as she leaned down to him at last and touched his forehead with her lips. Then she straightened her shoulders, turned to Jack, and took his hand as they left the ward. Philip lay back on his pillows and prayed for sufficient grace to help him see this through.

Jack did not speak in the bus on the way home, for that unwanted thought had once again struck him. His loyalty to Emma had never faltered, and he believed her loyalty to him was just as sure. But he could not help but wonder as to the level of concern Emma had shown Mr Manners by his bedside; a concern which he would have perfectly understood, had it not been for the look that was exchanged between them. That look revealed perhaps more than they realised.

My God, thought Jack, *Emma belongs to me. No one may surely dare come between us.*

He remained noticeably wordless throughout the rest of the evening, much to Emma's concern, but finally dismissed the disturbing thought as only his imagination.

There is no one more honourable than the head. I am mad to think such stupid thoughts.

Emma, noticing how quiet he was, made sure to give him loving attention as she snuggled up to him that night. It was easy for her, as she had never rationed her love for Jack in the face of her love for Philip. It was as if the two emotions were in quite separate compartments in her heart. And neither man was in any way betrayed by that particular truth.

Winter had taken its grim toll on them all. A weakened Philip was sent home after five more days of recuperation—a time that had seemed most wearisome to him—and now, at last, the school, a living organism, could breathe again. Once more, the regime of discipline descended on both Emma and Philip. Jack Holt relaxed into his secure routine again. And Miss Hanson brought news to Philip's study a few days later that gave them all a refreshing sense of hope.

Chapter 17

The reception Philip had received on his return had overwhelmed him, and despite having to resort to two sticks instead of one for the time being, he was thoroughly heartened. As he visited each house during evening meal, the boys cheered him, to his embarrassment, and Edna, Alan, and Jim encouraged them. Best of all was the visit of his Upper Sixth class.

"Mr Manners, sir, would you believe we've been working really hard? Here are our essays on George Herbert you set us before you were ill. All complete." The boys all brandished the finished products in front of him, grinning.

"My, oh my. You wouldn't have finished them yet if I hadn't had to leave you to it. Thank you. Now you can go home for Christmas and begin work on Donne." He laughed as they all groaned.

The invitation that arrived a few days later was addressed to the headmaster and his staff. It was a summons to a Christmas dance at the home of Miss

Hollingsworth—the grand old lady of Shadworth—and was to take place after the end of term when school would be quiet at last. Philip's own feelings were muted on the subject, so aware was he of the weakness in his leg, but everyone else from Cook to Harriet was enchanted at the prospect of a proper Christmas party. It would be the opportunity for the village aristocracy to engage socially with the school community, and as Kath Hanson put it,

"Miss Hollingsworth is quite the lady of the manor, and she will know how to put on a feast. I expect she will engage Hagenbachs to cater. Mrs Holt will be spared for once."

At mention of Emma, Philip was jolted into action.

"Yes, Kath. Let Jack know the Holts are included, will you? Perhaps they would like to bring their daughter with them."

At home, he was surprised at Harriet's enthusiasm for the project, as her usual response was a lack-lustre attitude to all things social relating to school. But not this time.

"I shall buy myself a new dress for this occasion. To be able to dance again after being shut up with you all term will do my heart good." This comment left its usual cold grip on his heart, but he allowed it to pass without analysis. The thought that he and Emma might be together for at least a short time was enough to ease its bitterness. It would not matter that he couldn't actually join in the dancing.

Meanwhile, in Low Shadworth, there was also excitement. The villagers all knew and respected Miss Hollingsworth, and many of them were invited irrespective of their wealth. At Holt House, Florence was thrilled to be asked, and Emma promised herself one night of pure pleasure, letting go of her usual iron grip on her emotions for once, knowing she would not have to bake and slave over the hot stove.

This, of course, provoked thoughts of what to wear. Unlike Harriet, there was no money to spare for fripperies in her household, but if nothing else, Florence must have a pretty dress and, just perhaps, she might manage to sew one for herself. So, she went to her bedroom drawer where she kept any good material she had managed to buy off the market and dug out a length of pale blue muslin and some dark green taffeta. Between them, there might be just enough to make two dresses. She had inherited her ancient sewing machine from Jack's mother, and she got to work with a will.

When she fitted the blue muslin onto Florence's girlish figure, she was proud of her efforts, and Florence could not believe her good fortune. Florence was developing into a lithe and lovely young woman. Her curly hair would not be disciplined but she pulled it back and fixed it in a bun with hairpins. Her dimpled cheeks with their smattering of freckles made a pretty picture, and Florence was especially pleased when her father stopped in his tracks and admired her as Emma looked on proudly.

As for Emma's green taffeta, it was a close fit—tight around her waist and low in the neckline to squeeze every last inch from the material. But Jack's look when she and Florence did a mannequin parade for him just a day before the party was enough to assure her that she and Florence could disport themselves in any company. Emma felt satisfied that she looked like the lady she intended to be the following night.

With a thought that was unworthy of her, she thought of Harriet Manners and prayed that whatever Harriet wore would not compete with her own dress. She admonished herself for the thought immediately and reminded herself of her promise to be extra loving towards Philip's wife. However, she had determined that for one night, she would indeed feel free to enjoy herself and so she prepared.

She did not forget Maggie who was feeling very forlorn at Harry's absence and her own increasing waistline. She was drawing close to the birth now and did not feel she could attend the party with them all, but her mother and Emma conspired to make her a special meal to enjoy while they were away, and Florence promised to bring her all the gossip back from the evening. Maggie's resilience in her pregnancy was truly admirable, and Emma had grown to love her as her own daughter in the months that had passed since Harry's departure. She and Mrs Granger had also grown close since the marriage of their children.

At last, the evening arrived, and the hansom cabs were drawing up in Miss Hollingsworth's long drive, bringing the delighted staff from the school and Harriet and Philip themselves. Even Kath Hanson had bought herself a cherry red, woollen dress and looked every inch Philip's proud secretary. The heads of houses were resplendent in their evening dress, though Harriet outdid them all in a long, golden silk gown and necklace given to her by Philip many years earlier. The memory of that gift and her pleasure when she'd received it struck him painfully. But he had congratulated her on her beauty before they'd left, and she had warmed in her manner towards him at least a little as he limped slowly into the great hall with her beside him and only a single stick at last.

The villagers had mostly walked, but Leonard Thomson and his wife had come in their very smart new automobile which fascinated Jack as they approached the front door. Miss Hollingsworth greeted everyone and led them into the feast spread out on long white tablecloths. Hagenbachs of Cranston had excelled themselves, and they all tucked in heartily. The dance hall itself was festooned with garlands of pink, white and cream, interspersed with huge wreaths of holly and ivy. It was truly magnificent, all agreed. Florence let out a breath of wonder. Only Emma was unmoved, searching for a sight of Philip, whom alone she wanted to see.

The repast complete, the musicians began to play as the couples dispersed themselves around the floor. Florence blushed crimson with delight as farmer Tempest's son, Ned, asked her to dance. Emma had to smile to herself as she watched but then her eyebrows shot up as she saw Mrs Manners dancing with a tall and incredibly attractive younger man; one she had never seen before.

"Who is that man dancing with the head's wife?" she asked Jack, who was about to lead her onto the floor.

"That's the deputy head of Fox House who's been newly appointed for next term. He must have arrived early. Geography, I think. Mrs Manners certainly has made his acquaintance," replied Jack as he swung Emma into the dance.

Emma sought a sight of Philip as she was whirled around, and then at last, she spotted him. He was standing with Miss Hanson, leaning hard on his stick against one of the huge pillars that supported the high ceiling. His face was a study as he watched. She felt cut to the quick as she read his mind. She knew he would be watching for her but that he would not be able to avoid the sight of his wife flirting on the dance floor so outrageously with the newcomer, magnificent as she was in that golden dress.

Mr Firbank, her well-loved boss from the station, was approaching Jack and herself to ask her to dance, and so Jack left her to take Miss Hanson's arm. Kath coloured with pleasure as she allowed Jack to lead her onto the floor, but Emma saw that Philip was now left alone at the edge of the celebration.

"Excuse me, Mr Firbank, but I must just see to something. Forgive me," she said as she withdrew her hand from his shoulder. The old man was untroubled. He would never question Mrs Holt.

She hurried across to where he was standing—the man she loved with all her heart—risking everything at that moment to reach him. The people on the dance floor were oblivious, she knew, all preoccupied with the dance.

"Emma. Emma. Take care, my dear," he whispered, but she took no notice. She clasped his arm and pushed his stick to one side, then pulled him to her so he could lean on her with one arm around her waist. It was irresistible. They stayed close to the edge of the dance floor and moved very gently to the rhythm of the song. She was holding him very close to steady him, and he felt her breath against his chest and her waist still slim from all her hard work. Slim, despite her age. He cupped it closely in a kind of relieved ecstasy. The taffeta clung to her breasts, and he longed to touch them.

"Emma, you don't need to be shuffling around the dance floor with this cripple. Hard to believe now, but I used to be a very good dancer long ago at Oxford." He gripped her round the waist tighter as he thought of those carefree days.

Emma assured him that dancing with him gave her a joy that nothing could surpass. "We two people shuffling, as you put it, are more than content. If only we could stay this way," she whispered.

"But, my darling, you know we can't. The dance will be ending, and people will see."

"I know this," she said, "But no matter what happens, this love of ours must keep you from loneliness. Promise me you will never feel alone as I saw you just now before I reached you."

"I do know that whatever comes of all this, we can endure it, as long as we also stay true to the others for whom we are responsible. But now, Emma, I must be the headmaster of the school. I *must* play my part properly. Give me back my stick and let me lean on the pillar again. You must find Jack, my darling. We must be careful."

As she walked away, she took one last look at him leaning nobly and oh so steadfastly by the pillar and was glad to see that Miss Hanson was returning to his side as Jack was to hers. Harriet had moved away from the new teacher and was sipping champagne by the supper table with her eyes sparkling. Jack said nothing to Emma but rather firmly took her arm and walked her to where Florence was chatting animatedly with Ned Tempest.

"Mother, Ned has asked me to have lunch at the farm on Christmas Eve. Do you think I might be spared from home?"

"Of course, my love," said Jack in unison with Emma, though he added, "Just as long as he sees you home before midnight."

"Thank you, Mr Holt. It will be my pleasure," said Ned, and he smiled such a sweet smile at Florence that her parents could not resist.

Eventually, the party came to its close and the guests dispersed, some to their cabs, some to their expensive cars, some on foot plodding back home along the country lane. All this was not before Miss Hollingsworth had thanked them all for coming and not before Philip and Dr Thomson had given the vote of thanks to her in their turn. Emma was reassured as she saw him safely back in his role as the head of the school.

The snow was beginning to fall as they walked back to Holt House. Florence half danced her way along to Maggie's cottage, but Jack was surly and silent. He had much to think over and he could not speak of it to his wife. He found himself yet again with that nagging doubt he had felt the afternoon of their visit to the hospital. It had reared its ugly head again. He had watched them as he'd danced with Kath. Because he could understand something of the strength of their friendship, he knew it would seem untrusting of him to ask her what she meant by the dance with his friend. Yet he felt very much in need of a drink that night before he could comfortably get into bed with this woman he had loved for so long.

As for Harriet, she was lit up with the pleasure of the dance with Godfrey Langdon—the new member of staff—and felt no compunction in regaling Philip with his virtues in the cab on the way back to school. He listened to her patiently. She had not been so animated for some time, and he could forgive Langdon much if he caused her some joy. He himself was relieved that she had not commented nor even noticed him with Emma on the dance floor, though he was sure Kath Hanson had not missed it.

Enough now, he thought as they drew up to the house. *Tomorrow is another day.*

Chapter 18

Neither Philip nor Emma slept much that night, though the village lay quiet in the frosty moonlight, and the school—empty of all its pupils now, with shadowed, echoing corridors—had no reason to disturb its head. Only their thoughts kept them both awake.

She dared not think about the dance with him. It was too painful whilst at the same time something rich and special to be treasured and kept in the innermost recesses of her heart. However, she was anxious for Jack, as he had not engaged in conversation with her as they'd gone to bed and she knew she had been dangerously close to showing her feelings for Philip that evening and must really make it up to Jack. He must not be allowed to feel in any way neglected. He needed her always to be her own loving self towards him.

It's second nature for me to love Jack. I've shared my life with him for so many years. It's easy. But I need to be more careful. And I can't imagine how I'm to deal with this yearning for Philip that haunts me all the time.

She had managed to compartmentalise her feelings so far but did begin to wonder if she could go on loving both men so much whilst maintaining such a precarious balance. Would there ever come a day when she would have to make a choice?

She determined to put her mind to the Christmas at home which she always masterminded for the whole family, though this year could not be the same with her beloved George gone and Will and Harry in France. She had so hoped at least one of the two might get Christmas leave, but it was not to be. All the troops were on full alert this year of 1915, as the Germans were increasingly using the deadly clouds of chlorine to advance. They had Ypres in a firm grip, and the British trenches along the established line were constantly threatened by German advances under the foggy poison.

For his part, Philip lay in his lonely bedroom, reliving the joy of being able to hold Emma in his arms, albeit fleetingly and under the stress of maintaining a professional face. Yet it had been such a comfort and such a reassurance that her love for him matched his for her that he was able to tell himself that God's grace was sufficient for them both and would help them through. Lines from George Herbert struck him afresh for he had been teaching his sixth-formers Herbert's poetry.

Love bade me welcome; yet my soul drew back, guilty of dust and sin.

But quick-eyed Love, observing me grow slack from my first entrance in,

Drew nearer to me, sweetly questioning if I lacked anything.

'A guest,' I answered, 'worthy to be here.' Love said, 'You shall be he.'

And how did it end?

'You must sit down,' says Love 'and taste my meat.'

So I did sit and eat.

As he was falling asleep that night, this poem and its final words reassured him.

Perhaps my dust and sin are not unforgivable and this love that we have is not profane but a pure and lovely thing.

The morning came to them both with a shock of activity. Harriet—spry and sparkling—announced her mother and father were arriving imminently to spend Christmas with them, and this filled Philip with dread. This would test his spirit and his will. He retreated into the school Meeting House and prayed for strength to keep his patience and his integrity towards Harriet in the face of her father's criticisms of his views. No doubt, they would go over the same arguments all over again and would come to the same absolutely opposing standpoints in the end. He would manage his frustration by getting down to marking the boys' essays on

Herbert away in his study. Even Kath would not disturb him, as she had gone to her sister's for Christmas.

As for Emma and Jack, they received a letter from Will grieving sorely that he had no leave.

My dear mother and father,

I cannot tell you how disappointed I am to be kept from you and from home this Christmas. Life here is pretty grim most of the time, though I expect the cook will try to make something we can call a Christmas lunch. Captain Montfort is leaning on me quite a bit now I have the stripe, and that does me good most of the time. But the poisonous gas has affected several of our men, and they have had to be whisked away for treatment. It has terrifying consequences, Mother, and I am more afraid than I care to be.

Anyway, I hope to meet with Harry sometime over the holiday. Albert and I and a few of the lads are hoping to take a brief trip over to his base to see him and others. That will be wonderful if we can do it. He seems fine from messages I have from him and from others who have seen him. He's excited about Maggie's baby. It won't be long now, will it? Being an uncle will maybe help make up for all this horror.

Take heart, Mother. Don't be grieved from what I say. I'll be alright, I promise. I send all my love to you, Father, and of course to Florence. If only George could still be safe.

Yours, Will.

After she finished reading, Emma stood and began to pace the kitchen. She couldn't bear to sit still any longer. She pulled on her coat and went out to the garden. She shivered in the freezing winter air and yet was glad to feel the icy chill.

I'm pleased to feel the cold for it's nothing to what you are suffering, my own love, my son. Why do men need to murder their fellows? How am I to bear this? She paced round and round the chicken coop where the chickens clucked and pecked unknowingly.

You don't know anything, you funny, feathered things. Why should you care? She drew a deep sigh and straightened her back. *Come, Emma, pull yourself together. You have to arrange a Christmas whether or not you have the joy of your sons.*

So she busied herself in cooking the Christmas delicacies to try to forget all the heap of emotions she felt. She was relieved that Jack seemed to have emerged from his dour mood and was once more his steady self, calming her fears over the boys. And Florence was delighting in her friendship with Ned Tempest, no longer a slip of a girl but a charming young woman in her own right. She was a great bonus to Maggie who relied on her increasingly as the baby drew near. Florence had some of her mother's quick perception if she suspected someone to be in trouble and had an easy and sensitive way of comforting anyone's troubles. Maggie and she made a very good team.

Christmas day arrived, and in the School House, Harriet and her mother cooked while the bishop presided at the table with his usual arrogant opinions about the course of the war. Philip tried earnestly to listen patiently whilst sustaining his own pacifist position. However, Philip noticed somewhat anxiously that the bishop got a little too hot under the collar as they discussed it and again, so Philip changed the subject to quieter topics to spare him. Meanwhile, he gave Harriet all his attention as best he could, and she seemed to relax a little in her frostiness towards him. As the Christmas he had dreaded drew to a close, he reflected that the effort with his father-in-law had not been in vain and they had spent some congenial time discussing the bishop's work in the diocese of Worcester—a position of which he was very proud.

Philip was thankful that his leg was healing well and giving him less pain. He knew he could not afford to start a new term still weakened. Marking the sixth-formers' essays in his own study had given him peace and pleasure as he'd seen how well the boys had tackled the subject he had set them.

At Holt House, the Firbanks had been invited to join them for Christmas lunch, along with Maggie's mother, so it was quite a jolly affair in the end. They all made a huge effort to forget as best they could the fears from the front, and Mr Firbank was business-like in his old way as he told Emma how busy the station was going to become in the New Year. He had no intention of letting his assistant consider herself superfluous to his needs. Indeed, he really knew he could not do it all without her help. He had written out her new timetable and presented her with it as he was leaving. She looked at it somewhat askance, as it would take up a great deal of her time on top of the cooking and washing for school. But she took it with the pretence of a smile as they all said their farewells.

As Boxing Day dawned, a new event took over all other business. Maggie went into early labour at only thirty-eight weeks.

Florence came running for her mother at five-thirty in the morning, and Emma hastily dressed and hurried to the cottage to see what was happening. Jack followed at his own pace and set about lighting the cottage fire. Maggie was clutching Florence's hand very tightly and her anxious eyes were fixed on Florence's face as if to find some comfort there. She was scared. Her waters had broken, and her bed was soaked through. Contractions were regular and very painful. Emma knew they must get the village midwife, Mrs Townsend, who worked under Dr Thomson, and Florence was given the task of fetching her. She swiftly returned with her, and Mrs Townsend immediately took charge, much to Emma's relief. She gave out her orders in short sharp commands while Emma stood by Maggie's head and talked softly to her, gripping her hand tightly, especially when the contractions were at their height.

"This baby is coming early, and I've a feeling we should call for the doctor himself to finish the birthing, Mrs Holt," whispered Mrs Townsend. "There may be the need for forceps and stitching, I think, but the doctor's an expert, never fear." No sooner had Emma told this to Florence than she ran down to her father who was kneeling beside the fire, coaxing the flames.

"Father, get Dr Thomson. Maggie needs him."

Jack was off at a trot. He was usually phlegmatic in life's trials, but this rattled him badly. The sounds from the bedroom of Maggie crying out in pain spoke to his softer side. Leonard Thomson took one look at his old friend and hastened to pack his doctor kit. The midwife greeted him with all the details that were causing her anxiety, and he hastened to Maggie. Sweat was covering her hot, sweet face, her hair was damp, and her eyes were scared. The contractions were coming swiftly, and as he examined her, he could see that she was making little progress despite her pain. Maggie would have to bear the agony of those contractions until her body could make a way through for baby.

"Mrs Townsend and Emma, stay with me. Florence, get lots of towels ready but stay with your father downstairs. Hold her hand tight, Emma. Maggie, I want you to take deep gasps of air while you hold off from pushing. It is too early to push. Mrs Townsend will check and tell you when it is safe to do so."

Jack closed his eyes as he heard the screams. It was as if time had stood still while Maggie squeezed Emma's hand to breaking point. She managed to whisper to Emma she wanted her own mother to be with her too. Downstairs, with a pang of guilt, this exact thought entered Florence's mind as well. She flew out of the cottage door and hastened to fetch her.

The moment came when Maggie's time to push at last arrived, and her screams were exchanged for a baby's cries just as Florence rushed back in with Maggie's mum in tow. From the kitchen below, the three heard the newborn cries and looked at each other in utter amazement and thankfulness.

In the bedroom, Maggie lay back against the pillows exhausted as the doctor carefully, and with extreme fastidiousness, stitched the torn birth canal and washed his hands at the water ewer close to the bed. Mrs Townsend watched him, full of admiration at his dexterity, knowing that the joy and relief of the delivery and the pressure of pushing she had endured would be enough to anaesthetise Maggie—a mystery of childbirth which never ceased to amaze the old midwife. She wrapped the baby boy in the blood-soaked towels and handed him to Maggie.

Dr Thomson stepped back from his handiwork very proudly as all the family now stepped into the room. "Why, we have three new grandparents here to celebrate. Congratulations, Maggie, you were a brave wee lassie indeed." The good doctor shook hands with each of them and then set off for home, leaving Mrs Townsend to put the finishing touches to his work with instructions as to what to do for Maggie and a promise to return the next day to see the patient and the baby.

"Your grandson's name is to be George after his uncle," Maggie managed to articulate as her eyes closed in sleep. The tears flowed down Emma's cheeks as she took in such thoughtfulness and love from the exhausted girl. She took the baby in her own arms and tenderly kissed his little forehead.

"*You have to do with things dying; I with things newborn,*" she quietly repeated. Jack had quoted those words on the day they'd heard of George's death and, at that, Jack smiled at her, unable to speak.

It was not the conclusion to Christmas 1915 that they had expected but it had its compensations. Harry Holt got his legitimate leave after all, and Harriet's parents left for their home, much to Philip's intense relief.

Chapter 19

Harry's homecoming was more than welcomed by the little family with its newest member, especially as Maggie was much weakened by the difficult birth and was prone to quite severe "baby blues" as Mrs Townsend called them. She found it hard even to smile as Harry wrapped her in his arms, for poor Maggie could find very little pleasure in the joy everyone else seemed to be feeling. Even the arrival of the new Tansad pram which Emma had carefully saved up for with her station earnings left Maggie cold.

Emma and Florence, meanwhile, were completely engrossed in knitting little baby clothes and the square napkins so much required. The muslins Emma had stored up ready were quite insufficient to manage with and so their knitted efforts were much needed. It was astonishing how quickly tiny romper suits and leggings also appeared, much to the amazement of Harry and Jack. Indeed, George was a complete delight to all in every way, and his father could hardly bear to return to the front at the end of his all too short leave. He had even taken a hand at bathing little George who'd managed a windy smile for him.

Harry was a man of few words, unlike Will, and never shared the details of his life with the French army in Verdun. He stored his fears away in some private place deep within himself and threw all his energies into concocting dishes to tempt the officers for whom he cooked. This, he said later, helped to keep him sane during the hours of the repeated, heavy onslaughts to which the enemy subjected the French base in their attempts to capture it. Harry took a pride in the knowledge that Verdun remained impervious so as he once more stepped onto the train at Shadworth Station to return to the front, he kept up his quiet, competent manner in front of his beloved wife who was clutching his arm as if to prevent him from leaving her. It was another of those farewells which penetrated deep into Emma's memory for the rest of her life.

Meanwhile, Florence took a pride in keeping little George perfect despite the many dirty napkins and soaking bibs, and she worked hard to bring Maggie out of her gloom and begin to look up at the sunshine again. Gradually, Maggie emerged from her despondency, her sweet nature overcoming her pessimism and returning her to her former self.

Emma thanked God for this, as she was worn out by the added strain of managing the two homes and baby as well as her school and station duties. Fortunately, term had not begun, so the call on her for delicacies and clean blouses had not yet added to the load. But Jack was already back at work in the school garden, preparing the frosty ground for planting when the time came. He was the proudest grandfather in the world, and Philip, meeting him one early January day on the path to his study, could not help but smile at his friend's boasts. Once again, Jack had thrown off his doubts and returned to his normal equilibrium. The arrival of George had secured it.

"You'll see him soon, sir, I'm sure. Emma is bound to bring him up to school on one of her daily walks. She is like a girl again, pushing the new pram like old times with our own children."

This gave Philip's heart a wrench of pain as he thought of all that might have been in his own life. *I must not indulge myself in this 'if only' thinking which gains nothing and helps no one*, he told himself.

He congratulated Jack with real affection, nonetheless hoping that Emma would indeed bring baby up to school soon and thanking God himself that Jack seemed not to have been aware of the intimacy of the exchange between the two of them at the dance. He would have been horrified had he had access to Jack's thoughts that night. However, innocent of that, he was able to remember their time together as a great pleasure very precious to him.

It was unfortunate that the day that brought Emma with the Tansad to school, Harriet was ensconced in his study, poring over the timetable for the new term. Kath Hanson, newly back at work in preparation for the arrivals, had been astonished to see her, as such visits were now much less frequent. Yet Kath suspected her of hidden motives. Was she looking for Godfrey Langdon's classes? Kath had observed Harriet's pleasure in dancing with him at the party. But then her thoughts were interrupted by a knock on the door, and she opened it to the sight of Emma holding a small baby, wrapped up to the chin in woolly shawls and sucking his thumb noisily.

"I thought you both would like to see baby George, Kath. Is Mr Manners in?" exclaimed Emma who had not noticed Harriet standing there. Harriet looked on askance with that air of haughty superiority which she had perfected over the years. Emma was stopped in her tracks.

"Mrs Holt, this is not a nursery to which babies can be brought willy-nilly. The head is doing his check of the house rooms, and Miss Hanson has better things to do than coo over new babies. I presume this is the new addition to your family?"

Kath came to Emma's rescue hastily. She herself, regardless of Mrs Manners' attitude, opened her arms to take the baby just as Philip arrived back from his expedition. Emma stood aghast at the woman's coldness, pale with dismay, then stepped back to let him pass her to enter his room. He took one look at his wife's face and summed it all up in a second.

"Whatever is the matter here? Mrs Holt, is this your new grandson? How delightful to see him. Jack has been telling me all about him. Look, Kath. Look, Harriet. What a beautiful baby he is. Oh, Mrs Holt, you have a new lease of life, I am told." He smiled, and her heart melted before his very eyes.

"Why, Harriet, are you not delighted with this small addition to our community?" He spoke very pointedly to her as if to warn her that her attitude was absolutely out of bounds.

She pulled herself together and responded in parting. "He's very sweet, yes. But I must be on my way. The returning members of staff will be expecting me back at the house. I'm having a small drinks party for returning staff. I didn't tell you for I know how preoccupied you are with the new term."

His face showed his surprise at this and he looked at Kath to see if she had any knowledge of the event, but Kath was already absorbed in her enjoyment of the baby who had opened his eyes from the depths of his covers to look around him. Philip abandoned himself to the same pleasure, and they both congratulated Emma, whose cheeks had got back their colour.

"Do you think I could hold him, Mrs Holt?" asked Kath.

"Of course you can," she replied and gently picked George up, handing him to her.

Philip stood quietly and watched this performance, the while looking at Emma with unspoken and unaffected tenderness. The baby snuffled a little in Kath's arms and she hastily handed him back to Emma, content to have had the opportunity.

"I'd ask for a go myself but I don't think I'd feel very safe to do so." Philip smiled. Emma took his hand and held it to George's little fist, whereupon the little fingers unfurled and wrapped themselves around Philip's finger. He was thrilled at that, and Emma threw her head back and laughed at him. She and Kath enjoyed seeing his pleasure, but Emma knew she must play her part carefully. It was so easy to fall into the easy comfort of their relationship, and Miss Hanson was no fool. It was time to go.

"I really must go," she said. "His mother will be wondering where I've got to."

Philip, too, was aware that he must return to his professional demeanour, and as she squared her shoulders to leave, he merely said, "Well, Mrs Holt, thank you for giving us the pleasure of meeting this little chap. I shall tell Jack you have been."

She left, wincing at the pretence she'd had to adopt. And he, in his turn, also winced inwardly. As Kath returned to her typing, she feared for all she had perceived that morning.

At home, Harriet entertained the returning staff to a cold buffet of which Philip had been quite unaware, and she once more savoured the presence of Godfrey Langdon as she presided over it. It was something of a salve to what was the unhealed part of herself for she had felt her childlessness bitterly that morning and had wanted to hit out at those more fortunate than she. If only she could have shared that with her husband, she might have found him compassionate and understanding in ways she had long lost sight of. But instead, she flirted with Godfrey and allowed her prejudice against the Holts to ferment.

I told Philip I didn't care for a baby anyway, but still, I would very much have liked to have my own little one to love. That Emma Holt seems to glory in her grandson and there she was, expecting to parade him in front of Philip. How dare she trespass in his study like that? Who does she think she is?

Meanwhile, as January wore on, the war machine rumbled more and more intensely as the ugly stalemate in the fields of France strangled the young men in its thrall. The war that was to be over by Christmas 1914 had descended into a futile morass of slaughter. Generals Haig and Joffre began to plan new rigours by which to end it all in a victory. Now protests against the war were being organised by critics of the generals. A peace march in Cranston one Saturday attracted many of the villagers to join in, and they went home bloodied after encountering anti-pacifist pro-government mobs on the town's streets. There was an atmosphere of violence close to the surface, and antagonism between neighbours reared its head even in Shadworth, for there were both those who thought the peacemakers were cowardly and those who were appalled by such loss of life. And overall, there was a dread of conscription. Women were watching the papers fearfully in case their sons should find themselves without a choice but to go out to the killing fields.

But Generals Haig and Joffre knew they must have more fodder for the front lines. The ghastly, dreaded announcement of conscription for all single men between eighteen and forty-one as from March, and for married men as from May, lay like a death knell on the hearts of mothers, wives and lovers across Britain. And in the Quaker school in Shadworth village, there was both horror and dread. Philip's male staff would be decimated: Alan Lorimer and Jim Fletcher—his main standbys for everything in the pastoral area; the new deputy, Godfrey Langdon. All were called up along with several other younger members of staff. Only the women staff could be left to hold things together. Philip felt a quiet despair and futile rage at this news, nervously watched by Miss Hanson.

The generals' second ploy was the inception of the plans for a major great offensive centred on the

Somme. Will, under his captain, knew something major was in the pipeline and was aware of his captain's reluctance to discuss it. Their time in the dugout with the men was claustrophobic, stinking and lice-riddled. The grog took care of the men's fears for only a brief time before they were once again overtaken by the almost surreal situation in which they found themselves. There was real anguish among them, and it was always heightened by letters from home where gentle, ordinary things still prevailed. Then the thought of going over the top into no-man's-land seemed more of an unspeakable option than ever. Will found himself biting his fingernails like he used to as a child with the anxiety of what was coming, and he looked at his hands, appalled that they were bitten to the quick and yellowed with nicotine from the hastily smoked cigarettes they all puffed when they could get their hands on them. The futility of gaining only a few yards of ground to the accompaniment of snipers' bullets and machine gun fire from the opposite trenches induced in him a kind of stupor. The sight of his comrades dead close by—men who had been smoking with him in the preceding hours now irretrievably lost in the work of a tragic moment—was almost too much to bear, and Will became resigned to his own probable fate. Will's captain, Ralph Montfort, a man of aristocratic birth yet very much one with his compatriots, confided in Will that the plans would involve a huge onslaught on the enemy front line and an undercover initiative to cut the wire around them in readiness for the British attack.

"But," said Ralph, "How can anyone be sure the wire is cut properly and in the right places when all around lies the thick, merciless sludge of French farmers' fields and the danger of being seen? God, Will, I sometimes think Haig and the other top brass have no concept of the realities we face every day. Where will they be when we find ourselves swamped out there as target practice for the enemy? It will be a miracle if we survive."

Will shuddered at this and shared Ralph's sense of the utter hopelessness and inevitability of it all. That was a truth he would never write home about. Yet he was glad his captain felt he could confide in him.

But neither man knew the date that was being set in the higher echelons of power: July1, 1916. The conscripts would all be in place by then, and the generals believed it would, with heavy bombardment and a full out attack, bring victory. So they thought, while the young men and their older brothers suffered death as an everyday occurrence.

Meanwhile, the enemy was assaulting Verdun in a bid to take it from the French, and there was heavy bombardment where Harry Holt was serving. This was to go on for many months through February to December, and thousands of men would die in the effort of holding the town. Will was terrified every time a word came from Verdun in case it should mean another brother was lost. But John kept alive despite the onslaught almost as if he had willed it so. He wanted so much to play a proper father to his little George. And no matter how hard they tried, the enemy could not take Verdun.

In school, from March onwards, Philip had to mastermind a whole fresh timetable by which to manage all the classes without his male teachers. Every member of staff who was not called up had to take a greater share of the teaching. Without his best colleagues and his deputy, he was forced to take charge of Ayton and Fox Houses himself, though he thanked God Edna Wright wasn't going anywhere. While Alan Lorimer and Jim Fletcher made their preparations to leave, discipline issues that had been dealt with in the jurisdiction of each head of house now fell in the main to Philip. The boys were restless in the face of the news that came through daily, and some of the older boys were using the younger ones as scapegoats for their feelings. To these boys, Philip gave the full might of his anger and punished them by restricting their freedoms. They usually left his study shame-faced and apologetic, but one particular boy was expelled for his repeated insolence, much to Philip's abject grief. He was weary but determined to maintain his school's highest standards, and he desperately wished his wife would be a more present aid to them all. As it was, she was devastated that Godfrey Langdon was going, having only just begun to enjoy his attentions, and found no incentive to play even her usual small part in helping her husband in the life of the school.

The men of the village had banded together to go as a group to their billets. They seemed to have a courage in the face of it that was remarkable, and their differences were forgotten. Now it was no longer a matter of choice and the younger ones, Ned Tempest, Florence's new beau, and Dr Thomson's son, James, had none of the fervour for battle glory that had sent Harry Holt and young Firbank to enlist. Florence had spent every possible last minute with Ned before his departure, and they had drawn very close. Ned reminded her of her beloved father—steady and capable, phlegmatic and reassuring. She felt completely bereft that this stalwart, beloved young man would no longer be able to court her as he had been doing assiduously since the night of the dance. And Florence was terrified that he would be lost out there at the front as so many young men had been. She was not alone. There was much weeping among the families as they prepared for the moment of departure. And still, they all felt compelled to show a brave face as the time drew near.

Of course, that moment came to them all, and Emma, Mr Firbank's stalwart assistant, found herself on duty very frequently as train after train, carrying the recruits, passed through Shadworth. She found it acutely painful to see the families—and not just the mothers and partners—embracing their loved ones as they boarded the trains, posies tucked in their hat bands, the love tokens given to them by those whose tears were falling. Florence herself was quite desperately clinging to Ned as he prepared to board, and Emma watched him as he took her daughter by the shoulders, looking her squarely in the eyes as if to strengthen and reassure her till the very last minute.

Please let Ned stay alive, thought Emma. She noticed Mrs Manners waving with a handkerchief to her eyes, and the thought struck her that perhaps she was grieving over the man she had danced with so flagrantly at the party. But that thought was soon forgotten at the sight of Philip himself shaking hands with his beloved colleagues as they boarded the train en route to Sheffield and from thence to Charing Cross where they would catch the train taking them to the ferry across to France and their assigned billets. He looked so tired and so solemn; she longed to rush up to him and reassure him, but she kept a tight hold on herself, surrounded as she was with neighbours and friends and with Florence, stricken by overwhelming sadness. She could only be grateful that Philip, and of course Jack, were just too old to be conscripted.

Philip saw her and saw her firm resolve. His love for her was all too painful, yet he knew he must try to match her resilience. The trains departed, bearing their cargo, the days of parting came to an end, and all returned to their own private places to grieve and watch and hope.

Chapter 20

Spring had come to Shadworth slowly and tenderly as if to alleviate some of the cruelty of the hard winter frosts. It could not remove the pain that every person was feeling in different ways, yet whenever Jack spied the tiny shoots of the crocuses he had planted in the school garden peeping through the dark, frozen soil or spotted a robin watching him from a nearby tree, its head cocked to one side thoughtfully, he remembered Browning's words:

God's in his heaven, all's right with the world. It was a sentiment he had been brought up with by his mother long before, and he recalled the words sadly.

How I wish I could believe it, thought Jack ruefully.

He shared this thought with Philip on one of his walks down to examine Jack's handiwork, walks which were always a brief respite from the teaching timetable he had set himself and the daily dread of receiving telegrams from more bereaved parents of his boys.

"Is it really alright, Mr Manners? Is it really?"

Philip only managed a wry smile at Jack's question.

He always hoped he would encounter Emma with the pram and the little one on these visits, but he was rewarded with little sight of her in this period for she too was heavily employed helping Mr Firbank down at the station. Indeed, he knew it was better that way in all honesty, yet a sight of her would have given him a modicum of pleasure.

Then came a letter from the MP to whom he had written after George's death at the hands of the firing squad. He had had no reply from him at the time, but clearly his protest then had not gone unnoticed, and now he was being summoned to London to a Commons committee on March 28 to discuss the procedures for Court Martial once again, review the death penalty for desertion, and analyse the protests that were being voiced about the war. In Shadworth, someone had scrawled graffiti on the side wall of the row of terraces where Maggie and Florence had their cottage: *Stop the bloodshed now*!

This graffitiing enraged Jack but he agreed with its sentiments. And Philip was fully aware that the generals were being attacked in the media by men who had been at the front and invalided home. These were the intelligentsia of the country, one of whom was Siegfried Sassoon whose poetry was pillorying the generals in protest at the huge losses out in France. Now those in the inner sanctum in Westminster wished to air the grievances and reassert their control. And indeed, plenty remained steadfastly on the side of the government. In High Shadworth Church, the vicar was preaching patriotism almost every Sunday, much like Harriet's father in Worcester. It was a rift that cut right through society, and still the death toll grew.

Unsurprisingly, therefore, Philip was very pleased with the invitation, for he felt it might be the opportunity to state again the sacred precepts of his Quaker faith that violence and bloodshed were contrary to God's law and the teaching of Christ. He knew what a battle was being endured by men who were pacifists called up for service under conscription. They found themselves treated with utter contempt as shirkers and cowards. Philip had a letter from Graham O'Connor, one of his English students and a fervent pacifist who had suffered under brutal questioning of his position. He wrote how he had been "*slapped around*", much to Philip's horror. Each man was made to face local tribunals to convince its members of the deeply held beliefs which prevented him from taking up arms. And he knew that such men were faithful and that their consciences could not and should not be denied. He knew how earnest Graham was in his faith and prayed nightly for him and all the others. Unless they were absolutists who would have nothing to do with the war at all, they could be sent to serve as stretcher bearers and field hospital workers.

Lord, let them be accepted and allowed to keep the faith.

Miss Hanson proudly brought him the letter with the House of Commons insignia but watched very anxiously as she realised the journey to London in a day would take a toll on his weakened leg. But Harriet arrived in his study at the news cock-a-hoop. For once, she looked at her husband with admiring eyes. She had not entirely forgotten their time when she had pursued him in Oxford, how she had admired his brilliance then and how she'd felt he could meet her hopes for a position in society worthy of her. The youthful and charming girl she used to be had evaporated as their life together had taken a quieter, less dazzling path. Harriet still longed for her husband to stand out as a figure in society, never comprehending that his Quaker school with its reputation stretching across the country was of itself an outstanding achievement. This was a success she could and should have enjoyed and shared.

"Philip, how wonderful that they are calling on you for your advice. Are you not pleased to be invited? You'd better not be parading your pacifism though. That can't be why they've asked you."

"Harriet, that's exactly why they've asked me and what I must do. If they want backing for their deadly policy, they should invite your father," he responded.

Miss Hanson winced as she watched Harriet's face change at his answer. *Oh, sir, you could have been gentler with her. She is pleased for you.*

"Philip, can you never compromise with your wretched Quaker principles? Why are you so stubborn?" She flounced out of the study, huffing with utter frustration.

Kath saw his look of tired sadness and once again wished she could shake some sense into Harriet Manners. "You will need to catch the earliest train on that day. But it will be too much to try to return on the same day, surely. Shall I book you onto the 6:00 a.m. and get you an early return next day, sir? I'll book you into the St Pancras Hotel overnight for you'll need to get a decent night's sleep," said his secretary.

"Yes, please, Kath. I think you're right. It's getting very close to the end of term, and there's still so much to do. I've got my work cut out."

Before Philip's day arrived, however, Emma got the news in the village that Mr Firbank's grandson had been reported killed. She and Jack hastened down to see him and his family that evening and found them in a kind of dereliction of themselves. The lad's mother was distraught, and the Holts could do nothing more than sit beside them in their grief, much as Emma had done the day the lad had joined up.

Mr Firbank was fretting terribly about his work, knowing trains had to be flagged and managed without respite for sorrow. Emma promised him she would go down there and man his post for him till he felt better. Jack looked at her somewhat askance, aware of how much else she was undertaking daily. Yet Emma knew she could flog herself for at least a few days till her boss could manage his duties again.

Thus, it was that at 5:30 a.m. every morning, she found herself on duty with one other railway man only, working to the timetable. On March 26, she saw Philip limping towards her down the platform, and her heart missed a beat. He had told Jack about the meeting in London, but Jack had been so preoccupied with his own work that he had not told Emma. He was carrying his suitcase in one hand, his stick in the other.

Regardless of the few observers close by, she hastened to him. "What are you doing here this early, my love?"

"Oh, my sweet girl, hasn't Jack told you? I'm going to Westminster to a Commons committee reviewing court martial procedure and military discipline. You know I wrote to them protesting after George died. And, anyway, what are you doing here too? This is not your usual time."

"I'm in charge for the interim until Mr Firbank is fit to come back to his duties. His grandson has been killed, and he's lost all heart for now."

As she spoke, she heard the whistle of the oncoming train in the distance and had to regretfully hurry back to her post. He smiled at her all dressed up in her official uniform, managing all the work, and thanked God for her energy and her grace. The steam from the encroaching engine almost hid her from his sight, and the onrush of the smoke made him gasp. He knew she had somehow stripped all selfishness from herself there on the platform as she pursued her relentless duties, and he felt again the ache of love for her. As he climbed onto the train with some difficulty, he looked back at her, and she raised her hand in farewell.

"I'll see you early tomorrow, God willing," he mouthed as the train steamed on its way past her. All his resolve to be firm with himself dissolved at that moment, and Emma, watching the train receding into the distance, knew it and gave a sigh of deepest regret.

No one will see me if I cry here, and I want so much to let my tears flow down my cheeks and soak me through. I love you, Philip Manners.

And the tears came but silently.

The word Philip applied in his head as his meeting proceeded was "justification". He felt utter frustration that he was not truly being listened to and was a token presence intended to put the case for compassion without real engagement with it. Over and over, the main participants insisted there was an absolute necessity to maintain the death penalty in order to ensure that the young men in the trenches could have no doubt as to the consequences if they ran away. The deterrent of a firing squad must apply. Philip reminded them that it was reported how many of the young men awaiting the firing squads refused to be blindfolded in order to demonstrate their courage and deny their cowardice. He told them of his own experience with the story of George Holt. But they repeatedly insisted that pacifism was a weak and cowardly means to shirk responsibility. Conscientious objectors must accept the realities of war and be prepared to face severe punishment. And they remained adamant, justifying their policy, and disregarding his arguments. He felt it had been a huge and futile waste of his time and angrily left them to check in at the hotel, where, in his inhospitable room, he raged inwardly throughout the night with barely a wink of sleep at the fruitlessness of his effort.

Why did I bother at all? he thought as he stood on the cold and crowded platform the next day, awaiting the train for Sheffield and Shadworth. He was weary, his leg ached, and he had achieved nothing. Deserters would go on being shot, the war would carry on, and a generation of young men—some of whom he had taught and treasured, golden boys who deserved to live and make the world a better place—would perish.

So, as he got down from the carriage, grey and exhausted, he had no words with which to greet Emma who was watching for his return, herself worn out from all the extra hours she was serving for Mr Firbank. There were many other passengers alighting at the same time, so she could not show her emotion at the sight of him. A look alone had to suffice that day. It was not lost on him, however, and he knew she wanted to share his trip with him as much as he longed to share it with her and that she would have been at his side if she only could.

At home, Harriet tried to coax out of him why he was so angry, and he was gratified that she was showing some concern. Even if some of it was out of guilt. She was very anxious for the man whose company she had begun to enjoy before he was conscripted, and despite all the pressures they were under, she and her small group of female staff, whom she had continued to entertain, had been sewing and knitting warm scarves and socks to send out to the front. He recognised something of the old Harriet he had married that morning and reminded himself that both he and Emma had sworn to be most careful in maintaining their love for their spouses.

"Thank you, Harriet, for all you are doing to keep the women on the staff happy. They're all under pressure with such a heavy timetable. And thank you for your war effort. I am grateful," he said to her over breakfast. "I can't tell you how difficult the meeting yesterday was. No one paid the slightest attention to what I was trying to point out to them."

He had hoped she would respond with sympathy, but she just shrugged and busied herself clearing the table. "You might as well accept, Philip, that your pacifist views are not well-regarded or appreciated when all comes to all. Father has tried to tell you."

"Please leave your father out of it, Harriet. He and I have agreed to disagree." He left the table, picked up his briefcase and stick, and headed out to his study. On the way, he passed Jack tidying up a clump of snowdrops. He stopped. He knew Jack would share his frustration.

"Do you know, Jack, how angry I feel? Those men in their mighty offices in London don't give a damn for the ordinary boys fighting for their lives out in France. I might as well have stayed at home as try to persuade them to give up the firing squads."

"I can believe it, sir. At least you tried, and I know you had our George in your head when you set out to speak to them. I thank you for that, sir."

"Oh, it's the least I could do, Jack. I'm just grateful to have someone who agrees with me." He limped away, still furious, and banged the study door, causing Kath Hanson to look up alarmed.

At Holt House, Emma felt so besieged by the weight of her responsibilities that she had no time for the old yearning that lay deep inside her. Her recurring dream of dancing with Philip at Miss Hollingsworth's ball and the feel of his arm tightening around her waist haunted her on many nights, but she awoke to the realities of every day and strengthened her resolve to work even harder. Nor did she allow herself to fret over Will and Harry. She could not believe that God would take another one from her and somehow managed not to panic over them, simply going about her many duties resolutely. Nevertheless, it was a great relief to her when, at last, soon after, Mr Firbank returned to his duties and relieved her of the extra work she had had to do.

Little George, now passing three months, was a sweet infant, and she delighted in him. Maggie was proving a competent and adoring mother. Her strange and unwanted feelings of depression had gone, and with Florence staying in the cottage with her, the two of them had made a warm and welcoming home. They had only the little money Florence earned at the local village shop—a job she thoroughly enjoyed. And they both knew Emma was behind them whatever came along. Of course, what little she earned in her very exacting task at the station she was setting aside to give them to augment their small income.

In between her duties at the station, Emma was still expected to launder and iron the staff's blouses. She comforted herself with the knowledge that she could transport them back to school folded on George's pram, allow Jack to see his little grandson in passing, and hope to meet with Philip en route. Perhaps it was not surprising that she often achieved just that. Philip frequently walked down to the school gardens and shared news from the front with Jack as a way of exercising his leg, and the thought that he might meet with Emma gave him a purpose which he hardly dared admit even to himself.

Philip's pleasure in baby George on these occasions was almost as great as the child's grandfather's. The terrible vacuum in his life, the fact of his own and Harriet's childlessness had never left him, and so he delighted in seeing the child. Indeed, for him, George reserved the special accolade of laughing delightedly whenever he saw him—a small bonus that Emma treasured up in her heart, a kind of relief in the painful discipline she had imposed on herself. And whenever Philip returned to his study after these encounters, Kath Hanson could hardly help but see the pleasure he took in the child when he talked about him. She gazed down at her typewriter, pleased for him, yet with a sense of foreboding too. Miss Hanson was a wise old bird.

As March turned to April, the trees were in gorgeous blossom, and in the school gardens and the gardens of the village, the daffodils were flaunting their frilly skirts while the gentler spears of the tulips were piercing their way through the soil. In Ron Tempest's fields, the lambs were being born. A year had passed since young Charlie Hopton had been awarded the treat of his visit there. He was growing into a fine and confident schoolboy now, but he had not forgotten the Holts' kindness, and he made it a priority to visit Jack in the garden whenever he got the chance.

Easter came and went, and the school itself returned to something more like normal after the many vicissitudes of the term that had brought such changes. Philip arranged a special meeting during the vacation with Edna Wright and with the deputies he had appointed to Fox and Ayton houses in order to check that they were managing with the much heavier demands on them in the absence of Alan Lorimer and Jim Fletcher and the other male staff. They arranged for the older boys to be given extra responsibilities as prefects to help manage the dormitories in the evenings. The other idea that Philip had was to set up a regular evening quiet time in the Meeting House for any boy to come and sit in a peaceful atmosphere in the quiet of the spirit to pray and relax. His colleagues all agreed with him that this was a very good idea to be implemented when summer term began.

As the meeting closed, his colleagues all sat in silence as if they were already in the Meeting House themselves and wondering what the future would bring: the future of the school but also the future of their friends and boys they had taught who were in the fields of northern France fighting a war that had begun to feel increasingly pointless. What, after all, did the assassination of a Grand Duke have to do with them?

Chapter 21

Summer term began, and soon the wheels of study were once again set in motion. The news from the front brought with it more and more names of fatalities and wounded. Philip found himself increasingly sent for by the house heads to comfort boys with nightmares, boys whose brothers and fathers were out there. He became accustomed to sitting beside sobbing and terrified boys whose fears for their loved ones had turned into horrific dreams. Somehow, he had an ability to bring solace where none had been expected, and as he stroked hot foreheads with a cool hand, he was able to restore them to softer sleep.

He encouraged many of them to take advantage of the quiet hour in the Meeting House, and he himself often went there to pray for them all and for himself in his own need. He was racked with his sense that he could find, in all honesty, no real excuse for himself in desiring Emma, another man's wife, yet the character of the love he felt for her as of something sacred and, in a paradoxical way, perfectly chaste and natural, continued to assert itself.

We would never hurt Harriet or Jack after all. We are giving love to so many others in our life's work, she as much as I. So how can it hurt for us to have just that special care for each other? God help me, and I pray He may.

The green buds of spring flourished and opened to fresh effulgence. Jack's hens produced multiple eggs in a glut of fecundity. Little George began to crawl and gloried in the chickens, often as not frightening them out of their wits as he descended on them. Emma would stand at the back door watching him with delight, rubbing her soap-sudded hands on her apron as he got himself filthy with the dust. Maggie, sipping hot tea in the kitchen, would laugh as she allowed him to frolic in the fresh air. They tried to shut out thoughts of Harry and Will, knowing it was no use to fret. But the casualty reports constantly reminded them of the terrible dangers.

In the drear dugouts of France, Will and Ralph Montfort, his captain, shared talk of what was afoot. Ralph knew that July 1 had been set for the huge offensive that was coming, of which every man would be a part. He shared his huge misgivings once again that it seemed their leaders were ordering them to go over the top all guns blazing and bayonets to charge straight for the enemy lines. The two just looked at each other with a sense of impending doom. A smug General Haig had prophesied this would bring about the end of the war.

Will left the dugout to find Albert who was on sentry duty in the trench. Will offered his friend a cigarette he had managed to save from the rations, and together they smoked and mused. The nicotine brought a small measure of comfort as they breathed it into their lungs, but the ugly grey sludge where their boots rested and the echoing booms beyond the trench were unremitting and conducive only to black despondency. They talked in a desultory fashion.

"I've had a letter from home full of my mother's anxieties and instructions that we must keep our feet dry and warm," said Albert. "Will, I'd so like to tell her how I'm feeling. I think I've got foot rot with the wet that's soaking through my boots. Some hope of keeping dry and warm!"

Will had to smile at that. He knew his own mother was constantly fretting for him and sometimes felt he could hardly bear to think of home at all. He watched the long tail of a huge rat slither into a nearby hole and shuddered. "It sounds as if your mum's letters are just like my mum's. Wouldn't it be a relief to share the truth sometimes? I'd like to be able to warn them something big's coming soon, but I don't want to frighten them. It's not long now before it all kicks off, you know, Albert."

As July 1 approached, they received their final orders from headquarters. They were to go over the top in broad daylight and charge the enemy lines with bayonets ready once the artillery had ceased their unremitting bombardment. The wires protecting the enemy trenches were to have been cut by stealth on the previous night before the attack, so enabling them to get close to the front line.

What Will found most horrific was the command that came with these orders: kill without mercy and use your bayonets to knife the enemy close up, straight into their stomachs, faces, hearts. Thus, yard by yard, the enemy trenches would be overwhelmed and defeated, or so Haig believed. Before the final hour, Will wrote home to Emma and Jack with words that warned them of what might come without actually articulating his innermost fear of the consequences of such an action. And he comforted himself with the knowledge that at least Harry was in Verdun and absent from it.

What ensued day by day during the Battle of the Somme was an unmitigated disaster of catastrophic proportions. No one had reckoned on the huge depth of the enemy trenches nor that the barbed wire defences would still be intact. The efforts to cut the wire by night had failed dismally. The enemy used machine gun fire as they advanced, and it rattled incessantly, mowing down the young, often raw, recruits as they approached. They fell like dominoes toppling row by row, and those who returned each day to their own dugouts felt it some kind of miracle of survival. Albert and Will with Ralph somehow survived, but their dead mates whose bodies lay out in the fields of France were in a blood bath. They found themselves hugging each other like frightened children each night, knowing it must be repeated the next day and the next. The dread of day following fearful day struck Will to his heart, and he often sat in the dugout in front of a sheet of blank paper, longing to express to his father and mother the homesickness that overtook him on many a night. Yet Will, strong and unselfish, resisted these moments and pushed the paper aside, as empty as when he began, swamped in a desert of grief.

Despite these appalling losses, however, General Haig and his fellow officers insisted on continuing in the face of the reports, and their pride kept them from mercy and sense. Sassoon was to pillory them in his poetry.

News of the horror arrived in Shadworth and Shadworth Quaker School; news of the nineteen thousand dead in the first days, numbers which were to increase to one hundred thousand by the end of the battle, with only yards gained to show for it. The villagers all gathered each morning beside the junior school's noticeboard to scour the lists of casualties, in dread of finding their own sons. With Will's letter and the reports from the front, an appalling foreboding engulfed Emma. Florence and Maggie tried to calm her and used little George to keep her cheerful with his antics. When confronted with George, his grandmother had to hide her terror and wear her mask of confidence.

Jack shared his concerns about her with Philip on one of Philip's walks down to the school gardens. Philip and Jack were of course equally horrified at what was happening. Philip was using the quiet time in the Meeting House for himself as well as for the boys in need, and he hesitatingly suggested to Jack that he might allow Emma to come and pray in the Meeting House if it would help her. He was aware of his own agenda in this offer, but he spoke of it only really to bring Emma some relief if he could. Jack nodded in acknowledgement of the idea and told Emma of it that night.

"You should go, my love, if it would only give you even a minute's relief from your anxiety. I know how scared you are for our boys. Go and put your feelings to the Lord," said Jack. He himself did not often stop to pray and would, in any event, have felt uncomfortable in the Meeting House. Jack personally felt himself close to God whenever he was nurturing the gardens in his care.

The Creator needs a bit of help from those who love the work. And Jack knew Emma needed an anchor amongst the storm of her feelings as he made this generous gesture, though he knew she would surely meet with Philip there. Yet he was content to encourage her, having convinced himself of the absolute integrity of both Emma and the headmaster. Emma was surprised that he would suggest it but much appreciated his intention. She could not help but admit to herself that the thought of seeing Philip seemed like a small ray of hope in the darkness of her emotions.

"I shall go tomorrow, as I'm not on duty at the station then," she told Jack, who nodded without a word.

The next day, she cycled up to the fingerpost at five o'clock, Philip's set hour, parked her bike outside the kitchens, and hastened to the quiet room. She had always loved this space. Perfectly plain with its white walls, upright chairs, and single cross on the wooden table at the front, next to a lectern where notices were given out and prayers just sometimes spoken out loud. It was totally unlike her own Methodist chapel with its pews and large pulpit and robed choir. She liked both but found a greater sense of peace here. She slipped in beside Philip as he prayed there along with several boys whose families were also out in France and who had found his special time of spirit-filled silence helpful in their distress. Some sat with their eyes wide open, others with heads down and fists clenched in fervent prayer. He felt her next to him with a surge of joy but contained himself, conscious of the urgent prayers all around him. He gently put his hand on top of hers as it rested on the back of the chair in front.

"Be steady, my love," he said so quietly as to be no more than a breath.

She let her head drop, closed her eyes, and allowed the peace of the place to fill her. Knowing the man she ached for was right beside her was in itself a comfort, but she spoke to God in her innermost heart asking Him to keep her beloved Will safe despite the killing fields wherein he found himself.

Lord, I'm selfish and ruthless for my boys. Let no shell or bullet get my sons, Lord. Look after all those who are suffering out there, but, Lord, it's Will at the Somme you must keep safe. Will Holt, Lord. Will Holt, Lord. And, Lord, let it all be over soon.

Philip could feel her shaking as she prayed, and he knew how important it was to let her without doing more than sitting silently beside her. Some of the boys were getting up and leaving the chapel, some with tears streaming down their cheeks. He smiled at each one as they looked across at him, and they nodded in acknowledgement and silent thanks. And at last, the room was empty save for Emma and himself.

"Emma, sweetheart, it's time to hand it all over to God now. The hour is ending, and I have to visit the house dining rooms to check all is well. You must go home too." She opened her eyes and looked back at him so very, very sadly that it was almost too much for him to bear. But he was resolute. He pulled her to her feet and there, regardless of the setting, kissed her gently on her forehead, then held her next to him for a mere moment before taking her by the shoulders.

"Emma, where is your wonderful spirit? Where is my bravest of brave women? You have done your utmost in prayer. Now you must let God be God. Leave Him to deal with it."

"Philip, oh, Philip, how can you be so trusting? How are you so faithful? Can you really believe it will all be alright? Could you just give me a little of your peace? Being here next to you has helped, but how I wish I could stay with you. I'm afraid my faith isn't as strong as yours."

"If you only knew, Emma. If you only knew. But you *do* have faith. There's no one more capable than you. Come, my sweetheart, we have to play our parts now. Please show me you haven't lost your courage."

She laughed then, a rather wry laugh, but enough for him to feel reassured that she was ready to resume her duties.

"My bicycle is waiting, sir. And you are a stern task master. Thank you for that. I expect it's just as well." She turned on her heel and left him.

He sat back down with a thud, frowning. *Emma, if you only knew how weak I really feel.*

He sighed, then stood back up, straightened his back, and limped slowly out of the Meeting House. He looked in on each school house in turn as the boys were eating their suppers, and they all acknowledged him with pleasure. From thence to his own home and to Harriet who greeted him with little warmth but with interest enough to ask how the boys had been at quiet time. Even Harriet felt their anguish for their loved ones. She too was horrified at the awful news from the front.

Chapter 22

The weeks dragged by. Somehow, the summer lost itself in the angst that held sway, and the holidays passed into autumn term. The new students arrived to begin their school life; new sixth-formers came into the classes for the Highers; Miss Wright took over the teaching of Physics in Jim Fletcher's absence; Philip undertook to teach History as well as his own English classes to maintain the excellent standards of the school despite its depleted staff; young women were appointed as teachers to help fill the timetable. Kath Hanson was heard to say, "I don't know whether I'm on my head or my heels."

Harriet kept up her group of women knitting socks and balaclavas by the dozen to send to the front, and between them, they sent numbers of their blouses to Emma for her fastidious laundering. This, alongside her station duties and her time with baby George, gave her little opportunity to rest, but Jack encouraged her to go and share in the quiet hour whenever she could. It had been reinstated by Philip for the boys, and this was a kindness from Jack which pierced her heart and conscience keenly when she stopped to think about it.

These times became very precious to both Emma and Philip, though they often had much to do comforting the boys who were most upset in the pews. Emma had a knack of knowing what to say to set them thinking fresher more hopeful thoughts. Philip soothed them often with a mere touch on their bowed heads. But these times of quiet sitting beside each other gave them the strength to keep going.

But worst of all were the lists of dead and wounded which kept on coming day by day. They drew a huddle of women, all wrapped in their woolly shawls shivering, if not from cold then from absolute fear. Dread hung in the air, and Emma saw it most clearly in her role as assistant station master. Train after train laden with wounded soldiers came through Shadworth Station as she flagged them through. She saw the faces at the windows of the coaches, faces half stupefied, looking out in desolation. She saw the bandaged heads stained with dried blood and eyes which had seen too much to bear, unfocused on the reality around them. She found herself almost overwrought with the horror of it as she recounted what she had seen each day to Florence and Jack. Always, always at the back of her mind was Will, and she thanked God daily that he was still safe and that Harry was in the French headquarters in Verdun cooking rather than on the front line.

As the Somme offensive drew to its final days at the end of November with little ground gained, due to the futility of it and the huge losses it incurred—they said 100,000—Philip called his staff together to discuss the possibility of a remembrance service in the school hall for all those who had died, whom the students mourned for, but also sons of the village. He discussed it too with Jack and with Emma, but all agreed it must be a sombre time of quiet in which every name of their dead could be called out. Even Harriet was supportive of this as she too scoured the lists. Philip sensed it was to make sure Godfrey Langdon's name was not on it, and he forgave her this, glad that she had found someone she could admire. What that meant for his marriage, he didn't stop to consider for he knew his own perfidy all too well.

The date set was November 30, 1916. Tragedy was to strike that very day before it could take place, adding to its abject pathos. News that Jim Fletcher had been killed in action in a skirmish out in no-man's-land came through to Kath in the study, and she threw her arms up, appalled at what she had to announce to Philip and the others. As Philip walked into her room, he saw her face and half limped, half ran to her.

"What is it? Tell me quickly, Kath."

"Our own Mr Fletcher killed in action, Mr Manners. How can the school bear such a loss? Such a man."

Philip allowed her to cry on his shoulder while he stood still as a statue and let his mind picture his well-loved colleague gone from them. He felt a mixture of fury and of bitter grief whilst holding Kath steady. He proffered her his handkerchief, and she restrained herself at last.

"We must be practical, Miss Hanson. We must still go through with tonight's service, agony as it will be to have to add such a name to the list. And I must contact Jim's parents. They are not getting any younger, I know, and he was always anxious about them. They will be utterly bereft. Come, Kath, we must try."

And so, the people gathered, many from the village and many families of those who'd belonged to the school. Emma and Jack walked up to school silently through the foggy November night. Philip had gone down to the gardens to tell Jack the news, and somehow neither Emma nor Jack could articulate all that they felt. Jim Fletcher had been everyone's friend, full of fun and full of love for his pupils. Edna Wright, Jim's close colleague, half walked, half crawled to the school hall to take her place beside the head, and her shoulders kept shaking with grief. Harriet stood beside them, grim-faced, and the people looked up to the rostrum as Philip began to speak. Emma felt a pang of acute jealousy at the sight of Harriet possessing him as *she* never could, then took a hold of herself angrily.

Emma Holt, you have no business to allow such feelings. You know the rules we have set ourselves. She is at her rightful place. He hasn't even glanced in my direction, playing his part as he always does. She knew this to be the only way, and she leaned on Jack as she listened to Philip talk.

"Friends and families gathered here this evening, I welcome you to this time of remembrance with a heavy heart. We are here to remember those who have given the ultimate sacrifice for their country and to thank God for them. The names I will call out are not merely names for us but beloved ones whose deaths have lessened us, whose dying has brought us all to a grief that will forever be a scar on our own hearts. We celebrate their lives with our silent prayers that they have gone to a higher and better place, to the hands of the Almighty. Let us be still and allow God in His mercy to hear our prayer."

Philip allowed silence to fill the hall then as in the Quaker way, and each one gathered there bowed their heads, envisaging their loved ones. Every student of the school thought back to the head of Fox House whose good humour and kindliness and wisdom had enhanced their lives. There was the sound of stifled sobs all around the hall.

He read out the names, beginning with James Fletcher, then name after name of young men taken in the prime of their lives in the barren, crater-pitted sludge of Flanders Fields. Mr Firbank and his wife clutched each other's hands as he read their grandson's name. Young Jacob Hill wept beside his mother as his brother's name was called out in the growing list. Emma knew the boys in the chapel whom she had tried to comfort and noted the world-weary, sad faces of their mothers and fathers, though some of their fathers had become only names on the list too. For herself, she could only pray her own fervent prayer for the safety of her own boys and picture in her mind her own dead son, cruelly taken by a British firing squad.

At last, Philip stopped. There was complete silence in the hall. Then he broke the silence with a spoken prayer of commendation into God's hands and turned to his group of school musicians specially gathered for the task. They played the tune to the hymn "The Lord's my Shepherd" slowly and quietly, then closed the service with "Abide with Me". There was another silence till at last people began to collect their belongings.

Many villagers and students' parents gathered around the head and his wife. Harriet played her part to perfection for which Emma could not but be pleased for his sake. Yet it made Emma groan inwardly with a kind of hopeless resentment. She told herself it was beneath her to feel that way and angrily berated herself for being such a fool as to mind.

"Let's go home, Jack," was her response to this but she had not reckoned on her old friend and boss Mr Firbank. He caught them as they made their way to the door and tearfully, grief-stricken though he was, extolled the praises of the head and the opportunity his thoughtfulness had given them all. She nodded dumbly for she wanted so much to claim Philip for herself. Jack shook the Firbanks' hands and affirmed everything they were saying. She looked back at the rostrum where he still stood overwhelmed with people and, try as she could, she could not catch his eye. Miss Hanson was still standing beside him and watched as the Holts left. She saw Emma's glance and felt for her, for she felt certain she had guessed what was in her heart.

For Philip, it was more than anything a huge weariness that came over him. He knew he had given his best for the people, but he also knew he could not bring Jim Fletcher back, no matter how much he wanted to. His regret was remorseless. Harriet had astonished and pleased him that she had taken her proper place at the front but she was not Emma. He knew Harriet had been playing the role of compassionate lady at the service, but equally he knew she could shrug it all off without another thought. That was the difference between them, and he judged Harriet harshly and somewhat unfairly in comparing the two. What is more, he had had no opportunity to see or speak to Emma or to Jack that night, and he sensed that Emma would have felt the hurt of that.

The evening finally came to its close. The doors of the hall closed on the people. He and Harriet returned to their home, but neither Philip nor Emma slept that night. He tossed and turned and went over and over in his mind the events of the day, the death of his friend, and the burden of his illegitimate love. Emma shed tears of frustration on the pillow next to Jack who was oblivious in a deep sleep. She even felt angry with Philip for showing her no attention, though she knew very well he could do no other.

Does he really care for me? she thought. *Why on earth should he love me, close on fifty, a mere washer-woman, a station lackey, a maker of fancy cakes? I offer him my very self, but how worthless is an offering that cannot be consummated because we must be faithful to others? Oh, I am sick unto death.* And her tears continued to fall, until at last, from sheer exhaustion, she fell into a troubled sleep.

Chapter 23

There was no relief from these feelings of utter frustration in the days to come. News that the Battle of the Somme had come to its bitter end with little progress in the war and little territory gained pointed to the futility of it all. Instead, the agonizing number of dead, the young men of a generation, led Philip into a state of keen anguish and anger that such loss was so hopeless. All his Quaker principles, principles that had guided him all his life, endorsed his strong conviction that he had been right in condemning the war in the first place. And he felt completely helpless in the face of so much suffering and loss around him—boys bereft of fathers and brothers; staff members grieving over lost fiancés; villagers like Mr and Mrs Firbank bemused and in pain from loss.

News of the fate of the soldiers at the front came with other information about the appalling state that many of them were left in. Their orders before the offensive had been brutal. The order to kill without mercy, their bayonets in the faces of the enemy, had had a terrible effect. Will had been right to dread it. He had found himself face to face with one enemy soldier and had knifed him with full force in his stomach as they had been told they must. *No mercy.* Will could do no other than kill him first before the enemy killed him. He would never forget the way the scarlet blood had gushed out of him in a ghastly fountain that splashed Will's face as it sprayed upwards.

Back in the dugout, he had been violently sick. Ralph, though he was his superior, had become a friend, and they shared their experiences of the horror. As he was retching what felt like his whole guts that night, Ralph had come and stood beside him, handing him a glass of water to rinse the ugly bile away. They had shared a lot of time together in the dugout through the long, hard days and exchanged confidences. Ralph had talked about his wife freely to Will, and Will had found himself envying Ralph having such a loving partner.

"If you envy me, Will, I envy you of your family back home. Whoever else has a mother who is a station master and who makes delicious cakes by the dozen all on the same day? And your dad, well, he sounds like the backbone of the village. When this is all over, I'd like to meet them. My parents are too busy fraternising with the rich and famous to bother writing to me. But I do thank God for my lovely Laura."

These horrific orders and their fulfilment in action left them all with terrible memories, not least Will. But worse were the physical reactions that affected some, and Will became fearful for Albert, his friend from Cranston. The newspapers reported boys with stomach cramps and facial tics, unable to sleep at all or else tormented with nightmares reliving their experiences. At headquarters at the front, this could not be ignored. Military hospitals were set up to deal with this very alarming syndrome—shell-shocked troops so stupefied and traumatised that they could no longer deal with daily living, requiring urgent hospital treatment with help from trained psychiatrists. The hospital at Craiglockhart became very famous, for it was there that they sent the court-martialled Sassoon whose words and poetry had so anathematized the generals. Philip read of these events in the newspaper and felt a huge pang of sympathy for a man he very much admired for his outspoken courage. The hospital that was set up in York for the same purpose, however, was much nearer to home, and he determined to pay it a visit and see for himself the men so disabled.

Philip hardly dared think of Emma, knowing she would be terrified of losing her own boys and unable to stand the thought that he could not really offer his comfort except for in the few brief moments at the end of his quiet hour. And to his deep distress, she had not come at all after the memorial meeting. Nor did she attend again as the weeks drew near to the end of term and to the Christmas holidays; holidays all the staff were longing for in their exhaustion. And Philip knew that would be the end of the hour until the boys returned. He had to content himself with chatting to Jack and asking politely after her and baby George.

Emma, in her turn, was striving to hold her courage and her belief in Philip's care for her. Her despair on the night of the service had never quite left her, hence her determination to try to keep away from him. Yet the desire to see him and love him was a torment. Day by day went by in a numbed state, clinging to the routine of cooking, washing, caring for George, and her station duties. That she had to get up in the morning and deal in a systematic way with all the calls on her was a kind of dull comfort, and this anguish was always underpinned with her thoughts and prayers for Will and Harry. Miraculously, the lists remained clear of their names.

I should be thanking God for their safe keeping and indeed I am, she thought, *But I am overwrought with this unasked-for love I am carrying.*

Then at last, as if to break this time of deadlock and as term ended and boys returned to their homes, letters arrived, and with them, the snow. It was a pitiless snow, heavy and unrelenting, descending on Shadworth in huge white globules and then massing furiously in the wind to create blizzard conditions. The school closed its doors. Miss Hanson donned her Wellington boots to struggle through to her office for one day only then to announce to the head that she was hibernating and that he too should do the same, especially as she could see his leg was paining him in the struggle across the icy paths and in the face of the onslaught. Even Jack withdrew into Holt House and left his beloved school garden to look after itself.

But Emma had to keep up her station duties as trains of troops with saddened, weary faces at the windows continued pushing through the harsh weather. It almost broke Emma's heart. Philip felt utterly inadequate in the face of it all and worried himself endlessly about Emma, knowing she would never give up and stay in as he had been forced to do.

Then the letters started to arrive. The first was from Will.

December 20, 1916

My dear Mother and Father,

I cannot tell you how relieved we all are still to be alive after the offensive on the Somme. Ralph, my captain, and I were convinced no good could come of it, and oh, Mother, we were right. Perhaps one day I'll be able to tell you about it. In the meantime, thank you for your wonderful letters which bring me such encouragement despite everything. Ralph, I think, envies me them, though his wife, Laura, writes to him.

But my worst news is about Albert, my friend who comes from near Shadworth. I've told you about him. They took him to the casualty clearing station because he started having awful nightmares about the battle, screaming out so loud that none of us could sleep for the noise. I tried to sit by him till the nightmares left him but even waking he just could not stop shaking. Father, you can imagine how bad I felt, can't you? In the end, Ralph reported it and he left still trying to hold on to me. I believe he's going from the field hospital near us back to Blighty, we think, to a new military hospital that's been set up for this kind of thing. It's in York, so not too far from home.

Mother, if I can get a bit of leave, I'd really like to visit him, as it's not so far away. See what you think.

I had news of our Harry a day ago, and he is fine, still cooking for those Frenchies. Maggie will never need to cook again—he loves the work. But the French are battling hard to keep the enemy out of Verdun, so it's not a picnic over there. Don't worry Mother, he's coping. You know our Harry!

I've got to close, but please pass on my best love to our Florrie and Maggie and kiss baby George for me.

Your own Will.

This gave both Jack and Emma some comfort at news of Harry, but the news of the horrific aftermath of the offensive and what it was doing to the men, and to Will's friend Albert in particular, rendered them speechless for some time, and they just looked at each other appalled. The terrible lethargy Emma was feeling was even more leaden after this. Despite it, however, she began to plan how to get to Albert if Will should get leave.

Then Maggie received a letter from her beloved Harry for whom she prayed earnestly each day and whom she longed to see.

December 20, 1916

My darling Maggie,

Oh, Maggie, I miss you something awful, and I think of you all the time, you and our baby. To think I am missing all this precious time and he will be growing up without me. His first birthday due and I just can't get leave. I'm very taken up with my cooking duties, and the chaps do seem grateful for it. I can't wait to come home to you and cook you one of my new concoctions.

Mother writes me that you've got a lot of snow. Same here, and it doesn't make it easy for the troops to keep the route for supplies open. They call the road that we're protecting the Sacred Way. Fancy that, Maggie! It's that important. But you mustn't worry, pet, I'm still alright.

I love you, Maggie.
Keep smiling. Harry.

The mention of George's birthday coming straight after Christmas gave Maggie and Florrie a renewed zeal, and they began harassing Emma that she must try to organise not only Christmas, quiet though it must be, but a birthday party for the little boy. When Florence discovered from Ronald Tempest on one of her many walks down to Tempest's farm that Ned had got Christmas leave, she blushed with pleasure and vowed to make sure Ned would have the excuse to come to the party. She had helped when she could, planting new crops in the fields which had lain fallow the previous year. And beside them were the very fields where, the year earlier, they had all gloried in the potato picking. The girls got Jack on their side to stir Emma up, and he was only too glad to do anything to rouse her out of her lassitude.

"I shall kill one of the chickens for the Christmas table, Emma, even though it will be a strange Christmas with the village so cut off and so many of the lads gone to war. You can make something with that, surely. Then we'll need some of your special little cakes for George's birthday. Maggie and Florence are going to make him a cake with candles."

Emma nodded dumbly in assent, but Jack was determined to snap her out of this strange melancholy which he could not fathom. He knew it was her fear for her boys but had no conception that it was also the pain in her sore heart for Philip.

"Maybe I'll take another chicken up to school if I can manage through the drifts. Mr Manners will likely be needing something for him and his wife, as the school is so cut off. What do you think?"

Emma's heart warmed at this idea, and she thought again of how fortunate she was to have a man like Jack to care for her. She must not allow her deep love for another man to damage her long-held love for Jack.

Unbeknown to the Holts, at the school, an urgent missive had arrived for Harriet from her mother in Worcester. This was to cause something of a bombshell in School House and turned Jack's idea on its head.

December 21, 1916

Dear Harriet,

I write to let you know Father has had a severe stroke and has been taken to Worcester Infirmary. It happened last night, and I am quite wretched. The snow is so heavy, and I know it will be difficult to get here but I am alone, and I do wish you could come and be with me. I know Father would like to see you more than anyone else in the world, so do you think you can leave Philip for a while and come and help out? He can surely manage without you, and I need you.

If you can come, let me know your train times.

Love, Mother.

Philip watched as Harriet opened the letter. She turned pale and quickly lowered herself into the nearest chair as if her legs could not hold her. He hastened to her and took the letter. As he read, she leaned on him in the old way she used to as her tears fell. He held her close and kissed her forehead.

She looked up at him pleadingly. "Philip, I must go to them. I can't bear to think of Father like that and Mother not knowing how to cope. How can I do it? Are the trains running through to Sheffield in all this snow? I could get a connection there for Worcester and a cab to take me to Mother."

Harriet had never seemed so fragile as he looked down at her, and he felt how important it was for them to sustain a level of care for each other. Indeed, he glimpsed in her at that moment, albeit briefly, the young Harriet as she had been in Oxford—vulnerable, worshipping her father in those youthful days, spoiled, and adored by him. He, Philip, had been an interloper in that close relationship and yet she had fought against her father to marry him. In the end, the bishop had had no choice but to give in to her wishes.

Poor Harriet, he thought, *she has regretted that wilfulness for so long now, and I could never quite match her expectations.* He looked down at her lovingly and promised her to do all that was needed to see her on her way.

"Whatever you want, my dear. I only wish Kath wasn't holed up in her cottage, for she would get things sorted with the station straight away."

"Philip, of course *you* need not come. You had much better stay here to see to school matters and look after things. I can do this, and Father will not take comfort seeing you, I'm afraid." He knew she was right but this awkward truth was painful to accept.

Nevertheless, this was no time for regret, and he hastily set to work sorting out train times and helping Harriet pack all the necessities for the journey. He searched for the convenient morning trains, praying they would not be cancelled due to the weather conditions. He found one to connect to the Midlands, God willing—an 8:30 a.m. train to Sheffield. He smothered the thought that Emma might just be on duty there though it would be like finding water in the desert if she were.

"My dear, you must sleep now to be ready for the journey in the morning. Come to my room tonight, love. Let me at least keep you comforted for tomorrow."

She assented with a strange look but allowed him to tuck her in his bed, so long empty of her, and fell asleep from weariness and anxiety almost instantly. He lay awake next to her for a long time, praying for the grace to give her the care she needed without selfishness on his part. There were a great many regrets running through his mind as he watched her sleeping.

If only we had managed to conceive a child. If only I had not been crippled with this confounded leg.

He knew full well his damaged leg hadn't helped. He thought ruefully of the bike he'd bought for himself in Salisbury so that he could get around efficiently. *I loved that bike,* thought Philip. But the day the brakes had failed as he'd been racing down the hill back to school after a meeting in town had left him unconscious in hospital. He had crashed headlong into the high wall which bordered the school and his knee had been smashed. The patella was badly fractured and would forever remain a terrible weakness even after it healed. Already then, Harriet had been finding it difficult to be sympathetic though she had managed it at first. But as she'd found herself with a permanently crippled husband unable to carry on his duties for many weeks, and then sporting a walking stick, she'd grown weary of being kind.

Perhaps if her father could have been more reconciled to our marriage and given me an inch of encouragement. And now he's sick and reduced. I am sorry for that.

It was something of a relief when morning dawned and he was able to wake her but more especially for the fact that a thaw was clearly underway. Water was dripping from the roof and huge clumps of snow were falling heavily down on the path. It meant that the walk to the station with her suitcase would be less strenuous; the walk he had been dreading through the long, sleepless hours, thanks to his maddening crippled leg. He had known full well no cabs would be running in the aftermath of the terrible snow.

So, they set out, she holding on to his arm in an almost childlike way—a phenomenon Philip could not help but note. Her suitcase dragged him down, but he struggled on, and eventually they reached Shadworth Station through the puddles of melted snow. As they walked, he reassured her that school would be fine and that he could manage perfectly well. She must devote herself to her mother's and father's needs without a passing thought for home. She looked up at him then and remembered with a pang what he had been to her in the old days in their early married life. The memory stopped her short for a moment.

Oh God, if only things could have been different.

To Philip's intense relief, the station loomed before them, and there was Emma ready to signal the earlier train to depart. She gasped as she saw them and his heart lurched, but Harriet, completely unaware, set off to the ticket office and bought her ticket as he and Emma gazed at each other. The returning Harriet interrupted the moment of quiet intimacy.

"Mrs Holt, I believe," said Harriet. "Do you work here then?"

"I'm the assistant station master for the interim, yes," she responded, "But I hope as good as any man." She saw the smile flicker across Philip's lips at that and smiled at him with all the love she had gathered up over the barren weeks just past.

Harriet was hardly listening, of course, and merely asked if the train was on time and if her connection in Sheffield would be secure. Philip explained the need for Harriet's journey very quietly, and Emma realised how anxious Harriet must be feeling. Her natural warmth and compassion came quickly into play, and she touched Harriet's arm and assured her that the trains were running in the thaw quite normally. Indeed, the Sheffield train was due, and she had to be ready on the platform without more ado. Nevertheless, she could hardly suppress the thought of the implication of Harriet's trip, and she felt an unworthy and illegitimate sense of relief.

She watched as the train pulled into the platform and saw him ushering her on with her suitcase. He touched her forehead with his lips and held her hand tightly as she climbed into the carriage. As Emma saw the man she loved carrying out his responsibility to his wife in his usual loving and conscientious way, she warned herself sternly once again of the reality of the situation.

The platform emptied and the train pulled out, waved on its way by the replacement station master.

Once her duty was over, Emma pulled him into the empty waiting room.

Oh, thank God it's empty.

Its grimy windows, still frosted over from the cold, gave them protection from the world outside for a few brief minutes. He felt the relief wash over him after her long absence in the late autumn and took a tight hold of her. She rested her head against him and shared the moment.

"My love, where have you been?" he uttered into the rough cloth of the cap perched on her head.

"I just felt so inadequate and so unworthy of you after the memorial. I could not get even a glance from you. You were so much the exalted head of the prestigious school. It all seemed so hopeless and pointless, for what can we do, my love? And who am I to dare even think these thoughts of such a man as you?" she whispered into his coat.

Philip abruptly pulled back with a look of such injury and almost anger that she gasped. "Emma, you must not talk like this. How can you? You are more than my equal in courage, endurance, and plain common sense. You know I want you with all my heart and, God forgive me, I have no right to desire it. Harriet has had to go and stay with her mother to help her with the bishop and here I am, having only just handed her onto the train, so utterly glad to see you. I am angry with myself for loving you like this, but I will not deny this moment." He pushed back the hair that had crept out from her cap and kissed her with all the repressed passion of the weeks of abstinence. Yet she had to break away from him reluctantly.

"Philip, you take my breath away, my love, but my 'plain common sense', as you call it, is already demanding that I get ready for the train coming in from York. I cannot delay here with you, much as I long to. And, Philip, look at you, you are worn out from the trek in the thaw. It can't be good for your leg. And what are you going to do for your Christmas alone? God, Philip, it's all too much. It tears me apart." This all came out in a tumble of words and tears, and she shook her head as though with the movement she could make it all go away.

"Jack was going to bring you one of our chickens to share with Mrs Manners, but you must come and help us eat ours. Besides which, it's George's first birthday the next day, and you should come and celebrate. Will you come, my dear? Please say yes, for I can't stand to think of you all alone."

"No, my dear Emma. That's too much to ask of your family and indeed of Jack. I shall just walk to The White Swan for Christmas lunch of which I am perfectly capable. But perhaps I really could come to George's party if you think Maggie won't mind me?"

"Oh, yes, you must come. Perhaps that's the best and safest arrangement though it will break my heart to think of you by yourself at The Swan. Oh, Philip, what a tangle we're in."

She kissed him gently and sweetly, and he tasted her salt tears on his lips; salt tears which were indeed bitter to him for there was absolutely nothing to be done but for her hurriedly to return to her duties and for him to take the hill back up to school slowly. His leg was throbbing uncomfortably again, but at least he had the certainty that he could see her in just a few days. After the long spell of absence, this came as a quiet solace.

Chapter 24

On Christmas day, the chicken, whose demise was grieved over by Florence, was in fact delicious under Emma's expertise, but she herself ate it without enjoyment so anxious was she that Philip was eating alone. However, her family noticed with great relief that she had found her vitality and was busy again managing them in her old way. This was truly thanks to the thoughts of George's party and the visitor to it whose presence she knew would light up everything for her. Little George always cheered her, and they all partook of the pleasure together when he took his first faltering steps on Christmas day itself.

Jack himself had suggested Philip be invited to the birthday and had an extra suggestion, typical of his thoughtfulness.

"Emma, can we invite Miss Hanson to come along with Mr Manners? Now the thaw has at last come, she has emerged from her cottage and is getting back to work, preparing for the new term already. She would

216

love to see our little George, I know. Do you think Maggie will mind these two interlopers coming? She does not know them as we do. And of course, Florence wants Ned to be there too."

Emma had to smile at this and knew quite well that sweet Maggie would be only too glad to share with the two of them. Maggie and Florence had baked a cake and placed a candle on it, and George had joined in the fun, much amused by the measuring and stirring.

Philip's leg was troubling him painfully, and he was delighted that Kath would be accompanying him down the lane to Low Shadworth. He was very afraid of it causing a fall or another infection and of course wanted to hide this fact from everyone. Kath would give him confidence on the way down. He had had a lonely time by himself at The White Swan while other merrymakers were celebrating around the hotel's large tables, full of hilarity. He also knew that Kath's per-ceptions were always alert, so he would have to take a firm grip on his emotions in front of her, never mind Jack. However, the thought of seeing Emma made the slow days pass more easily, and he felt unusually light-hearted as Kath called for him on the day.

Florence in particular was delighted that Philip was coming as she talked to her mother that morning. "He's so kind, and I always feel perfectly comfortable with him. You'd never know he was so important. I'll never forget how good he was to you and to us all the day we got the news of our George's death. And I've seen him in the gardens when I've had the baby in the pram. He doesn't have any children of his own, and I think he really likes George and so does dear Miss Hanson."

Emma nodded wisely in response to this comment and awaited his arrival with an expectant joy she hadn't felt for some time.

The tea she had prepared met everyone's expectations, and it was a jolly party which gathered around the table. Maggie showed all the motherliness she had acquired over the year in her handling of the small but determined little tot who exercised his newly discovered skill and tottered round his visitors quite unabashed. He smiled with utter innocent pleasure as the candle was lit and "Happy Birthday" sung loudly as he and his mother blew it out together.

Philip sat back in the old, grey armchair by the fire, exhausted more than usual by the trek down. *Thanks to my confounded leg.*

George, to Philip's enormous delight, toddled to him on his fat little legs and held out his arms to be picked up. He dandled him on his good knee as he observed the others all chatting as if they had managed to forget the awfulness of events in France. He watched his upright secretary laughing at something Jack had said and was humbled by a very considerate Florence who had decided to look after him for the afternoon. Her own visitor, Ned, simply watched her adoringly, and

Philip couldn't help smiling at the picture Ned made of such young love. He had asked Ned about the front and how he was coping out there, and Ned had confessed to being very afraid.

"But, sir, I couldn't be a conchy. The sergeants treat them like dirt when they're helping with stretchers and such like instead of fighting, and some of the men make fun of them," he confided. "I know you believe in being a pacifist, sir, but you'll have to forgive me for what I'm saying."

"Of course, Ned." Philip smiled. "I understand, and I'm sure you're doing your best out there. Needs must, I know." He felt glad to be able to reassure the boy and glad to see he was making Florence very happy. But best of all was being content in Emma's home as if he was a part of it and getting to enjoy the sight of her in her element, caring for them all. He knew she was loving him as he was loving her and simply relaxed for once in the warmth of it.

Emma, for her part, rejoiced in seeing the colour back in his cheeks after the look of exhaustion he'd had on arrival. Seeing him talking to the little one as naturally as any of the family made her almost feel like choking with the emotion of it, but she held it together, as she was also very mindful of her kindly husband. She was unutterably grateful to Jack for his patience and willingness to share the occasion with the two visitors. The partnership they had built over all the years was indeed resilient, and nothing could alter that fact. But it was difficult not to watch too avidly the man in the armchair with whom she had fallen so deeply in love. Occasionally she saw Kath Hanson watching her and had to pull herself up with a jolt. And Kath, in her turn, inwardly prayed that no harm should come of that relationship which she had watched develop over the years.

Be careful, Mr Manners. Be careful, Mrs Holt.

At last, the time came for George's bedtime, and Maggie rose with Ned and Florence to take George home to their cottage. She took him off Philip's knee, and Philip glowed with embarrassed pride as George protested loudly. Then came the moment for Philip also to rise to his feet and join Kath at the door to give their thanks to Emma and Jack for the day's joys. He allowed himself to take Emma's hand in gratitude.

"Jack, it's so dark now. Will you walk these two back up the lane with your torch?" Emma asked. "I'm fearful they may stumble in all this wet."

"Nonsense, Mrs Holt. Kath and I will hold each other up as we need to. You must not bother Jack."

"Nay, Mr Manners, it's no bother. What kind of a host do you make me out to be?" Jack laughed as he put on his overcoat.

The old pain returned to Emma's heart as the three left. Such sadness that things could not be any different, but also a sense of shame knowing that her thoughts would shock her loving family if they only knew.

That night, she once again silently cried herself to sleep in frustration and sad regret. Yet Philip, truly worn out, slept soundly despite the pain in his leg and dreamed of her deeply, only to wake with a grim jolt as he faced the reality of the situation all over again.

Chapter 25

December swung into January, and the winter still had the land in its iron grip. Fog and frost seeped into the fields and lanes as the trees stood eerie sentinel over them, their dark branches emerging into the air spookily from the frozen grey ground. Ron Tempest's black cattle huddled together at the foot of them, their breaths like white clouds against the gloom.

Term was due to begin on January 7, and Philip held his usual preparatory staff meeting, aware of what duress all would be under without Alan Lorimer and Godfrey Langdon, but in particular, without Jim. So much, once again, would have to rest on his own shoulders, though he was enormously thankful for Edna Wright. Considering the circumstances, however, they were unusually cheerful, and everyone tried very hard not to acknowledge the awful gap left by the death of Jim Fletcher who had always been the life and soul of the company. Then two letters arrived.

The first letter was from Harriet, and its contents left Philip with something of relief but also a question as to its implications.

January 3, 1917

Dear Philip,

I trust you are managing well in my absence. I write to let you know I will need to remain in Worcester with Mother for the interim, as Father is only making a very slow recovery despite being allowed home with a stand-by nurse in attendance. He is very frustrated at his lack of mobility and unable to articulate his words very well as yet, though we are assured he will make progress in time. I feel awfully upset seeing him like this, as does Mother, for you know he has always been the one to lead and speak out on every subject imaginable. I do hope you will understand that my place really is here in Worcester.

I must tell you though that I have had a surprise visitor to the rectory which has cheered me and Mother enormously. Godfrey Langdon, your newly appointed deputy, who, sadly, hardly had time to make his presence felt on the staff, has been invalided out of the ranks for a short time to convalesce from a nasty bout of glandular fever he caught at the front during the offensive on the Somme. We met in the high street quite recently and it turns out that he lives with his parents close to our house and will be returning in a few weeks

*back to France. In the meantime, we are helping pass
his time and getting to know his parents whom Mother
seems to have taken to. Father is very comfortable with
him despite his disability. Godfrey has asked me to pass
on this news to you and his very best wishes.*

*I will write again when things look easier for my re-
turn.*

*Yours affectionately,
Harriet*

A wry smile played on Philip's lips at this missive
which said much more than it professed, knowing as
he did how Harriet had lit up at Langdon's attentions.
He knew he should be the very last person to judge
Harriet's behaviour. At least her absence took the
strain out of his leisure time, and he need not fret that
he was keeping her waiting and angering her when he
was occupied in his study. He dared not admit to himself that it felt much more peaceful without her.

The second letter was a challenging and interesting
one. It came from his MP whose earlier intervention
had led him to the meeting in London, fruitless though
that had been.

January 7, 1917

*Dear Mr Manners,
You may remember our correspondence of a year ago
concerning the court martial procedures and the man-*

agement of the war. I was glad you were able to attend the meeting in London at that time in order to share your views. I was only sorry that you had such little encouragement and that the status quo remained as indeed it still does.

However, I now have another request for your consideration. The government is much perturbed at the news from the front in every respect, but one matter is a cause for some specific concern. There are many reports of troops who are not in any way physically injured but who are suffering some kind of serious emotional trauma as an aftereffect of the battle. We have set up several military hospitals specially to cater for this kind of illness. The one in Edinburgh you will have read about as it has housed the outspoken poet Sassoon. But there is one now establishing itself in York not too far from your area, and I have been asked to see whether you could visit it and report back to us as to its effectiveness.

I know you have your hands full with the students and without your male colleagues who have gone to the front, but if you could spare a weekend, perhaps in your half-term break, to meet the staff there and write a report on it, we would be very grateful. We would very much like to know how these cases are being handled in the hospital and whether it is likely that these men can be fully rehabilitated.

*My colleague, Arnold Rowntree, MP for York, who
is himself head of Bootham Quaker School, would be
pleased to meet you there and discuss the situation.*

I await your reply with thanks in anticipation.

Yours sincerely,

Frank Jacques, MP

Philip received this epistle just as all the boys were
returning and in the full flood of activity. Despite this,
he gave it some careful thought and was inclined to
take up the challenge, pleased to be able to help if only
in a small way. Moreover, he was aware that Arnold
Rowntree was himself a Quaker and he welcomed the
opportunity to discuss with him the whole subject of
conscientious objection.

Only recently, he had read how Rowntree had secured the reprieve from the death penalty on the 'Richmond Sixteen' absolutists—those men imprisoned in
Richmond Castle for refusing to do anything for the
war effort, who had been kicked, beaten, and starved
there. Philip knew how Kitchener, Secretary of State
for War, had made certain that "absolutists" should be
marked out for particularly vicious treatment and had
them sent, totally illegitimately, to France where they
would inevitably be shot for treason and desertion unless they capitulated. But the sixteen had maintained
their courageous refusal to act against their pacifist beliefs despite being left to rot in a disused fish quay in

Boulogne, from whence they would be taken and executed.

Philip had read how, by an extraordinary stroke of good fortune, one of the sixteen had managed to throw out a coded letter to Rowntree, his own MP, from the train carrying them to France. And Rowntree had spoken out in Parliament against this inhuman behaviour.

Moreover, the news reported that the sixteen had been saved from their inevitable executions by a stroke of pure chance. Kitchener himself, along with six hundred others, had drowned on board a ship which struck a mine off Orkney before he could implement their executions. He could pursue the "absolutists" no longer. The tragedy on board the ship allowed for the rescue of the sixteen—*an anomaly*, thought Philip, *which must lie in the mystery of God.*

He felt very strongly that he would like to meet Rowntree and here was his opportunity. Accordingly, he showed the letter to his colleagues who all agreed it would be something he could usefully do to see for himself the state of the traumatised young men who had gone through so much and assess the care they were receiving. His decision was strengthened by a circumstance he was not expecting.

On his way back home, he bumped into Jack and they exchanged warm greetings. As usual, he asked about Emma and baby George.

"Well, sir, we've had Leonard Thomson to look at the little chap. Emma was worried to death, as he had a temperature and would not eat anything. Maggie was beside herself, so we called in the doctor. He gave George a bottle of some mixture to bring down his temperature and checked him over and he's now as right as rain. But we could see the doctor was not himself at all. Indeed, Emma herself asked him what was wrong. It's as if she has a second sense about these things, you know, sir."

Philip nodded. He knew that this was part of the reason he had fallen so much in love with her.

"It all came tumbling out then. The doctor's son, James, is out there with Ron Tempest's son, Ned, and they've been at the front of the troops attacking the enemy lines in the offensive. Ned is fine, but James has been badly affected by it. He's so jumbled up with himself that they've invalided him out, and he's going to be sent to that new hospital we've read about in York when he's well enough to board the train back to Blighty. The poor doctor and his wife are hoping to visit him when he gets there but they are overwrought at present. I don't think there is anything worse than waiting for news. I speak for Emma and me in this. Knowing our boys are out there, in goodness knows what state, is hell, Mr Manners."

Philip put his hand on Jack's shoulder. He realised that he had his answer as to taking up the challenge of

Frank Jacques. Why, he could go with the doctor and his wife and do the visit whilst accompanying them on their very sad journey. It would be company for them and for himself.

He bid Jack his farewell with renewed determination to go, promising himself he would visit Leonard and Sheila, his wife, and discuss it with them both. What's more, he felt he needed urgently to see Emma and ensure she was coping and that George was better. So, having done his rounds of the houses and checked there were no homesick boys after the return to school, he returned home to write to Frank Jacques giving him his assent. Tomorrow, he would walk down to Low Shadworth and see for himself.

It was very icy underfoot as he began the walk to the station the next day in the hope of seeing Emma. He leaned heavily on his stick and felt his wretched leg really bothering him. But he had a purpose and was determined to pursue it. A train was pulling in to Shadworth as he approached. He was shocked to see the wearied faces of the injured troops en route to their designated hospitals as they peered hopelessly out of the windows. Yet his spirit lightened as he saw Emma pursuing her duties for Mr Firbank, buttoned up to the nines in the navy coat and crazy cap and still looking oh so beautiful. He struggled his way along the platform.

"Philip, what are you doing here? You should be resting your leg. I can tell it's painful."

"Emma, hush." He smiled. "I wanted to see you were alright and to check George is better. Is he quite back to normal now after the scare?"

As she nodded in affirmation, he went on, "I have had a letter about the hospital in York, and Jack told me about James Thomson." He told her the project and she gasped as an idea came to mind. Once the station cleared of people and they were alone, she voiced her thought to see what Philip thought of it.

"Will's friend, Albert, has also been sent there, and Will is taking leave if he can get it in this brief lull from fighting. He wants to visit Albert, of whom he is very fond, and for me to go with him. Perhaps we can share the trip with you and the Thomsons?"

"That would be wonderful," he said, taking her hand in his, "But we would have to think through how to combine everybody's needs. Does Will have some leeway as to when he can get away? And how would Jack feel? I'm on my way to see the Thomsons after this and can plan a date with them, though we must be sure Will can get a date himself first. Then we should get a place to lodge overnight for us all. But, darling, should we really consider doing this? I hardly dare allow myself the pleasure."

She loved him then for all the goodness that shone out of him and knew she could never match it. Yet she knew that such an endeavour would be not only a caring and compassionate thing to undertake but that also it would give them the chance at last to be together for a proper stretch of time. A stolen joy indeed.

"I will write to Will to get him to organise his leave, and you should settle it with Jack to check he is content for me to come. But, my love, another train is due, and I can't stop. The platform will soon be busy again, and we must be careful."

He kissed her then very gently in farewell, almost daring the world to see. She saw him wince with pain as he drew himself together and begged him to ask the doctor to look at his leg. As for Philip, with the prospect of organising the trip, he was beyond caring about his leg.

The visit he later made to the good doctor and his wife was heartbreaking as he shared their distress, but he was able to promise them he would do all in his power to bring them to their son.

As life and term moved on, the wheels were set in motion for the visit to York with everyone's agreement. Will was full of joy at the thought of leave, and the Thomsons found a renewed hope in looking forward to seeing their James.

Chapter 26

Ned Tempest had been given leave and arrived back at the farm as the spring of 1917 was bursting out in the meadows and the hedgerows. He was just in time to help his father with the lambing, and he invited Florence to come down and watch. She was much moved by the sight of the ewes struggling and birthing, sometimes with loud cries, and watched, enchanted, the newborn lambs almost immediately scrambling weakly to stand on their wobbly legs. While Florence gazed on, thrilled at the lambs, Ned drew near to her and kissed her. His kiss surprised her, she jumped with the shock of its suddenness and Ned hugged her to him.

"Florrie, my sweet, do you think we might make a go of our love? Do you think you would consider marrying me once this damned war is over, God willing?

Florence felt a huge joy surge up inside herself. She was humbled and thrilled that such a man as Ned should want her.

"Ned, I can think of nothing that would please me more," she said and kissed him again. She prayed that he would come safe and unscathed from it all so that this tryst might be fulfilled. They hurried into the farm kitchen and announced their news to the Tempests who hugged them and gave them their blessing. Florence could hardly wait to get home to tell her own parents. She knew Ned would have to go about it the correct way and actually ask her Father's permission for her hand, and moreover, she was longing to tell Maggie what had happened. Thus, Jack and Emma received the delighted pair at Holt House sometime later and were able also to indulge in a moment of unadulterated pleasure; a moment when fears and grief gave way to gladness.

Hard work from all staff and students alike continued at school, and Kath Hanson had her hands full with all the demands of her office. She wondered, as the weeks went by, when Mrs Manners would return but was more concerned with the head's health. She knew he was wearing himself to a frazzle with the demands on his time and that his leg was troubling him a great deal. And she also observed how intense he was in discussing the trip to York with the Thomsons and with Jack. She met with Cook in the school kitchens for a quiet cup of tea and was somewhat horrified when Cook commented on the way she had seen him look at Mrs Holt one day when she was bringing back the laundry.

"He's a lonely man, Kath. He must think a lot of Mrs Holt, don't you think?"

Kath, who had seen for her own part Emma's way of looking at Philip, retorted briskly, "He has got to know the Holts well this year with all the troubles they've shared. He and Jack Holt are good friends, you know, Connie."

"Don't get snappy with me, Kath," Cook answered. "I wasn't born yesterday."

The conversation closed, and Kath once again said a quiet prayer to herself that the head would not allow his affection for Emma to risk his reputation.

As for Philip, he was enjoying his lessons with the lower sixth boys who were studying John Donne, the poet who after years of philandering with women met his one true wife and then lost her to an early grave, finally ending his days as Dean of St Paul's. He was teaching them Donne's Holy Sonnets and demonstrating to them Donne's sense of his earlier sins which, Donne felt, prevented him from being truly redeemed. The boys, all of them very committed to their English lessons under their beloved headmaster, engaged with the work volubly, asking question after question about meaning and writer. He had a lucid moment whilst teaching them "Batter my heart, three-person'd God" with its last three lines:

"Take me to you, imprison me, for I,
Except you enthrall me, never shall be free,
Nor ever chaste, except you ravish me."

"What does that mean, sir?" they demanded, and he tried to explain to them the metaphor of a lover whose passion is only made truly pure by its consummation with the loved one. The passion and need for God, felt by Donne, required him to be completely abandoned to God if he were to be truly holy in God's service.

This was not an easy subject for teenage boys, but for Philip, it represented a truth about his love for Emma.

I pray that God will forgive me for this love I feel. I pray He will understand that I am trying so very hard to be faithful to all I believe in, to all the Quaker principles, to be chaste. And I hope He can understand that we are both trying to keep from injuring anyone by it. And yet I know how much I long to consummate this love for her and find the desire in me almost irresistible. And, oh God, it is within our reach now.

This thought shook him to the marrow, as he knew that the trip to York was to be accomplished in the near future with the blessing of Jack and with Will's leave successfully rubber-stamped.

The date was set for April 14, in the Easter vacation. He had himself booked rooms for them all for the night in the County Hotel in York at his own expense, given that he was receiving expenses from Frank Jacques for undertaking to make the report.

God help me to get this right, he prayed in the Meeting House night by night, sometimes joined by Emma, as she was still wont to come to the silent hour and share it with the boys in distress.

God help us both.

Chapter 27

Jack himself saw the party to the station with the loan of Ron Tempest's farm cart. Will was exuberant at his homecoming and the chance to see his old friend. He was quite overwhelmed at his welcome, especially at seeing his nephew who was now beginning to sound out his words and vociferously demanding to be played with.

Jack had carefully discussed with Philip the organisation of the trip, and Emma had stressed to him that he could come too if he wanted, but he had felt it not necessary for him to go and had given the trip his approval, even though he felt a small regret that he was not to be included.

"Aye, sir, of course you must go with the doctor, and Will'll love having his mother along. I'm sure it'll be a painful sight to see these poor lads in their trouble, but I've no doubt you can make some good come out of it. And my Emma—she'd do anybody good."

Jack trusted Emma's innate compassion and good
sense to support anyone in trouble. His suspicions of
her relationship with Philip had been shelved for, as far
as Jack could perceive, she remained as she had always
been—his own stalwart and best partner and friend.
Yet, at these generous words, Philip felt a sharp pang
of guilt that stopped him short for a moment. It was
all too painful. Indeed, he hardly slept the night before
they left as he thought of his friend. Accordingly, as
Jack saw them off to York, it was only Philip who knew
how ironic Jack's unselfish farewell really was.

"Take care of Emma, sir. Make sure she doesn't wear
herself out caring for everybody else." He embraced
Emma and then shook hands with Philip as he ushered
them all onto the train. Philip felt this request keenly
and the responsibility of it. All it represented lay heavy
on him. He promised himself to function as the good
shepherd of them all at that moment and was saved
from further self-doubt by Sheila Thomson thanking
him warmly for what he was doing for them.

They approached York Military Hospital for shell-
shocked troops by cab. It was a little way out of the city
in a quiet cul-de-sac but impressive in its own grounds.
Philip was met very officially by the medical superintendent along with Arnold Rowntree himself, who had
made every effort to come and meet the head of the
successful school in Shadworth, which had the same

Quaker foundation as his own school at Bootham. He had no doubt the schools would share the same principles. Both men were expecting Philip at Frank Jacques' request and, accordingly, he had to part with the others of the party at that point. Frank Jacques' invitation had come from his huge respect for Philip's work at the school and he had therefore sought his wisdom in visiting the young men so burdened by their experiences, yet not so much older than the boys under Philip's own care.

As Philip assured the others he would catch up with them on the ward they were visiting, he allowed himself one glance at Emma, who gave him a reassuring smile. Leonard Thomson had the last word as they parted their ways.

"Mr Manners, this is your opportunity to serve our troops in a special way. Remember, it is for the good of all those who are suffering that your report will go to the heart of the government. I personally would like to read it."

"We'll see you soon, sir," said Emma as she led the others to the reception point where they were shown to the ward where Albert and James were both being cared for.

The Thomsons hurried to James' bedside. Sheila stood transfixed, gazing down at her son, her hand to her mouth. James showed no sign of recognising them. His eyes were fixed on the ceiling but his hands kept twitching constantly revealing an inner stress. His father steadied himself as Sheila turned to him, shaking with emotion. He simply couldn't comprehend the strength of feelings overwhelming him.

"Sheila, we must both compose ourselves. You don't know how much he is noticing."

Yet James gave no acknowledgement, so disconnected had he become as a result of all the ghastly violence he had seen and done at the front. James' doctor had realised that Leonard Thomson was himself a doctor and had met them personally to take them to the ward. He was sympathetic as he told them that James had been suffering terrible nightmares, and he believed it was a result of James being ordered to bayonet the enemy in one-to-one combat. He had undergone hypnosis, and this fact had emerged under the treatment.

"What else are you hoping to do to help him recover?" asked Leonard with a furrowed brow. It all seemed so hopeless. His wife was already sitting beside her son, quietly crying in abject dismay. As she took James' hand to prevent it from twitching, she felt it move in hers as if he had, deep inside himself, some knowledge that his mother was there. This gave her a modicum of comfort, and she pressed the quaking hand gently. Both she and her husband felt they must sit beside him, simply silent, just to show they were there, for as long as they were allowed.

Meanwhile, Emma and Will had found Albert in an adjacent room. Their meeting was less disturbing, as Albert was sitting fully dressed on his bed, smoking a cigarette. He recognised Will instantly, with huge pleasure. Will was glad he had his mother beside him as he watched aghast as Albert tried to articulate to him all that was happening to him, unable to get his words out properly on account of a vicious stammer. Will found this heartrending, for his old friend had been the most cheerful and voluble and crude of all his colleagues at the front.

"The b-b-b-buggers don't give us m-m-much sympathy, W-W-Will," he stammered. "They've p-p-put me on some g-g-god-awful diet and all but told me to

p-p-pull myself together to get b-b-back to the f-f-front." His speech continued very haltingly between long pauses, and Will could feel his throat tighten with the emotion and the horror of seeing his mate struggling so.

"Albert, I need a cigarette, never mind you," he joked, but there were tears in his eyes as he spoke, and Emma knew how much this was mentally costing him. Together, they sat at Albert's bedside, feeling that their simple presence was all that was really needed. They conversed sparingly and a sort of peace prevailed there. But at last, they knew their time was coming to an end, and Will stood up and spoke.

"Albert, I have to return to the regiment in two days' time. It'll be full on then, I'm afraid. Try to get well here but take your time, that's my advice, and perhaps we'll end all this horror before you need to return. Get back home to Cranston instead, and you and I will celebrate someday soon in the pub at Shadworth."

"I h-h-hope s-so, W-Will. If only," said Albert bitterly and with great difficulty.

Will was feeling an awful dread about his return to the front. Ralph had told him confidentially that there was to be a new offensive out from Ypres to try to get the troops to the coast at Bruges and destroy the enemy submarine bases before they could stop the route up for good. It would be a large and dangerous move which awaited his return. Despite his own plight, Albert could sense his friend's trepidation at the prospect of return to the front and tried to articulate his sympathy. But it was taking him so much energy even to speak that Emma, seeing the effort it was taking him, took Will's arm and drew him away from the bedside. She was much heartened to see Philip limping towards them, accompanied by the superintendent.

"Say your farewells, Will," said Philip. "I'll collect the Thomsons." He turned to the somewhat austere figure by his side and said, "I think I've seen all I need and am incredibly grateful for your time. It has been illuminating to meet your MP and discuss a little of the plight of the troops."

"Thank you for your visit, Mr Manners," the other replied. "I trust you've seen the excellent work we're doing here."

Philip said very little in response but shook the other man's hand. He took Emma's arm and led her to James' bedside where the couple were still sitting silently beside their son. Emma leaned down to them and spoke very gently.

"We need to go, my friends. Can you say your good-bye to James?" She touched Sheila Thomson's hand where it still lay in James'. Biting her lip, the woman stood, kissed the young man's brow, and walked away weeping. Will was holding back the tears himself as he joined his mother. Albert had held on to him as if he would never let him go.

Philip led Leonard away as Emma and Will led Sheila Thomson from the ward. He spoke to them all reassuringly, "Let's not be too downhearted. I believe they are developing new techniques all the time, and I shall report all that I've seen. I know some of it was deeply disturbing for you, but time and patience will, I am sure, retrieve James from this terrible sickness of soul," Philip said. "You must hang on to his squeeze of your hand, Mrs. Thomson," he said, smiling at her. She nodded in acquiescence.

"Albert was close to being his old self nearly," said Will. "But that awful stammer has reduced him to a shadow of the man I knew. He kept shaking as if he couldn't control it. Do you think that will correct itself, sir?"

"According to the superintendent, they will try electric shock treatment if all else fails," Philip replied.

"Oh, I pray God something can be done before that's necessary. Such treatment would be brutal," said the doctor.

"Come now, my friends, let's go to the hotel, eat, and try to relax. We have a train to catch in the morning. School is calling me and work for us all, I suspect. Let's pray for all those we love and all those I've seen today, and trust it all to God," said Philip. As Emma watched him holding Sheila Thomson's arm, her heart pounded in anticipation of the evening.

They all retired early after dinner, as they were all exhausted after the long and stressful day they'd had. Will told his mother he was going to enjoy the luxury of a comfortable hotel bed after all those months of dugout accommodation, rats and all. She kissed him goodnight and closed the door of her room on them all with a shiver. She knew she had to be with Philip, and this was the moment she had waited for.

His door was unlocked, and she crept in as he was writing at the desk in his room.

"I feel a very scarlet woman, my darling Philip," she whispered. "I don't know how to deal with this. You'll have to help me."

He turned towards her and simply looked at her. She looked back as he got up and came towards her. Gently, he unpinned her hair, and the tangle of it fell down her back as he pushed its tendrils away from her face. She lifted her face to him then, and he took it in both his hands. All the deep longing they had for each other lay between them. Emma ached for him as, very softly, he began to undo the tight buttons of her blouse. His hands were trembling as he did so.

"So many buttons, my love." He smiled as he unfastened the last one. "How beautiful you are." He bent and kissed her breasts, caressing them with exquisite pleasure. Emma allowed her whole body to relax under his touch.

"You have buttons too," she said and began to undo his shirt. She was struck by the tenderness of his abandonment to her, so very different from the swift transition to lovemaking of her husband. The longing for each other was, by this time, extreme, and he held her to him tightly and kissed her with a kind of desperate passion. It was unlike anything she had ever experienced before, piercingly sweet and full of the pent-up desire of the years. It brought with it a powerful need to consummate it in all the fullness of their love. He lay down on the bed and pulled her down beside him. Then she could feel his hardness against her.

She held him close and tightly, longing to have him inside her at last. The pleasure it gave him was intense, the ache for her all but irresistible. And to resist cost him dearly. Yet she saw his hesitance in his face.

"Emma, we can't go any further, my love. How could we face Jack? How could I face Harriet and my staff? Emma, wait!" He uttered this plea even as she undid the last button on his shirt "Remember the vow we made to each other." But she had stripped off her stockings. "Emma, Emma, wait before I forget myself."

"No. No, Philip. Please don't deny me now."

As she pleaded with him, he knew this could not be the honourable Emma he loved talking in this way, re-iterating what in his heart he was also wishing.

"My darling," he began and kissed her again so gently as to bring the tears. "Try to understand. Who do we become if we give in to this longing? I cannot ravish you as I long to because that way is perdition. You must be chaste to me in your heart and chaste in your womb to Jack and your children. I can only possess you fully if we are both free. And, my sweet, sweet love, we are not."

"Oh, Philip, I can't bear to go back to that everlasting longing for you. I have known what it is now to be loved as you have loved me tonight." Tears dripped down her nose and cheeks, but she did not wipe them away. She was quiet as he held her. He could feel her renewed resolve, though the ache in his own body for her was almost overwhelming.

Emma pulled away from him. "My darling, God forgive me. I know you are right in what you say. I suppose there is nothing for it but to go on and endure this agony. But please let me stay a little longer just lying next to you. And let me at least comfort you where your leg hurts. I can see you wincing when you move."

And so, the two lovers shared their chance of being together and tasted the bliss of belonging to each other without, as they reasoned, fully betraying the others to whom they owed allegiance. They forfeited the ultimate pleasure for the sake of those others. Eventually, to enable Philip to sleep properly, Emma dressed and crept out of the room and into her own, where she lay awake for many hours. At last, she gave in to sleep but only just before there came the tap on the door from the hotel staff to alert her to morning and the realities of the day. Normality must be resumed. But nothing could ever be quite the same again after what had happened in all its melting sweetness and its accompanying frustration.

And indeed, normality came with all the practicalities of returning the sorrowful Thomsons to their home, and the painful knowledge that Will must return to the horrors of the dugout not knowing what prospect awaited him. Emma hardly dared look at the man she loved as they took the train home and were met by Jack, once more attendant with the transport as he'd promised. They all parted from each other at their different doorways, and she watched Philip slowly limping back up the school drive with a sense that the old, empty days were once again upon them.

As for Philip, he retired to his study, where Kath Hanson was still typing away, and sat down heavily on his chair. Kath knew instantly that something had happened and feared that it could only end in more misery. What she could never know was the powerful discipline it had taken Philip to withstand the longing to consummate his love. It was something of iron in his soul, and he hated that he had had to deny Emma what she begged him for. It was his wretched Quaker conscience, he thought wryly to himself, but she would be glad of it when she looked back on it and returned to Holt House and baby George. He knew for sure her undoubted loyalty, grown over years of marriage to Jack, would reawaken in the light of every new day.

Accordingly, he set about relating to Kath all they had seen at the hospital and started work on his report without delay.

Chapter 28

April 17, 1917

Dear Mr Jacques,

I have compiled my report on the York hospital and trust I have covered all the details you may require. Please find enclosed.

It was most helpful to meet with your colleague in Parliament who shares much of my view of this benighted war. He will himself, I am sure, fill in the extra details that struck us both so forcibly in the hospital. It was something of a harrowing experience to see those young men so devastated by what they had seen and done. It confirmed my opinion of the whole death-dealing enterprise.

The medical superintendent of the hospital was very helpful in showing me around the wards, the equipment, and treatment rooms. There, we found many young men suffering from what has been termed "shell shock"—trauma brought on by their experiences at the front with a range of symptoms varying in severity, as follows:

1. *Nightmares*
2. *Insomnia*
3. *Loss of appetite*
4. *Difficulty in speaking—stammering etc*
5. *Acute diarrhoea and stomach cramps*
6. *Hysterical facial tics*

It was extremely painful to observe the men under such duress from such a range of symptoms, and the nurses in charge of the patients confided in me that they were often themselves traumatised by what they have to deal with.

Treatments varied according to severity, the most dramatic being electric shock treatment which, to my view, seemed ruthlessly brutal. Indeed, general medical opinion remains sceptical about success. Certainly, I saw no evidence of patients recovering after such treatment.

Hypnosis had been known to help and often revealed what constituted the triggers for the trauma.

Massage and bed rest were much more palatable in my view, and, as I understand, this is a generally supported view. Again, some patients were clearly benefitting from this, but others continued to be tormented and incapable.

I must express my concern about one aspect of the hospital attitude as I saw it in the superintendent who accompanied me and in certain doctors I met in the process. They emanated a sense that all their patients were to be ashamed of themselves and that they must be, as the superintendent expressed it, "more manly" in their behaviour. I cannot condone this attitude which seems to me overly judgemental.

Rowntree and I had a very useful discussion, and I am grateful to know that there is such a member of the House able to speak out for those who are otherwise viewed with contempt. I thank you for giving me the opportunity to meet with him.

I trust the enclosed will prove helpful, but I do suggest that there is a need for a greater compassion for those deeply traumatised young men. Nevertheless, I would like it on record that there is overall, thankfully, the strongest will within the hospital to bring about healing.

Yours faithfully,
Philip Manners,
Headmaster

Philip spent two days thinking through his letter and the enclosed report, describing the wards, the patients, the staffing, and the range of treatments. Having covered all the ground he felt necessary, he gave it to Kath to type up and send to Frank Jacques. It had allowed him to concentrate his attentions on human need and to repress all the human need within himself. Then, at last, he sat back in the silent study and sighed heavily.

I must also be more manly, he thought sardonically. *Let battle commence.*

Once again, there ensued a lonely time spent in the darkness of the discipline he had set for Emma and himself. Emma returned to her routine duties at the station and at the wash tub, soaking and ironing the innumerable blouses of the staff. Jack was aware of a strange ennui in her, and unwanted thoughts of the York trip occasionally crossed his mind, only to be quickly dismissed. Her lovemaking was lacklustre, though he blamed himself for this more than his wife. He tried to understand that she was less pleased to succumb to his embrace, to which she normally responded warmly, because of her preoccupation with her two boys. And so, he convinced himself it was all to do with Will and Harry. Indeed, he knew that all that Will had been able to tell them about the war was frightening her to distraction. This happened to be true, of course, but much more than this lay beneath. Emma could not dismiss from her mind the sheer pleasure she had felt as she'd lain in Philip's arms, and no perfunctory lovemaking with Jack could quite compare with this memory. She felt an awful guilt about this and tried unconvincingly to show Jack that she was just her usual self.

In his turn, Philip devoted his whole time to the boys in his care and to sharing the woes and concerns of his staff. He was pleased to hear from Frank Jacques, who had passed his report to the authorities where it was being studied gratefully despite its firm pacifist perspective. He felt at least he had achieved something for the suffering soldiers in York, different from his efforts for the deserters at the London committee meeting. Then he received a letter which truly shocked him to the core.

He had not heard from Harriet for some time and had put this down to her caring for her parents without really recognising the length of time she had been absent. But Kath had realised and was constantly anxious on his behalf. Thus, the letter did not surprise her. Its contents were clear enough and sounded the death knell to his frost-bound marriage. She and Godfrey Langdon had formed a liaison in Worcester which had overpowered any feelings she'd had left for Philip. And she baldly announced she wanted a divorce. Godfrey was returning to the front now he was recovered, but he would be resigning his position as deputy in the school as soon as possible, and on his return, they hoped to marry. Now it was up to Philip to allow Harriet her freedom.

His reaction was a determination that he must go to Worcester as soon as he could. He was surprised to discover that he felt a sadness mixed with a flame of anger at her behaviour and her disloyalty to a marriage that had begun with such hope in its earliest beginnings. And then it became a rage with the man whom he himself had employed in his school. How dare Godfrey Langdon betray his position in the school? And yet Philip felt the pain of his own guilt. He too must himself bear some of the blame, knowing his and Emma's love for each other. He sat silent in his study with the letter on his desk till Kath could not resist asking him any longer. He slowly announced its contents to her and then lifted his hands in despair.

"That it should come to this, Kath. How have I allowed this to happen? Have I been so neglectful of her? I have failed Harriet."

Kath remonstrated with him at this, for she blamed Harriet entirely for the lack of love and care she had for so long exhibited. Nevertheless, she saw it was vital for him to ascertain exactly what Harriet intended and agreed he should go to her parents' home.

Thus, a few days later, he found himself facing Emma on the platform headed for Sheffield and the connection to Worcester. She was astonished at this news with all its implications, and she could see his face harboured his sense of failure. But the platform was busy and the grimy waiting room full.

"Come into Mr Firbank's office so we can have a moment's privacy." There, she took him in her arms and kissed him with all the passion she had for him, reassuring him it was not of his doing. As he felt her love for him, there he found the strength to go on to the confrontation that awaited him.

"Emma, are you sure it is not my lack of true concern for her that has caused this? Are you sure it's not because of us?"

"Philip, you have been more than considerate to Harriet these last few years," she answered sternly. "It is not your fault that she decided to leave you months ago and trespassed on her marriage vows. Nor is it your fault that she has shown you no warmth or care for a long time. And I know we have been close to trespass too, but, Philip, I truly believe we tried very hard not to bring any harm to Jack or Harriet. We both know how much it hurts to resist, but you keep on giving me the confidence to fight on, and we're not giving up on that, my darling. So now have a little courage and get on the train." As she spoke, she knew she must hurry to manage its arrival, and with one last look, she left him there with an encouraging smile.

As Philip arrived at Harriet's parents' home after the weary journey and the several connections he had had to make, he hesitated on the doorstep for a moment, then rang the bell. He was met by the bishop's wife, who ushered him in without a word. Harriet, pale faced and unflinchingly adamant, simply accused him of making an unnecessary journey. Her mind was made up, she loved Godfrey, and would have no argument despite her mother begging her to reconsider. He was surprised to find no shame or sorrow in her face or attitude. He could see he was already confined to the edges of her life.

"Harriet, you must understand the implications of what you are asking. It demands a humiliating requirement for evidence of your adultery with Godfrey before the authorities will consider my request. It is a sordid business and will be so difficult for your father and mother to bear. I can do nothing until such time as you show the courts evidence of such adultery. I can hardly dare to speak this out loud, my dear. Are you absolutely sure it is what you want and can bear to do? But if you can bring yourself to provide such evidence, I will surely do what is needed for your sake."

"I am ready, Philip. I'm quite sure about it, and I'll do whatever is necessary to be free to marry Godfrey. Surely you can at least make this possible for me."

"The disgrace of it, Harriet! How could you do this to your father?" said her mother. "You know how sick he is and how this thing will cause a scandal for him in the eyes of the church."

"Is the bishop at home?" asked Philip, wearily. He felt it incumbent on him to see the man who had never given him any support. Yet he felt pity for him in this vexed situation.

Harriet's mother led him into the bishop's sitting room where he was sitting in an armchair plumped up with cushions, the side of his mouth pulled at an odd angle downwards as a result of the stroke. Harriet joined them, taking up a position right beside her father's chair. Philip took his damp hand in his own and begged his forgiveness for any contribution he might have made to this sad outcome. The bishop drew breath to respond.

"Young man, Harriet is very much at fault, but I will not deny her happiness, and you were never able to make her content. It will be a notoriously scandalous business but so be it. Let us hope this man, Langdon, can do for her what you never achieved." As he spoke, his mouth drooped further at the corners, and a dribble of saliva fell onto his collar.

It was a biting response to Philip's humility though the bishop had a struggle to articulate it. Nevertheless, the acrimony that had always been a part of their relationship had not gone away, and Philip felt a great sorrow for it.

"Very well, sir. I shall return home and put the wheels in motion for Harriet to have what she has asked for. But, Harriet, you know what will be demanded of you and afterwards, even then, there will be a long period of separation before the law makes the divorce absolute. You will have to be patient. I will say that Godfrey has let not only me but the school down very badly in this. I will expect his resignation letter, which I shall show to the governors, and may God forgive us all.

Harriet, I beg you to reconsider what you are doing. Do you really want to admit to adultery, as you will have to? The scandal will drag you and your parents so far down. Think of them, I beg you, if not of yourself. Can you not remember happier days between us? Are you not able to return to your home and to your position as headmaster's wife? God knows, Harriet, I am terribly sorry it has come to this." He took her hand solemnly and looked at her with great sorrow, but she pushed him away, and he could see it was hopeless to pursue it.

"My mind is made up, Philip, and nothing now would make me return to your benighted school. Godfrey can give me everything I desire; maybe even a child, Philip. Who knows?" She laughed a brittle, bitter laugh.

At that last comment, Philip shuddered, for he knew she had blamed him for her childlessness though the doctors had indicated there was no way of knowing where the problem actually lay. He shook the bishop's hand once again, wishing him a full recovery with his continuing rehabilitation. He gave Harriet's mother a look of sad regret and kissed Harriet's cheek in farewell. Heaving a huge sigh of sorrow and yet relief that he had done all he could, he hailed a cab and left for the station, having been offered neither a drink nor any refreshment to help him on his way. He realised then that he was famished and that it had already been a very long day. Accordingly, he sat in the station café on Worcester Station with a coffee before embarking on the journey home.

As the train pulled out of Worcester Station, he thought very sadly of the death of his marriage. Images of Harriet, the young woman who had pursued him as he'd studied in Oxford, came to mind. Daughter of the vicarage close by to the portals of St. John's College, his alma mater, she had ensured that her father, as chaplain there, gained her entry to the formal dinners and the high table to sit beside the college principal and the academics who dined there. But her interest had lain in the young male students who danced attendance on her, for she was indeed beautiful. She had sparkled with charm then, and he had tried hard to resist. Yet she had been determined to conquer the brilliant Quaker student who usually avoided the rowdy celebrations and preferred to retire to the library to study his beloved Shakespeare. She loved a challenge, and his reticence had made him all the more irresistible to her.

He had to smile to himself as he remembered the evening he'd succumbed to those charms. She had followed him to the library and challenged him to leave his books and walk with her through Christchurch Meadows. And so had begun a carefree liaison. She was just a girl who adored dancing and having fun. She'd dragged him away from his studies to relax and enjoy the social life of Oxford. Philip, whose parents had died when he was only a small boy, brought up by a strict Quaker godparent, had found himself attracted by her beauty and, at last, had thrown his inhibitions to the wind. She'd considered him a very good catch and sported him as her favourite trophy until, at last, she'd promised to marry him. The fact that her father was very much against it, a high Anglican faced with the prospect of a Quaker son-in-law, had made Harriet all the more determined to make him her husband. She had always had her father wrapped round her little finger and had convinced him to marry them for the sake of her happiness. And so, they'd married in Oxford in 1892 as he'd completed his degree. There followed four years in Salisbury, where he'd taught at the grammar school there as Harriet filled her days playing hostess to the many adherents of the school.

I thought she would be pleased when I got the deputy headship in the Quaker school at Salisbury. Maybe she was for a while until the accident with the bike. That's when I damaged everything, not just my bike. That's when I became a patient and she got bored. But I did at least hope she would be even more proud to stand by me when I got the job as headmaster of Shadworth School.

He was jolted out of his reverie as the train pulled into Birmingham where he knew he must change for the last train to Sheffield and Shadworth. He felt absolutely drained of energy, hardly able to raise the effort to change platform and then mount another carriage. But at least he was heading for his home and the school he loved in Shadworth where he had, in 1904, been appointed its head. By then, he mused with chagrin, the light had already gone out in their marriage. Harriet had tired of the serious man through whom she had thought to gain prestige and status and had lost interest in sharing in the complete commitment of life and soul he gave to his students. She still wanted to have fun while his scholarly, conscientious nature reasserted itself.

But it was that awful accident with the bike when the rot had begun to set in. That's what finished it, in truth. He had needed to rely more and more heavily on his walking stick, and all the sense of fun they had once shared became lost in a quagmire of heavy teaching commitments and sleepless, painful nights. Well before Shadworth, all through the time in Salisbury, Harriet had already spent more and more time with wives of other staff and retreated from their marital bedroom, claiming he was keeping her awake as the leg troubled him.

I had certainly stopped being fun to be with, he thought sadly as he carefully stepped on to the Sheffield train. *God, what consequences the work of a moment can cause.* He frowned at the thought. *Even so, the bullet that struck the Archduke Ferdinand had set off the most appalling chain of events in Europe. My own suffering is nothing compared to the evils caused by that.*

Yet, as he thought of Harriet's acerbic words in front of her father, he knew for certain, as he had always suspected, what the major factor of the lovelessness that had then pervaded their relationship was. They had wanted a child, and no child was forthcoming. The doctors had all warned her that she may be unable to conceive, after many visits to the private specialist in these matters, and she had begun to pretend she had never really wanted to be a mother: "Anyway, what sort of a father would you be, always in your study bothering with your blessed school? We're surrounded by children and that's enough. And I'm just not bothered anymore. I'd rather be free of such responsibility. Think of all the mess they create. You would never be there when I'd have to change their nappies. Let me be, Philip. Stop trying to make it up to me."

Her voice resounded in his memory as the train drew nearer to Shadworth, and the love he had carried for her through the years and his rejected attempts to help her saddened him deeply. He knew she had been dishonest in saying she didn't want babies, and he knew she actually blamed him for their infertility, though the private consultants had been unable to give her any clear evidence of that. He had done everything in his power to share her sorrow and turn it around into a positive acceptance. Instead, she had turned away from him and from his bed and taken on the tone her father had always adopted towards him—an atmosphere of rancour and blame.

God, now it's really over, and I shall never be able to forgive myself for that, thought Philip. *I believe the writing was on the wall well before I met Emma Holt, but I pray God my love for Emma has not contributed to the damage. Perhaps it's true that I haven't tried hard enough.*

As this thought filled him with sorrow, he realised it was already past ten o'clock in the evening and the train was pulling into Shadworth. He knew he had to put this melancholy away and pick back up the threads of his life in Shadworth and his beloved school. As he stumbled down the carriage steps to the platform and called for a cab, he wished with all his heart Emma could have been on duty there. But she had completed her duties of the day and handed over to the night attendant. The very thought of her brought him a comfort he knew he should not indulge. He was at last untrammelled by the acrimonious atmosphere of his erstwhile matrimonial home. Yet he knew it could not make any difference to his and Emma's situation. He cared very much for Jack Holt.

His leg was throbbing painfully now as at last he reached his own front door. What he did not know was that Emma's anxiety for him had led her to beg Jack to go to the school and check he was safely returned.

"Jack, he's travelled such a long way to see that wife of his. Please will you go up to schoolhouse to see if he's alright?"

"He's a grown man, Emma. Surely he can look after himself, can't he? What is it to you?" Nevertheless, Jack grumpily put on his outdoor clothes and gave her a cursory peck on the cheek as he went out of the door, slamming it behind him. As he walked up the hill to school, Jack frowned. His doubts about the relationship which existed between the two of them surfaced yet again. But for the moment, he shrugged it off as something to be put to the back of his mind. He knew how much he enjoyed his own easy friendship with the head, so why, after all, should not Emma share that too? And indeed, when Philip opened the door to him at that late hour, he was glad of Emma's persuasion. For Philip was by then ashen with tiredness and the pain in his leg. Jack could see he had had trouble walking to the door and took action.

"Mr Manners, sit down and let me get you something to eat. You look half starved. Has it been a very arduous day? Emma told me about seeing you this morning on the way, but she thought you would have caught a much earlier train and was worried. She made me come, and I'm glad she did." As he spoke, he went to boil the kettle and found bread and butter on the kitchen surface which he handed to Philip. "Emma would have done better but at least this will do," said Jack.

"She need not have worried. I'll be fine. It was one of those days, Jack, and I can't tell you how grateful I am that you appeared when you did. I felt I was going to faint, but it was just because I've had hardly anything to eat all day. More fool me."

They sat in companionable silence as Philip consumed the bread, and Jack and he shared the tea. The irony of it did not fail to be noted by Philip who felt an overwhelming sense of gladness that Jack was his friend and that he and Emma had not completely betrayed him. Nevertheless, he knew also that they had gone, in truth, much further than was entirely honourable in their closeness and that their relationship should, in the future, be kept under strict discipline for Jack's sake. That truth cut into him, but he knew it to be the only way to keep faith with Jack.

On Jack's return to Holt House, Emma greeted him trying hard to be casual in questioning him but wretched inside. He reported what he had done, assuring her he had left Philip in good health and humour.

"It was a blessing I went, Emma. He was needing a little bit of company. He'd had a terrible day, I think. That woman he married, heaven knows how long ago, has been a thorn in the flesh for too long and has let him down now completely. He's better off without her in any case. Now he can do his job as head without her dragging him down."

There was a brief silence while Emma nodded quietly, yet Jack could see there were traces of tears in her eyes.

"You are very fond of him, Emma, aren't you? I find myself being a friend to a man who is so different from me in every way *and* different from you, Emma. You do know this, don't you? You will never do anything to damage us, will you, Emma? You know, surely, how much I love you." Jack took her hard by the shoulders and looked directly at her.

"Jack, I am your wife, and of course I know you love me as I you. You must never think I could do anything to hurt you. I beg you not to mention this again, Jack, do you hear me?"

Jack nodded slowly and smiled quietly. But behind his look lay an understanding of the nature of the admission inherent in her words. And she, as she reassured him, prayed for the strength to remain faithful and for the iron will she required by which to be the woman he trusted. But she held Philip Manners deep and close in her soul that night and knew she could never deny her love for him either.

Chapter 29

Term moved on, and Philip and Emma pursued their daily tasks, allowing all feelings to be repressed in the volume of duties that consumed them.

Nevertheless, Philip's lessons with his sixth form continued to challenge him as he taught them the syllabus set and, with it, Donne's wonderful love poems. How he felt each one as if it were his own. The boys fortunately had no idea what was going on in their teacher's head as he taught them Donne's Song:

Sweetest love, I do not go,
For weariness of thee,
. . . .
But think that we
Are but turn'd aside to sleep;
They who one another keep
Alive, ne'er parted be.

Oh God, thought Philip, *I am for ever parted from Emma* But then he turned back to the boys who were writing notes and studying conscientiously albeit somewhat reluctantly. He had every expectation of their success and prayed that the war would be over before they were old enough to be conscripted.

Emma, at her laundry, was pleased to receive a letter from Will, though its contents were far from cheerful. He could not tell them the news of the troops being moved up towards Ypres ready for the big offensive they had been expecting. All had been sworn to secrecy lest any information should pre-warn the enemy. But he did tell them the news that the Bosch were now using another more lethal gas in their attacks—mustard gas. Will regretted telling his mother this almost as soon as he had put the letter in the post bag, but it was too late anyway, for Emma had already devoured the newspapers which were reporting the effects of this new horror: lungs suppurating as the gas broiled and burned in their breath so as to leave a choking effect like drowning. She had found the details almost too much to bear, and she had at last simply stopped reading them.

But now she screamed out loud at the letter and looked around for Jack, almost, in her dread, oblivious to the fact that she had already posted him off to the school gardens. *Don't be such a fool, Emma Holt. He's at work. Pull yourself together.*

So, she read on and was glad at least to see that Albert had been told he would not have to return to the front given that his condition was still weakening him and unlikely to improve. Will was relieved for Albert but told her how much he himself longed to be able to come home at last.

Emma read and reread the letter, shedding tears at how helpless she felt in the face of Will's longing. But when Florence appeared with a letter from Ned relating his fears of what lay ahead, her mother had to pull herself together to assure a distraught Florence that they must keep praying for their loved ones' safekeeping and hold fast.

"Courage is what we must have, Florrie. Courage. It will do no good to be at home shaking with fear. We must carry on and make our home the haven they believe it to be for when they do return." She was as much talking to herself as she tried to assure Florence, for she was also afraid that they might never come home.

Part of everyone's salvation, including Philip's, was little George who was growing up apace. Maggie often took the pram up to the school gardens and called in at Philip's office more bravely after her initial shyness. She soon learned the times when Philip would be least occupied with staff and students and willing to enjoy a brief respite in the company of her little boy. Kath Hanson always welcomed her warmly and everything came to a halt while the little boy made straight for Philip's desk, delightedly. There, Kath had placed a small box of books he liked, and he sat comfortably on Philip's lap, listening to the tales of Beatrix Potter and the nursery rhyme book he knew off by heart. It did Kath's heart good to see her serious headmaster delighting in the little chap, laughing at his little ways, and putting on the voices of Mr McGregor and the sly fox who stole Jemima Puddle-Duck's eggs. When Jack knocked on the door to retrieve him and rescue the two of them, Philip had to hand him back to his mother and grandfather very regretfully.

George's grandma was his absolute favourite, and he had learned that when she was baking, he was allowed to help put the jam in the tartlets and then lick his fingers. Maggie remonstrated with Emma over this, but Emma was adamant. "A little bit of his sticky fingers won't hurt anyone, Maggie."

At the front, Ralph and Will were often in conversation as the time drew near for the attack. General Haig's plans were taking shape, and he had been bolstered by the taking of the Messines Ridge in June after setting mines at the end of long tunnels under the German front lines. Now, Haig believed, was the right time, and the bombardment of the German lines approaching Passchendaele began in mid-July.

"But, Will," said Ralph very privately as they sat together sipping grog in the dugout in late July, "The enemy must know what all that shelling meant. They'll be ready for us, and there'll be no surprise. I dread it,

Will. There's an open playing field for them—we have to attack over a flat plain. What will the ground be like after the bombardment? Our guns will be firing on positions that they've fortified ready. Then there's the mustard gas. If we get into trenches that have been infected with its aftermath, we can find ourselves choking to death. God, Will, I wish to God we were anywhere but here. But we must not let the lads know it."

Will simply looked back at his captain and friend. It was a hopeless look, and their dread was palpable.

Nevertheless, on July 31, it began, and while some troops did indeed gain ground, the section where Will and Ralph's men were fighting on the right flank made no ground and only stalemate ensued. Many of their colleagues were killed, but Will and Ralph kept up the fight and stayed firm.

Then the rains came as if sent from heaven to stop the bloodshed in its tracks. Yet, as the fields of Flanders turned into a quagmire of thick mud and stinking animal waste, still Haig pushed his troops to do more. It had been reduced to a war of attrition. Hand to hand fighting in a sea of mud was gaining very little ground. There were no letters home to Shadworth as Will and his men fought on bravely but with weary pessimism and horror.

Then the worst happened. As Ralph and he were standing together confronting the enemy, Will saw Ralph slip in the deep mud, and as he lost his footing, he sank into the morass of the swamp. A horse nearby had fallen too, and it was struggling and kicking out its hooves to keep its head above the slime as Ralph's cries were submerged under the surface of the stinking mud. Will shouted out to him to hold his hand up so that he could grasp it and pull him out. But though he pulled to the last gasp of Ralph's breath, he could not release him from the deathly hold the mud had over him. Will felt as though his arm would pull out of its socket with the effort to rescue his dear friend but it was indeed his heart that was breaking as Ralph drowned in front of his eyes. It was all in vain and Will felt he could hardly bear it. He lay down in abject despair and gave up with a heavy groan.

"No, you don't, sir," came two voices in unison. With bullets flying all around them, they dragged Will to his feet and hoisted him back through the quagmire that had once been a field, away from the front lines, to the safety of the dugout. There they attended to him. He was slimed all over with the mud and pained to his soul at Ralph's death. He staggered to the latrine where he was physically, violently sick and then lay back on his makeshift bed in utter wretchedness. His two privates, themselves grieving and mud-caked, just stood by wordlessly. Poor Will tried hard to pull himself together.

"Jim, get straight to the commanding officer and let him know what's happened. Tom, help me up so I can see what's going on." But the effort was too much for him at that moment, and the emotion overwhelmed him. The tears fell though he tried hard to keep them back. The thought of such a loss of a man who would no longer share with him the friendship that had grown and cheered them both turned his blood to water. He remembered how Ralph lovingly folded his letters from his wife and stored them in his trench coat pockets, and with that thought, he struggled to his feet.

"I need to check Ralph's trench coat; it's just hanging over there. I believe he has a picture of his wife in the pocket, and there'll be an address for her. I must write to her and send his belongings back home. Her name is Laura, I think."

They brought the things to him, and he looked long and hard at Laura's pretty face with great sadness. A picture of his own mother came into his head, and he felt an overwhelming homesickness come over him. He knew what his mother would say if she were only here beside him. "Courage, Will. I know you are strong, my son."

He pulled himself upright and gave the two anxious young troopers a wan smile. "You can leave me now, lads. I can manage."

Hundreds of miles away, as his mother was signalling a troop train through Shadworth Station, she felt a strange sense of closeness to her eldest son and looked up as if he were just about to walk towards her on the platform. It was a phantasm, she knew, but she stopped and prayed for him then and there as he was thinking of her in the dugout. So strange are the ways of love.

One other comfort came to Will that evening, and it was a felicitous coincidence indeed, for into the dugout strode young Ned Tempest who had been close by with his group fighting that day and had heard of the loss of Will's captain. They hugged each other closely as if they could not let go and felt a piece of Shadworth had come into the dugout. Visions of Florence and of Maggie and George were a kind of antidote in the midst of the horror of the circumstance they found themselves in.

"Never mind now, Will. We'll be going home soon surely. The Americans have at last decided to join our side and will bring welcome reinforcements. We must be patient."

"If only Ned! I am looking forward to a glorious wedding for you and Florence. Maybe Mother will make her cream horns especially for us." He had found the heart to look towards better things and it bolstered his courage ready for another day. Yet thoughts of Ralph continued to haunt him in spite of that, and he wondered whether his heart was permanently broken.

What they did not know that night was how long and drawn out the battle for the Passchendaele Ridge would be, for it lasted right through the cold autumn as far as November. Haig claimed success in the end as Canadian troops finally took the ridge, but what was gained was minor compared with the huge losses on both sides. Will and Ned and the troops serving and dying with them felt the utter futility of the enterprise.

Chapter 30

In his study at the school, Philip maintained a quiet and steady atmosphere of learning and of optimism. Though he was fighting the ache for Emma, which was sometimes almost intolerable, he served his staff unremittingly and taught English to his own classes and history to Alan Lorimer's to the best he could, given the additional pressures of the administration of the school. Divorce proceedings were continuing from Harriet's side, and he was corresponding regularly with Frank Jacques about the war. He felt very strongly that General Haig was so obsessed with victory that he had lost perspective of the appalling losses he was suffering. Jack had told him of what they had read between the lines from Will's letters. What's more, the lists of casualties coming through told their own story. Frank Jacques, fighting his corner in the Commons alongside Arnold Rowntree, found Philip's memos very helpful as he argued the cause. Philip went so far as to send Frank some words from the Peace Testimony declared in 1660, words sent to Charles II to set out the Quaker principle of pacifism:

We do certainly know, and so testify to the world, that the Spirit of Christ, which leads us into all Truth, will never move us to fight and war against any man with outward weapons, neither for the kingdom of Christ, nor for the kingdoms of this world.

Philip reread those words with great sadness, knowing as he did how far removed from their wisdom his world had moved.

The new intake of boys in September was swept up in the rush of term, and with them came a new wave of sadness of still more fathers and brothers lost in the battlefields of France. Young Jacob who had suffered such nightmares in an earlier time and Charlie Hopton both brought news to him of boys they knew who were mourning their loved ones and trying to hide their troubles. No one knew better than these two how much their headmaster would help them if he knew, and they both made it their regular business to bring names to him. Kath had to smile at them as they knocked timidly on his door every week to bring him their reports. So, he found himself once again visiting dormitories in the evenings, trying to soothe troubled souls and get alongside them in their unhappiness. He set up his silent hour in the Meeting House again where they could attend at will if they wanted a quiet opportunity to think and pray.

Once again, he had to admit to mixed motives, as he knew Emma would sometimes be able to avail herself of the chance to come if she could get away. George was particularly demanding of her time now that Maggie had her own little job helping with paperwork in the village school office.

If no other staff were present, Emma would creep in beside him and sit in silence next to him. This was a kind of sweet relief from the effort of their more usual wariness. Just to be close to her for that brief time kept Philip strong. As for Emma, she died inside every time she had to stand and leave him there. But she was getting to know the young ones who were regularly in the chapel as well as renewing her fondness for Charlie. It was not long in the autumn before she had several of them down to Holt House for their Sunday lunch and a trip with Jack down to Tempest's farm. Philip always came and picked them up in the evening and sat awhile with her and Jack, sharing the day and the news. This was a mixed pleasure, as it only served to make the necessity to leave with the boys a pointed reminder that he could not claim her.

One visitor to chapel made it even more necessary to remain studiously formal. Dear Edna Wright had lost her brother in the Passchendaele offensive and had confided in Kath her utter frustration at the grim resolution of Haig to continue the attack when there seemed to be little or no point. Even so, after her own quiet time in the meeting house, Edna often commented to Kath that she thought the head seemed very close to Mrs Holt, but Kath, with a determined air, remarked, "Well, it's quite understandable now that he and Jack work together with her to do what they can for the poor, wretched boys."

If no one was left in the chapel at the end of the hour and Emma had been able to come, they sat holding hands while she laid her head on his shoulder for a few moments like two lost children. That thought made him smile in spite of himself and, at those times, he would kiss her forehead very gently. Yet when she left him there, he remonstrated with himself to be more careful to keep a close lock on his feelings.

News now came from their absent head of Ayton House, Alan Lorimer. He wrote to both Edna and Philip to let them know he had his discharge papers already, owing to an injury to his back which had put him permanently beyond action. Accordingly, he was struggling to get back to fitness but was hoping to return to his post in January. This brought everyone good cheer as the weeks went by.

Before Philip realised it, another Christmas was approaching and, with it, a special birthday Jack had told him about. Emma was to be fifty on December 15—a date she had ignored for many years, being far too interested in the birthdays of others rather than her own.

After classes one Friday in late November, he limped down to where Jack was still working clearing out the dying, wintered plants and suggested that they might do something special at the school to celebrate this landmark birthday. Jack's first response was to dismiss the idea considering it had come from Philip and not himself.

Why does he think it's his business to throw a party for my wife? This is our family business. And once again, Jack felt haunted by the fear of what lay between Emma and the head. Philip saw the fear in his face the minute he suggested it and shrank back in horror that he had upset his friend.

You fool, Philip. You should have been more thoughtful. He immediately tried to remedy his error. "Of course, Jack, you probably have already thought of how you and the family want to celebrate. Silly of me to bring school into it. Forgive me."

At once reassured, Jack relented instantly. "Nay, Mr Manners, of course you and the boys she cares about would add something extra to the day. We shouldn't leave you and Kath out. It's a smashing idea, and to think what a grand surprise it would be for her if we do it here and not in her own kitchen. I'm very tempted."

And so it was settled. They agreed to set up, with Kath Hanson, a small celebration in Philip's study. It would be for just a few of Emma's "adopted" boys, Charlie and Jacob amongst them, and for Florence,

Maggie, Mrs Granger, and of course little George who was to be two himself within two weeks, not forgetting Cook.

Since December 15 fell on a Saturday, this party could be next day, after the usual Sunday morning meeting, and Philip promised to invite Cook and ask her to bake a cake for the occasion while Jack was to get the girls in on the secret. Connie was pleased for the invitation but raised her eyebrows at the reason for it. Kath, however, was quick to put the enterprise onto a safe perspective, explaining that it was perfectly natural for this particular group of people to give a little back to Emma Holt. If anyone deserved recognition, she did. Connie grudgingly accepted the point. Accordingly, she baked the cake and decorated it with one candle and cherries.

"We are all going to the school meeting this Sunday," announced Jack. "We should be thanking God for fifty years of a life that's so important to us all. To think, I'm an old man in comparison with you, my dear. I shall be sixty next year."

Emma had no idea what they had in mind but was only too glad to think of seeing Philip close to her birthday. They trooped up the lane to school and sat in the silent Quaker meeting while Maggie kept George busy with drawing books and sweeties, much to his glee. As the meeting came to its close, Philip stood up to speak. He glanced at the woman he loved so dearly and prayed for the right words to come; words that would express his love but with nothing that might give Jack cause for concern.

"As yesterday happens to have been a special birthday for Mrs Holt, I just want to have a few words before we leave. I want us to be thankful for the years of toil and hardship that have been mastered with strength and enlightened with God's Spirit. Today, let's be thankful for the many gifts we have shared as a community with the Holt family. You all know that we come to seek blessing for us all gathered here. And we have thought of those we love who couldn't be here today, at this moment fighting in foreign fields. May that blessing be for all those and for us as we celebrate today."

He sat down abruptly, hoping he had not said too much, but he was reassured by a stout handshake from Jack and a sweet thank you from Florence and Maggie. Charlie Hopton and Jacob had already gone up to Emma and hugged her, and Charlie had flung George into the air with many shrieks of delight.

"Come," said Kath, "Let's see what we can find in the head's study." She led the way back up the path to the birthday treat. Connie had helped her set it out, and it was a pleasure to see it.

"Oh my!" Emma gasped. "What have you all been up to? Jack, you should not have told them all. Mr Manners—Philip—you need not have troubled yourself with all this. Miss Hanson, Connie, thank you both so very much." Emma sat on Philip's chair and shook her head. The tears were brimming in her eyes, and Philip hastened to her side and took her hand.

"Happy birthday, Emma. No tears now, this is a celebration. Come here, George, and help your grandma to blow out her candle."

George did not hesitate to do as he was asked, and as they sang 'Happy Birthday', he clapped and blew for all his might. Philip picked him up then and felt all the pleasure of holding the little child. Kath watched him with tears in her own eyes, and Jack patted Maggie on the back as she stood by. The schoolboys were beginning on the food, and it was a jolly affair as if there was no war going on in Europe. Philip knew that Emma, for one, would not have forgotten it and hoped against hope that she would be able to relax from her worries for at least a short time. It felt strange seeing her in his chair as if she belonged to him, but he kept a stern hold on himself lest Jack should see a suspicion of it in his face. But clearly, Jack had thrown himself into the merrymaking, completely oblivious of everything else.

Florence could not help but think wistfully of the absent ones and knew that her mother was missing them too. But as she presented Emma with the posy they had made up for her, she whispered, "You must not be sad today. They will be thinking of us, I do believe."

"I thought you might like this, Mrs Holt," said Philip and handed her a package all wrapped up finely. "I think you will enjoy the poems." It was a book of Donne's collected poems, a gift inscribed: *To one who will appreciate the brilliance of John Donne. Happy birthday, from Philip!*

She opened it later in the quiet of her own bedroom and read the careful but deliberate inscription, written, she knew, with all the love he bore for her. And she held it against her heart as of a great treasure, then put it in its wrappings in her private drawer where no prying eyes could read it.

So, Emma's fiftieth birthday and George's second birthday were spent with a warmth that had grown with the years, acknowledged by all without a shadow to spoil it. Christmas 1917 was celebrated at Florrie and Maggie's small cottage at their insistence with Kath and Philip both included because, as Florence put it, no one should be alone for Christmas. Philip had tried to resist, but they would not take no for an answer.

God forgive me if I am allowing myself to indulge too much in this pleasure or if it should hurt Jack in any way, was a fervent prayer at this time, and he determined to ensure that he should not trespass too much on Jack's good nature. As for Emma, she simply allowed herself to relax in the joy of his presence and tried hard not to feel the frustration inherent in it.

Christmas passed and the balance of relationships was maintained intact and safe for the present. But for how long could it be sustained?

Chapter 31

After a warm spell in December, winter arrived in January 1918 with a vengeance. The snow descended on Shadworth unremittingly. It lay over the guttering and smothered the rooftops in deep drifts. The rooks in the elms were half frozen on the stark black branches where the snow had not lain and they set up such a cawing as never seemed to let up. In the gardens, the frail heads of the newly appearing snowdrops were engulfed in the snow, and the cold was intense. But spring term was upon them, nevertheless.

Philip knew how the cold had previously affected his crippled leg, and he was terribly afraid of a repeat of it as he felt the pain in his knee increasingly. He let no one know of this fear and maintained the smooth course of the new term as if all was well. One huge comfort was the return of Alan Lorimer to take his place once more as head of Ayton House. He was much changed from his grim time at the front—gaunt and haggard in a way Philip had never seen him before—and his back was still very painful so he stooped as he walked.

"Philip, we make a pretty pair between us, do we not." He laughed. "But, God, it's good to be back. My mother has been in such agonies of fear for me that she almost smothered me with love when I got home. Thank God for this place and the boys and you, Edna, and Kath. I've kept myself going by thinking of you all." He did not mention the absence of Harriet, having been taken to one side by Kath and instructed to avoid the subject and all mention of Godfrey Langdon. Nevertheless, he felt terribly angry indeed that the affair had left his very good friend alone, under the shadow of an unasked-for divorce.

He also saw the help Philip was giving to the bereaved boys who were far too many in number, and he made his own mind up to join the silent hour whenever he could. He met Emma there with pleasure, as he was very fond of both Emma and Jack.

He was fascinated by the relationship Philip and Kath too had established with Jack's little grandson, who appeared quite often in Philip's study for stories.

"You've become quite a family man in my absence, Philip," he joked. "He is Harry Holt's son, isn't he? Jack tells me Harry is out with the French troops in Verdun. That's a fairly gruelling place to be, I'm told. The French have managed to keep the Germans out of the town by every means in their power. They say they call it the town they cannot conquer. I suppose Harry is as safe there as anywhere. I hope to God the American presence there now will help bring this war of attrition to an end. We are winning, I'm assured. We are, if only Haig will keep his cool."

"Don't speak to me of General Haig," was Philip's reply. "He's a dolt as far as I'm concerned. He's kept the men fighting for Passchendaele for months despite any worthwhile gain."

But Philip also had other things on his mind. He visited the good doctor a few weeks later, as his leg was tormenting him badly. He was almost sure his knee was infected again, as an abscess had formed below it. He had bathed it conscientiously, but it simply would not go away. In the end, he knew he had to get professional advice. He kept it quiet from Kath and felt he could not worry Emma.

Emma was having a very hard time with little George who, at two and a half, was developing that trait they call the 'terrible twos'. He was adored by all but considered a handful in his behaviour. However, it was the diagnosis of childhood asthma that frightened them all and meant they all kept him, as it were, wrapped in cotton wool. Emma had got used to boiling kettles and warming his little chest in a steaming kitchen, as this helped him to breathe in an attack. Her kitchen walls were streaming with water regularly now as she managed his condition. But she grew frightened every time he'd start gasping for his breath, and Maggie was distraught.

"If only Harry could be home," Maggie confided. "I'm half sick of waiting for him."

"Take comfort, Maggie. He's tougher than you think," she reassured her. "And the news from the front is so much more hopeful now the Americans are helping us. Harry will be home soon, I pray."

She would not have felt so cheerful had she heard what Dr Thomson was telling Philip. Philip's own particular toughness was seeping away with the acute pain in his leg.

"Mr Manners—Philip, you will lose this leg if you do not rest it," threatened the doctor. "I'm prescribing the antiseptic you had before in hospital, and I'm contacting the hospital to send a nurse to dress the abscess. Take at least three days off and stay in bed to give it a proper chance to heal. And I'm not asking. That's an order."

As he picked up his bag to leave, he turned and added, "And, Philip, there's news of James. His mother and I are to bring him home at the end of the week even though he's still not really himself. At least he's communicating with us better though. His mother is very relieved. We'll have to see how he gets on. I shall be back in a few days' time to check up on you. Goodbye."

Philip thought long and hard of what the doctor had said. He felt utter dismay that he would have to confess to Kath and to Alan Lorimer that he was once again reduced to taking time to rest despite the huge pressures of the job. At least Alan was back and could carry the responsibilities for a short time. As for Jack and Emma, how could he add to their worries with his problems? He only knew he longed to be able to tell Emma and give in to his need for her for just a little while. Yet how could he give in to the desire for her now? He must resist it.

Kath took charge the minute he confessed to her the situation, and she herself decided to tell Emma, knowing as she did that this one person in his life was the one he needed at that time. Kath had long since recognised the love between them, wise old bird she was. But she felt quite safe in the knowledge that they could be safely trusted not to hurt all those others they loved. So, she carefully found an opportunity to tell Jack that Philip would welcome Emma's advice on his current predicament.

Jack took this message with a cursory nod though he gave Kath a questioning look which she returned with a reassuring smile.

"I think it would be much more effective for Emma to make him stop working rather than me, don't you think?" she said. "She'll know how to persuade him just like she manages to persuade the family when they're in trouble."

Jack thought about it for a moment, then shrugged his shoulders and left. He had a feeling that Emma would go scurrying off to school as soon as he told her, and this truth was somewhat uncomfortable. However, he did as he was asked and was satisfied that she took time to consider before reaching for her coat.

"Jack, I shall be back in time to cook supper and make sure Maggie has everything she needs. You don't mind me going, do you? You know how ill Mr Manners was last time this happened. We need to keep him from getting any worse. If Dr Thomson said 'rest', then he knows what he is on about. Jack, say you don't mind me going?" She kissed him fondly as a reassurance.

"Go, Emma, and do your best," he capitulated.

Without another word, she left. If she had not scurried out of the house, she certainly scurried up the lane to the fingerpost and along the path to his house, unable to help herself at the thought of seeing him, but also with a growing sense of foreboding about his health.

He was not there, however. He had struggled back to the study to try to get on with all the tasks that he knew he must complete before retiring to his bed. Kath was remonstrating with him as Emma knocked.

"Come in," he called and then looked in amazement and a wonderful relief. Here was Emma like some kind of angel answering prayer.

But it was late, and she would normally have been at home looking after the family. "What are you doing here, Emma?"

"Kath let me know you were in trouble, Philip and I felt I must come and check."

. "She should not have bothered you, my dear. Kath, you really had no right to take things into your own hands. It's not fair to Jack. You must let matters take their normal course. I will be alright if I rest," he said sharply and wondered what on earth Jack would be thinking if Emma ran to him at one word from Kath.

Neither of the women could doubt that he was truly angry. Kath was upset that he thought she had interfered and shown, in sending for Emma, that she knew their secret. Emma herself was mortified to see him so cross, knowing that he was thinking of Jack's feelings. Yet she knew he needed her, and her concern was all for him. She saw how white he was along the line of his lips and knew that it was not only his anger but real pain that produced it.

"Philip, please don't be angry with Kath. She only has your welfare at heart. Jack really didn't mind me coming up here. You should be resting, and I can see you are not." She went over to Kath who was standing

294 - JANE ALLISON

horrified at the reprimand and hugged her, much to her surprise.

"All is well, Kath. Leave this troublesome headmaster to me."

"Mr Manners, I am so sorry," said Kath, red to the roots of her hair. "I'll head off home now. And, sir, Alan Lorimer will have it all in hand until your leg recovers, you can be sure. Please do as the doctor has told you."

As she left, Philip, regretting his tone, smiled at her reassuringly. She knew she was forgiven. Then he turned his attention to Emma who was looking at him with a look of anxious concern. Nevertheless, she spoke to him strictly.

"Philip, I don't think I have ever seen you angry like that before. Poor Kath—she really didn't deserve that. I came and all you can say is, 'What are you doing here?'"

He had already regretted his reaction, and he held out his hand to her. "You know why I was cross. We don't want everyone to know about you and me. Kath knows too much, I fear."

"She is your best and kindest guardian. She only has your interest at heart." She held her arms out to help him up as he winced with the pain and then allowed him to lean on her, with his stick in the other hand. Together, they walked very slowly along the path back to his house, passing the school kitchen where Cook was busy clearing the day's meals away. She saw the two of them as they slowly laboured towards home. Her old suspicion was again reawakened. *Jack Holt had better watch out*, thought Connie, *though I'm sure Mr Manners wouldn't want to hurt him.*

Philip unlocked the door, and they entered the privacy of the house. He turned to Emma and embraced her like a parched traveller arriving at an oasis. "Too many buttons, Emma." He smiled, remembering the last time they had been alone.

"Too many buttons, my darling. But you must lie down and rest. Is this your room?" She led him, his leg throbbing intensely, to his bedroom and gently laid him on the bed. He was hugely relieved and allowed her to help him unresistingly. She knelt next to him and kissed him with a piercing sweetness that made him almost cry out with pleasure, his leg, for a moment, forgotten. But she was very aware that she could not stay long for Jack's sake and reluctantly stood up.

"Now, my dearest, I must go. Jack will be wondering. Are you going to be able to manage? I hate to have to leave you."

"The nurse will arrive in the morning, sent by Leonard Thomson, my love. I suppose I will have to survive all this though I have so much work to do."

"Stop fretting, Philip. You must let the healing work be done so you can be in charge again. Just, for once, let others look after the school. I'd stay if I only could, but I can't even come back and visit while you are still recuperating. I don't think that would be understood. I shall just have to trust to the ministrations of Dr Thomson till you are better. I know I'll be thinking of you all the time. God, how I hate this."

"Don't, Emma. You know you have to go."

Reluctantly, she left him, calling on Maggie and Florence to check all was well there, and thence to Holt House to cook supper, where she found Jack in a strange mood. He ate without asking about her trip, nor how Philip was, and she sensed his displeasure with her for going even though he had sent her himself.

Then, after supper as she was clearing the pots, he shocked her. He took hold of her roughly and kissed her violently as if to claim her for himself and no other.

"You are *my* wife, Mrs Holt. You will remember that, I hope. Don't ever deceive me, Emma. I would find that very difficult to forgive."

Emma took a step back, horrified at this revealing comment, and felt a terrible pang of guilt that her love for Philip had percolated itself into Jack's feelings and pained him. She knew also that Philip would be devastated to hear of it and would insist they be even more circumspect than ever.

"Jack, you know I would never leave you. Please don't say such things. Why, I am your partner in all things, not least as the mother of our boys and Florence, and George's grandma. Jack, surely you know this." She kissed him but so much more gently than his rough and angry embrace.

Jack shook his head very sadly and tried to compose himself. His enormous tolerance and patience, strained by the events of that evening, resurfaced, and he forced himself to put his arms round her comfortingly. Gradually, his natural good temper reasserted itself. For a moment there, he had felt a sense of real exclusion from Emma's love though he discarded the thought almost instantly.

He was trying hard to understand Emma's feelings which he could not help but question. He knew he had to trust her as he always had. Moreover, he knew the kind of man Philip Manners was. He liked and respected him as a friend in spite of the vast gulf of social background that separated them.

So, without a word, he turned to her and took her hand, leading her upstairs, and quietly pulled her down next to him on their bed. He made love to her there in the old, practised way of the years, and she did not resist.

"I love you, Jack, and I don't deserve you," she whispered. She knew this to be true and yet she knew that in her heart of hearts, she also loved another very different man.

Oh God, she prayed as she lay with him, *keep me from damaging Jack for I am most unworthy. Yet help me please to find my way through this maze in which I*

find myself. Keep my beloved Philip safe too, Lord. Help
us. I am tearing myself apart.

Night fell on Holt House and its inhabitants, and
on the single occupant of School House. And in their
perplexity, they all tried to sleep. Jack fell asleep almost immediately, feeling he had somehow stated his
claim and spoken up for himself. Emma laid awake with
no more tears left in her. She besought God's comfort though, in truth, she felt it far distant. Philip, in
his turn, tossed and turned with the pain in his leg,
unaware of what had happened on her return to Holt
House, only knowing how much he loved her.

And in the morning, Sister Wilson—the nurse the
doctor had requested—arrived to tend the wretched
abscess. She knocked and marched on in without waiting for an answer. She was sour-faced and harshly spoken and took no prisoners that morning or any other of
the mornings she dealt with him. He found it very difficult to keep his dignity in the face of her unyielding
stripping of his bedclothes and her washing the canker
on the leg with antiseptic fluid quite mercilessly. It was
agony in the acute stinging it caused, and the abrasion
left behind bled profusely. Yet he warmed to her strict-
ness by the fourth day, and she began to respond to his
patient endurance of her efforts.

"You are being extraordinarily brave, Mr Manners."
She smiled, much to his amazement. "I think and hope
we can say we have got the better of the infection now

so long as you keep up with the strapping I've put on your leg. I shall wait a week now before coming, and you can begin to walk as long as you're careful. Dr Thomson will be calling, I know." She shook his hand, and he felt a sudden lightening of the anxiety that had been so heavy upon him.

"Thank you so much, Sister Wilson. I do believe you've done me good."

"It's been a pleasure, Mr Manners." And off she went, sporting her supremely efficient medical bag. After she left, he had to smile. The awe-inspiring Sister Wilson apparently had a heart of gold after all. *I must tell Emma.* It was as natural as breathing to think that thought but then, remembering the actual reality of their situation, it gave him a stab of pain.

Meanwhile, Alan Lorimer and Edna Wright had not been backward in organising the timetable around Philip's absence and in beginning to make the requisite plans for the installing of a new deputy head for the school. Exam time was approaching once the summer term got underway, and Alan was aware that Philip was always meticulous in the arrangements.

Philip emerged walking very slowly and leaning on his stick. His weak leg was supported by Sister Wilson's strapping under his trouser leg. Around him, he saw the signs of the blossoming spring, so much of which had been planted by Jack Holt. Snowdrops had reasserted themselves despite the heavy blanket of snow they had borne and pale yellow primroses were peeping shyly amongst them. Buds of cherry blossom and almond blossom hung heavy on their branches, ready to burst out in a glory of pink. And as he walked into his study, he was infinitely comforted at the sight of Kath in her office next door with the timetable spread out before her, and Edna and Alan poring over it. They looked up in delight at seeing him and ushered him to his own chair.

"The commander is back, Edna." Alan laughed.

"Thank goodness for that." Edna sighed. "Mr Manners, we greet you."

Kath was visibly moved at this little cameo, and she rejoiced. Perhaps all would be well now.

They asked anxiously about his leg.

"I shall have to be sensible, I guess, or Sister Wilson will be chasing me. But no, my dear colleagues, I'm fine. Let's get on with managing our school."

They spent time then looking at all the applications they had received for the post of head of Fox House to replace Jim Fletcher. Alan had instigated it and set up the shortlist for interviews to take place as soon as possible before the end of term. That way they knew Fox House could have a new head in place for the summer term.

Philip's time now became consumed by the practicalities of the arrangements as well as beginning to think with his heads of houses about the following term. The interviews were set up for March 30, and Edna volunteered to accommodate the interviewees in Applegarth House. All the catering would be covered by Cook from the school kitchen and, accordingly, three candidates arrived, all of them women whose credentials were immaculate. Jack, busy in the gardens, viewed them all as they took their turns to enter Philip's study where he had a panel of several governors and staff awaiting them. Jack commented on this to Emma at home, and she astonished herself with a shiver of jealousy at the thought that Philip would be meeting younger and possibly more beautiful women. Indeed, Philip himself, with Alan Lorimer, noted how glamorous they all seemed.

But the final decision was down to the qualifications of Miss Beatrice Constable, who accepted the post gratefully. She had lost her fiancé at the front and was starting a new life for herself. Moreover, she had high marks in physics which meant she could take over Jim's timetable perfectly.

Emma, meanwhile, was labouring hard fulfilling her duties at the station, toiling at the laundry coming down from the school, and working without let up with little George. She was also determined to convince Jack of her loyalty whilst breaking her heart with the longing simply to go up to school and look after her beloved Philip. However, she was much heartened by a message brought by Jack that Philip was back at his desk and with the news that James Thomson was home, though he had not made a great deal of progress since their visit to York. His parents were in despair that he had no company of his own age.

After one of his slow walks down to where Jack was working, Philip had discussed this with him. Jack had greeted him warmly in the old way, revealing nothing of his outburst to Emma and had suggested that Emma might visit the Thomsons. As Jack put it, she had after all helped comfort the Firbanks and many of the boys over the months of this ugly war, a sentiment with which Philip wholeheartedly agreed.

"Do you think she might consider visiting them, Jack?"

"Why of course she will, sir. You know she would do anything to cheer Dr Thomson who is so kind to her whenever George is sick with his wretched asthma."

"Tell her I've asked, would you, Jack? Leonard Thomson is always very good to me too and has helped my leg recover from the ghastly abscess."

Emma rejoiced at this very small crumb of comfort from him yet knew she could not bear to stay away from him much longer. She would visit the Thomsons and then she could go up to school legitimately to see him.

It was a difficult visit and difficult also not to seem as if she were intruding on a family in sorrow. Yet she sat with the three of them, chatted about her two sons, and tried very hard to include James in the conversation. He was sullen and silent, and his mother told her he was having continual nightmares about all he had seen at the front. He brightened up a little when Emma told him that Ned Tempest had become engaged to Florence, for he and Ned had been together as they went out to join the battle. But he had a nervous tic which clearly upset his father to see, and Emma found herself aching with pity for them. Moreover, it brought back to her all that Will in particular was going through, having been beside his friend and captain at Passchendaele.

In the end, she excused herself and hastened home to write another letter of consolation and love to Will. She was less anxious with Harry, as she knew he had found a real satisfaction in his role in Verdun, but her Will was clearly still desperately sad at the loss of Ralph. As she walked home from the Thomson's, she asked herself again how she could find the resilience to hold everything together for them all with all the vicissitudes of every day, underpinned by the heartache she had as a permanent leaden weight inside.

"I shall write to Philip," she said to herself. *"Maybe that will give me some relief."*

Chapter 32

Holt House,
April 12, 1918

My beloved Philip,

My soul is in some turmoil, so I have decided to write to you and simply feel close to you as I write. I feel I have hardly seen you since I left you alone to recover in the hands of others. I found that very difficult to bear.

When I returned home that night, Jack was brusque with me, insisting on his husbandly rights and reminding me that I belonged to him. He did not mention you, my love, but I believe he was angry at my coming up to school late in the evening to see you. I tried to reassure him and felt such a wicked hypocrite knowing my heart was somewhere else. I do indeed love him as my loyal partner over all these years, and I reminded him of that. I think I reassured him, promising that I wasn't going anywhere.

But, oh, Philip, the irony of it. I feel it still as though I need to go to confession with a priest to beg God's for-

giveness. Then, in a kind of agony, I remember one must be sorry for the sin and repent of it to receive absolution, and indeed I cannot, my darling. I refuse to repent for loving you. Nothing can be done. I am defeated in the battle and keeping honourable is getting harder.

I must remain utterly calm and keep my brave face if I can, but I simply long to see you. I have been to see James Thomson and he is a sorry sight. His parents are grieving over him. I am using this to give me a reason to see you. Jack himself suggested this visit after all. So, do not be too surprised when I appear. And then maybe I could bring George to see you. He asks about you regularly and his talking is so good now; a matter of great pride to us all. There's another reason to come, and Kath would like that too.

But we must be cautious, I know, especially in the light of Jack's outburst. You must be careful in reading this letter, my love. It contains so much love, but you cannot reply.

Emma

On receiving this letter and recognising Emma's hand, Philip put it away in his jacket and kept it till he was in the privacy of his home. Kath Hanson noticed his look as he did so.

Please God it doesn't bring him more trouble.

As he read it at last, his head sank into his hands in dismay—nay, more than dismay—at the news of Jack's reaction to her evening visit. She had had to bear this all alone and had had no crumb of comfort from him. Furthermore, he was utterly helpless in the face of it. He too knew they must stay true to those who needed them and to their responsibilities in the community. He too felt he needed absolution and, like Emma, at the self-same moment, knew he would not repent of loving her, simply because he could not.

He limped slowly to the Meeting House that evening and knelt in the quiet of the empty space, actually glad that this was causing him acute pain in his weakened leg. The pain somehow denoted his penitence. There he fought with his feelings, seeking some light from the Holy Spirit to show him the way.

God, help me. I don't know what to do. I only know I must be strong to keep faith with all I represent here in school. I must stay loyal to Jack, never to damage him or his family. But I love Emma so much and I can't stop that. It's a sacred thing for me, and I won't believe it to be something unworthy or unrighteous. I don't want her to be unhappy because of me. I want her to have all the grace she needs to keep her whole and true.

He was silent then but a gleam of something like solace for him came into his mind in the words of Psalm 23.

The Lord's my shepherd, I shall not want.
He maketh me to lie down in green pastures.
He restoreth my soul.

Somewhat restored by that blessed thought of the Good Shepherd who would lead him from exhaustion to a fresh sense of peace, he stood and slowly limped back to his home. In the morning, perhaps she might come.

That night, he dreamed of her. It was a vivid dream. She came to him in her different guises: the over-worked laundry woman with her hair wet with the sweat of the wash tub, and he was pushing the tendril of hair from her forehead; the cook bearing her cakes to the school kitchen, invisible to the staff who took for granted the delicacies she had slaved over, and he was carrying the tray for her as she parked her baskets in the school kitchen; the fill-in station master in her uniform, cap on head, waving the flag for the outgo-ing train, and he smiled as he dreamed of taking her into the station waiting room and lifting her face to his kisses; the elegant woman in the green taffeta dress with whom he had danced, and he was holding her waist, feeling its slenderness in its stiff silky wrapping held tight against him. He woke with a start, sweating with the overwhelming pleasure of it even in his sleep. And then he groaned with the awful knowledge of its unreality.

He sat up in bed and looked at the clock. It was only early morning and school was still soundly asleep. He made himself get up and wash and dress in the me-chanical routine of every day, numbing his mind to the pain of the situation and the desire the dream had rendered even more acute. Once ready, he sat at his desk and made himself plan the summer festivities of the school for which he was responsible.

I am its head teacher, for God's sake, he thought. *They all look to me as an example and I fail the test. Work, Philip. Work now and be stronger.*

Later that morning, he limped over to his study and greeted Kath cheerily. There was another letter awaiting him on his desk and he recognised the very different handwriting. Harriet. Kath watched him as he read with a resigned frown and inwardly prayed for him to keep the composure she knew he could muster. He had not been appointed head of this establishment in vain, and she knew he could and would rise to the situation.

"Harriet tells me she has done all that is required to prepare for the pending divorce, Miss Hanson," he told her. "It has come to a sorry pass indeed, has it not? Harriet's solicitor has drawn up the papers, but I have to arrange a time to visit his named partner in Cranston to sign them, a Mr Wells. And Godfrey Langdon has provided the evidence needed which means that the wheels are now in motion for the final chapter. What a sad outcome. I know nothing can happen as quickly as Harriet wishes it. She is in a hurry; God forgive us both.

"Kath, can you make me an appointment with this Mr Wells as soon as possible so I can get this whole shameful business over with?"

Kath was quick to assure him that none of this was his fault and that it must be for the best. She began to set about contacting Wells and Bruin, solicitors in Cranston, to implement his request. He said nothing more but simply put Harriet's letter back into the envelope, his face stern. He squared his shoulders and returned to the business of the day.

"Now, Kath, can we type a letter to Frank Jacques? I have an idea—we should ask him to attend our end of term speech day and give out the prizes. He seems a good man and has much the same view of this terrible war as I. He seems pretty sure it is nearing its death throes now we have the help of our overseas allies, and we should make the end of this term a celebration of the school if we can."

He had successfully steadied himself and had set to work on all the issues of the day when there came a gentle knock on his door. It was a group of young second-year boys who had come to show him their work as the reward for its excellence. They had written poems about the war in their English class, the class taught by the young woman whom he had helped during the years with her discipline. She had turned the corner in her confidence and looked at Philip as some kind of benevolent saviour.

As the boys showed him their poems and glowed with pleasure, he felt very moved by their efforts and by the sight of the smiling young teacher beside them.

"Why, these are sensitively written, boys. I can see you have thought hard about what war does to people. Miss Kenning, can we put them in the end of year magazine? You have had such success with this class. Congratulations. Now let's pray we never have another war when this one ends."

Miss Kenning nodded her agreement of this sentiment as she beamed with pleasure at his words and the boys with her.

"Mr Manners, it's all thanks to your help and guidance that I am still standing here. I couldn't have done it without you. Thank you. Come, boys."

As Kath ushered them out, Philip felt an intense relief at this small gift of grace awarded to him. It reminded him that his work was not wasted and that he could still serve despite his own inner turmoil.

But there came the sound of a little boy outside in the corridor and his heart leapt.

"May we come in a minute if we are not disturbing you, Mr Manners?" came Emma's voice, and as she spoke, George scurried over to him and lifted his arms up to be picked up. Kath greeted them with pleasure as George settled himself on Philip's lap.

"Have you got a book, Uncle Philip? Will you read the story of the big pancake?"

"Why, Emma, he's talking so well now. How lovely to see you both." And he began to read the familiar story as the little one snuggled into him.

Emma stood quietly and smiled at Kath. It was a huge relief to see him at last and forget for a moment all the tangle of emotions they both were bearing. This small delight gave her a sense that perhaps somehow all would be well, and she allowed herself to relax in the warmth of the thought, impossible though in reality it was.

"Philip, I have seen James Thomson, and Jack has had an idea. The poor boy is changed almost beyond recognition but has calmed down from the worst of the trauma. It has left him totally unable to pursue his studies at university, but Jack thinks he could benefit from some gardening work alongside him. There is, as you know, plenty of work in the school gardens and in the maintenance of the buildings, and Jack thinks it would be a healing thing for him to be using his hands again. His parents are devastated but think, like Jack, that this would be a therapy. What do you think?"

As she spoke, George had slipped off his lap and was now pulling out all the books from the box Philip and Kath had set up for him.

"I think it's a wonderful idea and typical of Jack to have it. I shall tell the Thomsons myself that we shall be delighted to give him a job here as long as it's needed. Thank you for bringing this little chap to see us. We love to be visited, do we not, Kath?"

Kath smiled but, muttering something about sweeties, took George by the hand and scurried out of the study. She knew her presence was unneeded in that moment and thought it wise to get out of their way.

Philip took both Emma's hands in his and looked at her with all the long-repressed emotion of the weeks between. "My dear," he whispered, and she gazed back.

"I am just so glad to be with you even though it's so fleeting, my darling," she said. "Did you get my letter? It's been so hard to resist coming and so tempting just to give up the fight. Let's just run away, shall we? But, oh, Philip, you know I don't mean it. Of course we won't. God, forgive me."

"Emma, I do believe God will forgive us, but we've got to make this work. We owe it to Jack if nobody else. Perhaps, in a strange sort of way, we owe it to Harriet too. And I am horrified to read what happened the night you left me. Poor Jack. If I had known what he was thinking and what you were going through, I would have despaired. I know it's easy to say but there is still much we have to do to make others happier. I must maintain the school's reputation while you care for the world and your family as I know you do. Are you not, my darling, still holding the world up for everyone?"

He stopped then as he saw her face, the terrible look of sorrow printed all over it. He hugged her to him wordlessly, and she clung to him. Then he kissed her gently on her forehead and squared his shoulders, knowing full well that Kath would be returning with the little one and he must help Emma to regain her equilibrium. He sat back at his desk just as Kath returned with George, whose hands were holding tight to a sticky cluster of jelly babies. They laughed at the sight of him.

"Grandma, I've got sweeties. Look." He held his arms out to be picked up. Philip knew Emma would be unable to resist this.

"Thank you, Kath," said Emma, and Kath just nodded in response, as they both knew the thank you was for more than could be acknowledged.

"Goodbye then. Come, George. Let's find your grandad." She left, closing the door firmly behind her.

"Kath, to work!" he announced. "We need a staff meeting soon."

Chapter 33

While Philip and Emma were struggling to maintain their integrity in Shadworth, the war was proceeding at a greater pace. The German high command, aware of the imminent arrival of the American forces, threw huge efforts at the British and French lines, bombarding the trenches heavily, followed by assault after assault of freshly trained storm troopers, moving in, trench by trench, until the allies were forced to pull back.

Area by area, this tactic succeeded but never quite sufficiently to break the allied line though the suffering and bloodshed caused was huge. Yet the line held firm and a new allied commander took charge as the Americans were moving in. The new general, General Foch, now presided and launched a major counterattack on the enemy. As American and Australian troops with all the force of aircraft and tanks pushed with increasing power, the German hierarchy realised they could not withstand much longer. General Ludendorff, the German army commander, began to seek for an armistice as July turned into August and his men were increasingly facing a fearful and ugly defeat.

When will it ever end? thought Will.

Will I ever get home to see my son? thought Harry.

Will had never fully recovered from the sight of Ralph choking and being smothered in the morass of dense, slurping mud as he himself had frantically pulled and pulled to try and draw him to safety. It was the subject of his nightmares every night. He had managed to put on a brave front at the sight of Ned and for the sake of his men, which made the days manageable. That at least prevented his spirit from collapsing in on itself entirely. Yet at night as he relived again in his dreams the quagmire, the ghastly sound of Ralph gurgling as he tried to scream, and the mockery of his own arms aching with the force of his efforts, Will felt as if death would be a relief. Why could he not die as enemy troops attacked over and over again? What kept him somehow alive as others fell around him? Getting hold of cigarettes to soothe his shattered nerves was increasingly difficult, so Will puffed on the old fag ends he managed to pick up in the trench to give him some relief. Now his finger ends, yellowed and bitten, spoke volumes to his men about his state of mind. Had Emma seen his fingers or seen him as he woke each night sweating with horror, she would have descended into paroxysms of grief.

One thought kept Will sane: the promise he had made to himself that he would find Ralph's Laura and convey to her the strength and courage that Ralph had always shown even in those last moments. If he somehow survived, that would be his first task before he reached the haven of Holt House. And Harry, by now beloved cook of the French troops in Verdun, began increasingly to believe that he would indeed return to his lovely Maggie and his little boy as talk of an armistice became more and more optimistic. His role there had kept him from the cruel memories that Will suffered.

At home, Emma studiously kept her resolve to keep clear of the school and distance herself from the man she loved. She knew Jack would be there and able to keep watch over Philip, for she felt that was necessary knowing Philip's usual complete disregard for his own health in comparison with the needs of his school. The irony did not escape her that it was Jack she trusted with his well-being. She thought little of her own dedication yet served all who needed her, not least her own husband.

At the station, train after train was signalled through bearing injured troops whose dulled eyes saw only what they had escaped. What they didn't see as they looked sadly out of the windows of the carriages, was the joy of the glorious green of the summer and the fields glowing with the haymaking. Emma's heart missed a beat as she saw the bandaged heads still stained with dried blood and the crutches whose handles decorated the train windows like dead trees. And she thought of the mothers and lovers who would be receiving them home, full of joy at the coming reunion, only to be shocked by the ravaged state of so many.

"*God, bring Will and Harry safely home undamaged,*" she prayed, but knew in her heart of hearts that Will, especially, would be bearing scars which were deeply ingrained.

She washed and laundered the teachers' blouses just as she had always done, always accompanied by the little boy who adored her. She was constantly called in by Maggie and Florence whenever George's breathing changed to asthmatic gasps, and she'd sit beside his little bed and boil kettle after kettle to bring him relief with the steam. She had hot flannels ready in a minute's notice to apply to his weary little chest, and amidst his gasps for breath, he held her hand tightly. Maggie could never thank Emma enough, and Florence watched her mother and learned from her something of the sacrifice of motherhood.

Emma also regularly visited the Thomsons to make sure they were managing James' changing moods and to reassure them that he was thriving and busy in the school gardens, watched over by Jack. Sometimes she was so exhausted that Jack would find her fast asleep on the old horsehair settee. He would cover her with his old coat and smile to himself.

Sleep, lass. You deserve it.

Meanwhile, Philip had busied himself with the last weeks of the summer term and his plans for the grand speech day to which he had invited Frank Jacques. He observed with a great deal of pleasure Beatrice Constable's installation as head of Fox House and even more with the signs of a relationship flourishing between her and Alan Lorimer.

"Philip, have you seen the way Alan looks at Miss Constable?" whispered Edna. He and Edna were both thrilled to see it flowering, and he found himself envying Alan who had such easy access to the woman with whom he had fallen in love. He ached with frustration that he could not bestow on his beloved Emma all the outward bounty of his love. Instead, it was a secret thing only to be snatched at in moments of delight, rare and all too brief.

But having promised himself to stand firm, he found he had a perfect reason to summon her. The speech day was looming, and the staff had all agreed it should be a real celebration of the school in the presence of their MP but also an occasion to honour all the exam triumphs of the boys in the exam classes. Parents were attending from far and wide, and Cook was demanding she had Mrs Holt's help with the catering.

"You know, Mr Manners, I'm the first to say only Mrs Holt can make meringues and fancies of such delicacy and quality to impress a member of parliament."

Kath overheard this comment and quickly added her word to Connie's, knowing well what it meant for him. "We'll ask Jack to bring her, sir," she said. "He might bring little George to see us as well. You know perfectly well that Cook is right."

That was enough for Philip, and he allowed himself the luxury of expecting her though he made himself focus on the stack of work on his desk. However, he was to be disappointed. Emma knew that seeing him would only open their wounds, so she opted instead to visit Cook and ascertain her requirements privately. It meant a huge amount of baking and cooking in her kitchen at Holt House which she undertook with pride and anticipation. Her resolve was being broken even as she sweated over the hot oven, even as her back ached with the effort of lifting the heavy cake tins in and out.

On the day, I will enjoy the sight of him, and I will not have betrayed my resolve.

Chapter 34

What she had not anticipated was seeing him at the station on the actual day, meeting Frank Jacques from the London train with Beatrice Constable and Alan Lorimer beside him. It was extremely painful for her, as he was never alone for even a moment, and all he could manage was a brief smile at her as he greeted the visitor. She stood watching him in her station uniform, cap perched on her head, and felt all the indignity and stuffiness of her appearance as Beatrice glowed in the morning sunshine, auburn hair shimmering in the light, fur cape around her shoulders, laughing at some joke shared between them. Emma knew nothing of the flowering of love that had grown between Alan and Beatrice. She only saw Philip's hand on Beatrice's arm and his attentiveness to her. She looked across at the man whose love she should never have doubted and felt the fear and jealousy all over again, like a canker in her soul.

Oh God, thought Emma. *How can I go on living like this? And tonight, I must put on my white apron of servitude and bring out my god-forsaken cakes and be invisible again.*

She felt suddenly nauseated and, having waved the departing train off, fled into the station toilet to be violently sick.

Something in Philip made him aware that he had somehow trampled on her spirit by being forced to play the role of the good headmaster. This was bitter to him. He returned with his guest to school, reflecting grimly about his and Emma's situation. It was so doomed, so futile, so absolutely banned. He thought of the uniform and how he adored her in it, but the distance between them, self-determined by them both, seemed like a vast ocean.

God, help me, he uttered to himself for the umpteenth time.

Yet the afternoon of the prize-giving arrived and with it the assembly of the proud parents. Jack and Emma had both transported all the specialities to the school dining hall, and she now stood beside Connie, the table in front of them spread with the delicacies they had conjured for the refreshments. She observed proceedings as if from a long way off, trying to calm herself and revive her courage. Standing on the hall stage, Philip introduced Frank Jacques, who spoke movingly to the gathered audience about the efforts he had made with the head to convey to parliament the horrors of the war and the deathly treatment of deserters as well as the effects of shell shock. It was an impassioned speech congratulating the school and all its pupils for their achievements and their head for sustaining the cause of peace throughout the years.

It was Philip's turn next, and he stood, leaning on his stick, looking around at the boys for whom he had a father's love, and thanked them for keeping the school as a place of peace and a haven of concern for the world.

"We know how many of our boys have gone to war nobly and sincerely to fight for their country and its cause. I honour them today, though I continue to stress to all gathered here the Quaker belief which I follow myself, that the apparatus of war and of hate can never truly bring about human safety and harmony.

"But I have also today to remind you that this school is a place of very hard, studious work where many boys have achieved great success in their examinations, as well as many sporting achievements. They are today to be congratulated, honoured, and encouraged by our acknowledgement of their achievements as we award them their prizes. So, ladies and gentlemen, to the prize-giving."

Philip read out the names slowly, allowing Frank Jacques to shake each boy's hand and speak individually to them. But each and every one passed him as they clutched their award and bowed their heads towards him as if he was the one for whom they had the greatest respect. He had to hold tightly to his tears as he thought of Daniel Latimer and those boys whose deaths had prevented them forever from reaching the fullness of their potential. Beatrice sneaked a glance at Alan as she noticed it, and Alan squeezed her hand for a moment to say he too saw all that Philip was feeling. That squeeze came as a blessing to Emma looking on.

It's Alan Lorimer who has fallen for her. How could I have doubted Philip?

Emma watched him with love in her eyes, noting the tiredness around his shoulders. She thought how young and vulnerable he looked despite the greying hair at his temple, and she noticed him flicking a tear from his cheek.

You fool, Emma Holt. And as she thought it, he caught her eye and smiled across at her. For just a fleeting moment, the world belonged to them both and nothing could take that away.

Philip was met by parent after parent wanting to thank him for his care for their sons and by some of the boys whom he had in past times soothed from their nightmares in their dormitories. Now they shyly approached him to show him their awards. Young Jacob was among them—the child he had carried back to his bed after the news of his brother's death.

"Sir," said Jacob, "I'll never forget what you did for me on that dreadful night. Thank you, sir."

Others were remembering the quiet hour in the Meeting House where they had been given the opportunity to pray in their suffering. They too wished to thank him, and some of them asked if they might speak to the woman behind the long trestle tables in the white apron who had shared with them in those healing moments.

"Come with me and we'll find her. She is with Cook who also deserves our gratitude for all her work in feeding you all," he said and led them to where Emma was busily handing out plates for parents as they helped themselves to the fruits of her hard labour of the past few days. Charlie Hopton had beaten him to it, for there he stood beside her with Cook, helping with the serving.

"I've brought some thankful young people to greet you, Emma," he said, and her eyes shone at the sight of him. "Not forgetting our own school cook."

Frank Jacques approached from behind him and noticed her shining face as he himself thanked them for the wonderful feast they had produced. "I can see that a school is not only made up of teachers and pupils," he commented with a smile. "It relies so much on all those who serve it in so many other very important ways. You are fortunate, Mr Manners, to have such support."

"Frank, this happens to be our gardener's wife as well as Cook's standby," said Philip, "But she is also something of a mother to the boys here. They can vouch for that themselves. I can't thank you enough, Mrs Holt, for all you contribute to the life of the school." As he spoke, he gave her such a look of devotion that she couldn't help but blush.

Philip then led Frank Jacques away to where Beatrice, Alan, and Edna, with other members of staff, were also shaking hands with parents alongside Kath. They all congratulated the MP for his contribution as, at last, the day was ending. They bade farewell to the visitor, and Philip ushered him into the cab he had prearranged to take him to Shadworth Station for his return to London.

"You have a very special school, Philip," Frank said as they climbed out of the cab and Philip put him on the train. "All your concern for our troops has not gone unrecognised. Very best wishes to you for the new term when it comes. And pray God we see the end of the war soon. Goodbye."

As the train pulled out of the station with Mr Firbank himself acting in his own role as station master, Philip closed his eyes in a silent prayer of thanks that the day had gone so well. He felt utterly exhausted. He smiled a wry smile as he thought longingly of the other station master whose absence there and in his whole life was felt more keenly every day.

Chapter 35

Between August and November, what became known as the Hundred Days Offensive took place, finally bringing Germany and her allies to their knees but not without the devastating loss of many more young lives. The German commander, Ludendorff, knew that the end was inevitable and that he could do no more. Accordingly, he pleaded for an armistice to be managed by the Americans who were demanding the abdication of the Kaiser. His army and its allies were in tatters—confusion and chaos ensued.

Will, Harry, and Ned found themselves unbelievably still alive, albeit shattered, exhausted and changed irrevocably by what they had experienced. But they saw that light was dawning at last, and when the Kaiser finally abdicated in early November, the armistice was marked on the eleventh hour of the eleventh day of the eleventh month. Amidst the wreck of so many lives and the devastated landscape of France and Belgium, peace and freedom could again flourish.

School had continued quietly all the while as Philip kept a steady hand on the tiller. The new first-year boys had arrived and settled into the gentle routine that Philip had maintained throughout. His heads of house stood side by side with him as he announced the news that the war was over. The boys gave an almighty whoop of joy which seemed to refresh the atmosphere of the whole school. In the Meeting House, they celebrated peace at last, the peace that had always been Philip's most treasured priority. Boys flocked to be there each Sunday to breathe their relief and their delight at the hope of new beginnings.

Jack, in the gardens, nurtured the very late roses, and they continued to glow with colour throughout this time. James Thomson's nightmares began to fade as he learned with Jack the lessons of horticulture and assisted with some of the routine school maintenance jobs. James found enormous pleasure in the company of the stalwart and patient gardener who encouraged him as he nurtured the plants. But he noticed Jack rubbing his chest sometimes as if in some pain and breathing heavily when digging, so he offered to help with the heavier tasks whenever he could.

"Thanks, James. I'm not as young as I was," replied Jack, admitting he was grateful for the bit of assistance. Philip rejoiced to see the friendship growing between the two of them, as did James' parents who would, from time to time, visit him in his study to drink coffee and talk, sharing their hopes and fears. And James did not comment to any of them that he was keeping an eye on Jack.

Little George, approaching three years old, was often in the garden with his grandad. James and he became firm friends. But there was no friend more beloved of George than 'Uncle Philip' whose study door was left permanently open during this time so that boys and staff could visit him whenever they wanted.

It was to Emma's huge relief that she realised her boys would finally be coming home, and with them, Florrie's beau, Ned Tempest. Yet she could never relinquish the grief in that corner of her heart that belonged to the other George; her beloved boy so cruelly killed. She allowed herself the pleasure of sometimes meeting with Philip when Maggie and she walked up to school, and she contented herself with seeing his health improving, his limp less pronounced, knowing he was not unhappy and lonely, save for that yawning gap there was in the life of each of them. But their fidelity to the task in hand kept them strong, and they thrived in these weeks as they worked for everyone's sake. Kath Hanson saw it and was thankful, though she suspected what it might be costing them.

So, Emma, gradually now shedding some of her duties for Shadworth Station as the menfolk began returning to their posts, set about preparing for the homecomings. She helped them decorate Shadworth Station with bunting, she took to singing as she worked, and the kitchen at Holt House resounded with the old Methodist hymns with which she had grown up. Jack laughed at her singing "Will Your Anchor Hold" at the top of her voice as she pummelled the washing in the boiler with the peggy stick. He related this fact to Philip and Kath on one visit to the study with George, and they all enjoyed the thought, especially Philip who decided he could at least write to her and maybe even walk down to see her. There were small crumbs of comfort that sustained them both.

In France, Ned, Harry, and Will planned their return with an eye on the orders for demobilisation. Soon after, Will and Harry found themselves among the most fortunate troops to be allowed to go home early, having volunteered for service almost at the beginning of the war, though it had been to their parents' grief. Ned was less fortunate and had to await his discharge papers until his company had satisfied all military and medical requirements.

On his release, Will had one very important promise to keep, a promise he had made to himself as a covenant with Ralph. He was determined to visit Laura, Ralph's widow, whose address he had retrieved from Ralph's wallet in the dugout. Thus, as Harry was already en route for Shadworth, Will set out for a place in Hertfordshire, a small town called Baldock, wherein was a Catholic convent school at which he knew Laura taught. Ralph had often regaled him with stories of her pleasure in teaching English there and of the girls she loved under her care. He had also spoken of her great beauty. Will, whose life until that time had never included any particular young women, now found himself quite nervous at the prospect of meeting one whom Ralph had adored. He looked more than once at the photograph of Laura he had taken from Ralph's pocket.

By God, she's lovely, he thought to himself. This was not to trespass on the sacred nature of the covenant with Ralph, but nevertheless, Will couldn't help a feeling of nervous anticipation at the prospect of seeing her for himself.

Accordingly, he had written to her and arranged to come to her convent school at the end of her Christmas term to talk with her about Ralph's final hours, to relate to her how much she had been in Ralph's thoughts, and mention how often he had spoken of her. On December 15, the date of his own mother's birthday, Will stood on the steps of the convent school and watched Laura come down to greet him. He was overcome with an emotion he had never encountered before. She was truly beautiful in a shy and gentle way, with her black hair pinned up in a demure chignon. Her eyes were expressive of the sadness that had swallowed her at Ralph's death and her finger still carried Ralph's wedding ring. Will took her hand and looked at the ground, speechless.

"It is more than good of you to spend time on your way home to see me," she exclaimed. "Let's go to mine and you can tell me all those things which I need to hear, no matter how unbearable."

And so it was. She made Will tell her of the deadly morass that had smothered her husband and how he, Will, had laboured unsuccessfully to retrieve him from its grip. He shuddered as he recalled it, but she listened bravely, without a tear, and insisted on the details of it, then of the dugout and of their alliance within. He told her how they had both known the futility of the venture out there in the ghastly battlefield and how that knowledge had bonded them as almost brothers. At last, she gave in to her grief. She leaned her head on his shoulder and wept great gasping sobs of loss and heartache.

"Have you parents to go to for Christmas?" he asked her.

She shook her head. "There was only Ralph and I. My parents are dead."

It was a moment of absolute, unrehearsed impetuosity that overcame him then. "Come with me to my parents' home for Christmas. My mother would welcome you with open arms, as she always does anybody who needs comfort. Say you'll come."

Laura simply nodded her acceptance of the offer so lovingly made and thus Will's fate was sealed. He was completely infatuated already and meant to honour Ralph's memory by returning his wife to a fresh happiness.

Would Ralph have minded? he later asked himself. But he knew deep down that Ralph would be at peace now at such an outcome. So two people, not one alone, returned to Holt House two days later and surprised Emma as she was feeding the chickens and humming to herself.

Of course, Will was right in assuming her hospitality, and Laura was to benefit from it. As for Harry, he was overwhelmed at the sight of the almost three-year-old who greeted him at Maggie's cottage door with his thumb firmly in his mouth and his soft toy rabbit clutched to his chest, big-eyed and wondering as his mother threw herself into the stranger's arms and squealed with delight. The reunion with Maggie was all that Harry could have hoped and dreamed. She was sweet and shy with him at first but then she kissed him so passionately she made him gasp.

"Who's that man, Grandma?" asked little George. "Why is he kissing my mummy?"

Emma had to suppress a giggle as she explained that this was his own daddy who'd come home to them. "Why don't you go and give him a big hug, George? I bet he'd like it."

Philip found himself standing at the fingerpost on that particular day as Jack was leaving the school after work. He wanted simply to look down to Low Shadworth as he had many times before, just for a little while, to feel closer to Emma. Kath Hanson had already gone home to the quiet of her cottage. He had been astonished by two visitors to his study earlier that day—Alan Lorimer and Beatrice Constable. They'd had a special request for him.

"Philip, Bea and I are going to get married. She's accepted this old man, somewhat unbelievably, though she tells me she won't give up her teaching unless she has to. I need a best man, Philip, and I can't think of a better one than you. Will you do it for us?"

Philip had accepted this honour readily, astonished at being asked but so incredibly happy for the couple, but now he stood there thoughtful indeed, with a sombre face as Jack approached, aware that his head was troubled.

Jack stopped and looked questioningly at him. "Sir, is something wrong? You should be at home enjoying the absence of students."

"I'm fine, Jack. Just had a bit of a surprise I need to absorb. I've never been asked to be anyone's best man before. Mr Lorimer and Miss Constable are to be married quite soon, I gather, and I am to be their best man. In fact, it's wonderful news, isn't it?"

"But, sir, that is indeed good news." Jack laughed. "So, why so serious?"

"I am delighted for them. I just have to rearrange my thoughts a little."

Jack nodded and smiled as he set off again down the hill. Philip was left at the fingerpost, and again, the loneliness of his thoughts struck him forcibly.

What I really want is to take Jack's wife and ravish her. To hell with the consequences and my bloody Quaker conscience. She should not belong to anyone but me. But yet, all I can do is stand here wishing.

He groaned as he stood there leaning on his stick, reprimanding himself for the selfish, God-forsaken anger that was ripping through him and hurting hard.

I'm allowing myself to whine like a child who cries out, 'It's not fair' when he doesn't get what he wants, he remonstrated with himself. *I must pull myself together. But, God, how much I want to claim her for my own.*

With this thought, he shivered suddenly with the winter cold and realised he was still standing at the top of the hill with no overcoat and must indeed return home to his empty house. Though that, he knew, would only exacerbate the acute sense of aloneness he was feeling.

Had Emma known what he was suffering as she strove to keep her side of their promise, she would have dropped every activity and run up the hill to him. As it was, she was overwhelmed with jobs and demands—sons and their companions, a little boy pulling at her skirts, washing still to be completed, last shift at the station finishing off her duties. She barely noticed when Jack complained of the indigestion pain he'd been having.

"It's a nuisance when I'm trying to get the jobs done, Emma."

"Jack, you must go and get checked by Dr Thomson. Perhaps you've been drinking too much beer with Harry at The White Swan."

Jack just nodded gruffly at that. He was enjoying Harry's company on these trips to the pub. It felt like he was getting to know his son all over again

Philip contented himself that night by writing to her. He needed to tell her about Alan's nuptials and the demand to travel to Matlock immediately after Christmas to share with his friends in the wedding. He also knew she would half expect him to come to them for George's birthday tea and he would be unable even to do that. Christmas itself was to be with the Thomsons at their kind invitation, and he really wanted her to know exactly why he could not be at Holt House as he had been these last two years.

"Perhaps that's what the matter is. I know I cannot even enjoy being close to her this year." So, he sat at his desk and wrote.

December 18,

My darling Emma,

This must be the next best thing to seeing you, as I am promised to the Thomsons for Christmas and have to go away immediately after Christmas to act as Alan Lorimer's best man—an honour I never expected and hardly deserve. But the wedding is in Matlock, so I shall be miles away for little George's birthday and miles away from any chance of coming to you. I find myself more and more bereft, my darling.

I felt I must at least tell you once again how much I love and honour you. You remember that line in the wedding service? 'With my body I thee worship.' Or from Shakespeare, 'T'were a consummation devoutly to be wished.' In fact, of course, Hamlet is wishing for death. I am simply wishing for you.

Emma Holt, if I were not the head of a renowned Quaker school and you were not the wife of an outstandingly good man, I would run away with you to some island paradise and make love to you every day.

As it is, my dear, I am living in an unreal and forbidden dream as I know very well. So, don't let this letter upset you, sweetheart. I am perfectly rational most of the time. If you were to be on station duty when I leave for Matlock, you would see how reasonable I can be. But never forget, my beloved, that, all things being equal, you would be by my side at the school and as my wife. Nevertheless, I believe you really should burn this when you've read it, my love, for it expresses everything that can never be made public.

I am,
Your own,
Philip

He sealed the letter and typed her name and address with *Private* marked on the envelope so as to look business-like and impersonal and limped back out to the nearby post box to post it to her.

Then he went home, sat back in his study chair, and put his head in his hands. *God, forgive me*, he whispered.

Emma received this intense and achingly loving missive but ignored his final instruction which she simply couldn't bear to fulfil. Instead, she hid it in her secret drawer next to the book of Donne's poems he had given her for her last birthday. She shut the bedroom door lest any of the household should find her and then she lay on the bed and wept. Jack was out at Tempest's farm helping with the stacking of the fodder for the cattle, so she knew she could have privacy. She allowed herself the luxury of weeping in great waves of tears till her face was streaked with wet and her hair damp. Of one thing she was sure and that was that she would be at the station to see him off when he left for Matlock. Then she sat up, straightened her hair, washed her face at the washstand on her dressing table, and turned herself back into the competent hostess and mother. The Christmas she provided for them all would be its usual stunning and delicious offering, and she threw herself back into embracing the lovely girl Will had brought home with all the warmth of her hospitality.

Chapter 36

Alan Lorimer's wedding was all that he and Beatrice could have hoped for. Her parents had been devastated at her earlier terrible loss and were now much relieved that she had found such new happiness. Though Alan was an older man, they could see that he and Beatrice loved each other dearly, and they felt she would be safe with him. Their best man was quickly recognised as a man of some status in his own right, and his affection for the bridegroom shone in his speech. They knew he was Beatrice's boss, yet he had no arrogance or superiority and his whole bearing was one of a lovely humility. What they did not know was how, en route to them, he had been embraced as he'd stood on Shadworth Station by a woman in station uniform. Emma had found a sheltered space beside the signal box and had led him there, unable to hold back any longer. She'd kissed his face and his lips with an ardour that left him breathless, and he'd clasped her to him as if he would never let her go. She had somehow managed to renew his faith in what they were trying to do, whilst promising him her undying love. He had felt strengthened to the task once again though it seemed to hurt more and more as the days went by.

As the year drew to an end and 1919 dawned, Ned returned home to the farm at last and to Florence whose joy was complete. Now another wedding was being planned. It was to be in early spring at Shadworth Methodist Chapel and then in the Tempests' barn for the reception and an old-fashioned barn dance. Laura had had to return to Baldock to complete her contract at the convent school, but Will had already approached Philip to tell him that he was to bring home to Shadworth one who was a fully qualified English teacher and whom he hoped Philip could employ at his own school. Will was very shy about asking for this favour from Philip. But he was surer every day that he and Laura should be together. They had taken long walks along the country lanes around Shadworth holding hands and talking over all they had suffered but also sharing all about their childhoods. They mentioned Ralph at nearly every breath, for neither of them wished to forget what he had meant to them. And they laughed at the silly things they found they had in common.

"Do you like butter?" asked Will as he picked a buttercup and held it under her chin just as his mother used to do when he was little. "Yes, you do. Your chin is glowing yellow and that says you do."

Not to be outdone, Laura picked one too and forced him to let her reach up to him and check. He couldn't stop laughing at that, and they sat in the lane, observed by two brown cows peeping at them over the hedge. Then he pulled her to him and kissed her firmly on the lips. She returned the kiss ardently and sat up in the dusty road and laughed.

Meanwhile, Emma was engrossed in making Florence's wedding dress as well as suits for all the men and for George. Maggie was to be Matron of Honour and her own mother was making her dress. But as plans proceeded, a kind of grim miasma was creeping across the country and soon descended on Shadworth. Just relieved of the horrors of an excoriating war, now a new peril had begun to stalk Britain. A flu epidemic was the very last thing the nation could cope with, as many folks were underfed and sickly after such a long and arduous effort for survival. Resistance was at a low ebb. As these things go, it was a perfect scenario in which a potent virus could thrive. And the nation succumbed to it in large numbers. The people of Low and High Shadworth were no exception.

It started with fever and nausea, and people in the cottages clustered all along Low Shadworth's peaceful street and the boys up in the school sanatorium fell into its grip. For Emma and the family, its evil came home to roost. Maggie developed the symptoms, and George was sent with Florence to Holt House to keep him away from danger. The contagion, however, had been rampant whilst everything had appeared perfectly normal. Harry Holt was frantic—afraid for George and terrified for Maggie. He looked to his mother to wave her magic wand as she always had in the past, and she prayed for the strength to maintain the pretence of it and to manage the necessity of "holding the world up" as she had always called it over the years.

She herself took up residence in Maggie's cottage whilst the others kept their distance and cared for little George without her. Grandad Jack, with Daddy Harry, retreated to the school gardens to work harder than usual and keep him from fretting. In this small venture, James Thomson was a lifeline. He occupied George with silly ball games and Hide and Seek.

Philip and Kath Hanson very soon became aware of the situation, and Kath had to use every skill she had ever possessed to keep Philip from racing down to Low Shadworth to be at Emma's side, uncaring as to what anyone would think. She restrained him successfully by reminding him of his various duties, demanding he keep a calm and positive atmosphere of well-being within his study.

The study where, despite the circumstances, he tried to keep up with all the demands of his work became a haven not only for the schoolboys but for Jack and Harry themselves. The growing George found solace there with his thumb and his toy rabbit whilst sitting comfortably on Philip's knee. It became a helpful place of respite whenever he asked them where Mummy was. They would hastily walk him up to the study to get sweeties from Kath and a story with Uncle Philip. Kath looked on with relief that Philip managed to maintain his equilibrium at these times and play his part as comforter despite his inner turmoil.

He could hardly stand the anxiety of knowing the dangers of the virus yet being unable to do more than merely stand by. He resorted to the silence of the Meeting House where once again many boys and staff came at the silent hour to pray for their loved ones. The devastating effects of this evil flu hit the school three times as February came in. Three second-year boys developed pneumonia with complications. The warning signs of imminent death—dark spots on the cheeks, blue faces—became apparent. As their lungs filled with froth and blood, there was no room for oxygen, and they drowned from lack of air. This most appalling tragedy that took even younger lives than the war had done was heartbreaking, and the school descended into a dark gloom which shadowed every day.

It's as if I'm walking through a very black tunnel and can see no end, he thought desperately. *These young lives are wasted before they have even had the time to enjoy their childhood. It's unbearable.*

As Philip was forced to speak or preside at funerals for young innocents, in utter horror at such losses, Emma, and Maggie's own mum, Elsie, found themselves kneeling by Maggie's bed, holding her hands tightly as she too gasped for air, still praying for her beautiful little boy to stay safe and asking over and over for Harry.

At last, as Florence visited to check in on her as she did every morning and evening, her mother turned to her with only two words: "Get Harry."

Harry Holt arrived as the darkened spots and the strange blueness spoiled Maggie's comely young face. He laid his head on the sheet next to her as she struggled to breathe, and she at last choked on her final breath, her hand resting on him.

It was in these terrible circumstances that Harry Holt was rendered widower so young and so desperately bereft after surviving all the dangers of serving in Verdun. He looked round at his mother and mother-in-law and groaned in agony. Then the tears and the sobs tore through him as the others were shedding terrible tears of their own. Maggie's mother was beside herself, crying out Maggie's name in an unrecognisable voice. Florence had watched from the doorway and now picked up her skirts and ran to the school to find her father and little George. Kath met her on the pathway and led her into Philip's study where Jack was already sitting with George. She shook her head as he looked up at her, and the gesture told them all they needed to know, without words needed. Philip took charge then. He hugged a weeping Florence and gently led Jack to his own chair. Kath was sent to bring hot tea as he picked up George. The child sensed something was amiss and looked questioningly at him.

"I want my mummy."

"I'm sure your grandma will be looking after her, sweetheart. I think perhaps she has gone to be with Jesus because she was feeling so poorly. Now she will be all better. Trust Grandma to see to it."

"Can I see her with Jesus?"

"Maybe not, little one. But you can be sure she'll be safe with Him, and she'll be always watching over you like the angels in heaven watch over you. Do you think that'll be alright?"

George nodded and sucked hard on his thumb. To Philip, it was truly unbearable to behold, and he knew Jack and Florence were feeling exactly the same. Even thinking of the implications of what had happened made him tremble. But he had to square his own shoulders to help Jack.

"Come now, Jack and Florence. You'll both be needed back at home. Let me come down with you. I wonder if James and you, Kath, can look after this little one for a short while until I return?"

Kath came swiftly to the rescue while Florence searched out James. As he saw James enter the room, George gave a little cry of delight and was swung up onto James' shoulders and whisked away to the garden. They all looked at each other with relief but a relief darkened by an overwhelming grief at the loss of a mother who had adored her son and who had been adored by him.

"What on earth are we to do, Philip?" said Jack helplessly. "How can we give him all he will need and compensate him for the loss of that sweet lass?"

"Father," Florence broke in, "There are enough of us to manage, and I know Mother will take a lead in it. He adores her too and is always perfectly at home with us at Holt House. Maggie's mum will help too though she is in some dark desert of her own at present. Harry is the one we must pull together. He will crumble under this horror."

Philip was getting increasingly anxious as he listened, for his thoughts were down in Low Shadworth where Emma would be coping alone with Harry, Elsie Granger, and all the ghastly requirements of a death and its aftermath. He was all too familiar with the practicalities of a death: the undertaker, the death certificate, the funeral arrangements. And he knew his old friend, Leonard Thomson, would be needed to sign the certificate.

"Jack, Florence, we should waste no more time getting back to Emma. God knows, I pray she has not caught the contagion. Get the local cab please, Kath, as soon as possible, and let's go."

Florence glanced at him through her tears, and it dawned on her in a moment of utter clarity that he loved her mother and that his whole attention was focused on reaching her. She looked across at her father but saw he had no notion of this, for he sat as one paralysed by the shock of the appalling loss. She knew she would need to think hard about this revelation but put it to one side to consider when she felt more able to bear it all.

Philip drew Jack to his feet, and between the three of them, they led him to the waiting cab. The cottage door was open as they arrived, and Philip was relieved to see Dr Thomson already about his work.

"I've sent Emma and Harry home to Holt House while we do the necessaries and allow the undertaker to lay out her body in preparation for a funeral," Dr Thomson announced. "Her own mum won't leave her side, and we must respect that wish. But Harry and Emma can do no more for Maggie now, and it's best they are not here to watch the procedure. There will be time for final farewells to this beautiful girl when she has been made ready. Go and see them at the house and check that Emma in particular is not sickening. She's been under so much stress and her resources are down. She had a headache and desperately needs rest. I've given Harry something to calm him down but she won't take anything. Go. I'll finish off here. My wife is going to look after Elsie Granger when we can persuade her to leave Maggie."

Philip limped after Jack and Florence slowly up the road, which was no more than a stone's throw from the cottage, and followed them into Holt House. Jack hurried over to where Harry was lying on the sofa weeping, knelt beside him, and hugged him close.

My God, where is your mother? Philip was trembling as he looked across at Florence, and they hurried up the stairs where years earlier he had gone to her as she'd lain prostrate at the news of George's death. Now it was different, for she looked hot and feverish and was tossing and turning as if in pain.

"Oh God, Emma. You are sick, darling. Florence, go back and bring the doctor. He should have guessed a headache means trouble." He knelt beside her, wincing at the pain of his weakened knee, and took her hand. Florence took one look and fled for the second time that day.

Jack had been stood silently at the bedroom door and seen for himself Philip's intense anxiety. Jack clenched his fists as the truth dawned on him, a truth only suspected but now blatant and very, very significant. Philip rose to his feet to allow Jack to the bedside just as Leonard Thomson arrived, and Jack had to summon all his resolution to greet him and motion to where she lay.

"Look at her, Doctor. What are we to do now?" uttered Jack in a low and desperate voice, and Philip went to stand by his old friend. Jack was beyond anger or jealousy. He swallowed his pride and held on to Philip's hand as though the two were blood brothers.

The contagion, which Dr Thomson confirmed, had indeed hit Emma herself, for she had stayed beside Maggie day and night, nursing her with every ounce of her energy. It was a rapid decline so soon after Maggie's passing, and there was nothing for it now but to weather the deadly fever and fight for her own life. Philip knew there was nothing else he could do but pray with all the love he had for her that she would beat this. Emma was fighting alone now and past knowing who was present in the room. He took Florence's hand, and she managed a sad smile at him, nodding as a way of showing she understood.

"Mr Manners—Philip—I will stay by her with Father, and I promise you will know if there is any change. Please will you go for our little boy and get James to bring him home to us? He'll not understand where we've all gone. I'll persuade Harry he must help me look after him. He needs his daddy." She paused for a moment to think of the right words. "Thank you for your care for us all. I do believe my mother knows it."

"Florence, be assured she does. Bless you," he said with his own tears choking him. Then he shook Jack's hand warmly in departing; an action Jack did not reject.

"Prayers will do it, Jack. We won't lose her," he muttered and limped away.

Kath had already taken charge by the time Philip returned and, unbelievably to his state of mind, school was functioning smoothly and along its normal routine lines. James had already set off with George. The newly married Alan Lorimer, his old friend, came to see him soon after, and he quickly saw the lines of stress on his head's face.

"Is it George's mother that's gone, Philip? Oh God, that's truly awful. How are the Holts taking it, and what on earth will become of the little chap?"

"Emma Holt has caught it from the girl," Philip told him. "Pray God she will come through."

Kath glanced at Alan then, and he suddenly grasped the truth in a blinding flash. He simply laid his hand on his friend's shoulder and took a deep breath. "We need hot tea, Kath, please."

"Tea, the cure for all pain, eh, Alan?" said Philip with a quiet bitterness.

"Trust me, Philip. We'll have tea first then go through to the Meeting House and sit together."

Alan was as good as his word, and the two men prayed in silent companionship there.

Emma lay in the deadly fever for over two weeks, enduring searing headaches and difficulty breathing. One moment, she was shivering with cold; another moment, she was drenching the bed covers with her sweat. All moments, she was quite sealed off from reality frightening her family dreadfully. Florence disregarded all orders to leave her mother's bedside and stay at the farm. Much to Ned and everyone's relief, she stayed free of the danger, glowing with health. She managed to keep her father from drinking too much whisky to numb his pain and actually hid the bottle in her own bedroom. But she could not persuade him to eat more at any meal than a meagre sandwich before he would be up from the table again, pacing the garden, digging over ground that had been already thoroughly gardened, with short, angry bursts of energy.

"Father, come in. The dark's setting in, and you'll catch your death without your jacket. Father!" But it was always to no avail. Jack had a kind of rabid anger in his soul that would give him no peace.

Philip endured a torment up at the school that was, as he put it, worse than any torture that could be inflicted. Unable to be at Emma's side, he was left in a state of nightmarish darkness. Florence kept her promise to keep him up to date with her mother's progress and took time whenever she could to cycle up to school and visit him with Kath, albeit briefly, so that he was at least aware of how Emma was doing. But the lack of any sign of recovery over many days sent him into a spiral of distress. *There's something gnawing away at my stomach like some terrible parasite that's eating my insides.*

"Kath, I should go down there, shouldn't I? Surely I should, Kath?" But each time of asking, Kath shook her head sorrowfully, as much afraid for his health as for the sake of his maintaining his reputation in school.

There came a time, at last, when Emma opened her eyes and raised her head delicately as if she had just woken from a long sleep. "Have I been ill, Florence? Where are Father and George? Is everyone alright?" she groggily asked. "I feel so dreadful, Florence. Whatever has happened to me? And, Florence, I think I might be dying of thirst." And then, like some kind of lightning bolt, the truth hit her, and she looked in horror, eyes wide in disbelief, at Florence who was reassuringly holding her hand and smiling at her, relieved. Florence picked up and held to her lips the waiting glass of cold water for her to sip gratefully.

"Mother, you caught Maggie's flu, and we have all been terribly afraid for you." Florence hid her head on her mother's breast and the tears fell. "We thought we were going to lose you too. Oh, Mother, I must get Father. The others are all at the farm, keeping out of the contagion, but Father's in the garden digging as if his life depends on it. He's been like a raging bull."

"Fetch him, quickly, Florence. Let's put him out of his misery straightaway. I must get up," she said, trying to raise herself into a sitting position but falling back on the pillows with a wobble and a groan. Florence was gone in an instant and returned with Jack who embraced his wife with all the force of his outstanding relief and thankfulness. She returned this outpouring of love with love, but as she did so, she thought with a pang of horror of the other one who loved her and who would also be waiting in fear and trembling for news. He too must be relieved as soon as possible. She was overwhelmed by her own exhaustion and yet felt she must fight the lethargy left by the illness and emerge as quickly as she could to bring reassurance and consolation to him as well as to the rest of her beloved family.

"Florence, Jack, we have to let the others know all is well. There is so much to do and Maggie's funeral to manage. Oh God, how could I have gone down with this awful sickness at such a time?"

"Father, will you go to the farm for the others while I let Mother rest? She cannot run before she can walk." She touched him on the shoulder where he stood smiling down delightedly at Emma, and he was roused out of his reverie.

"I'll get them straightaway, love. Emma, thank God you're okay though." He hugged her hard again in parting.

There was someone else on Emma's mind. "Florence, I feel very anxious about the head and Kath too. They will have been waiting for news at school. Oh, dear me. What have I put them all through? If only I didn't feel so incredibly weak." As she spoke, she looked up at Florence beseechingly. Florence read the unspoken request and knew she must answer it if her mother was to be at rest.

"Don't fret, Mother. I'll just about manage to get up there and let them know if I go straight away and still be back before Father and the family." She fled to fetch her bike.

Emma lay back against the pillows. She could hardly bear to think of what Philip must have endured up at school, unable to be close to her and knowing how the flu could so quickly devour its prey. *Oh God, let Florence get there as fast as she can and save him from any more suffering.*

As Florence rode helter-skelter to the school, she smiled a wry smile. *I won't allow myself to think about that look on Mother's face. I need to think about what it means when I can be quiet.*

As she knocked on Philip's door, it was opened by Kath with very anxious eyes, and she could hear Philip in the middle of remonstrating angrily with a boy.

"How dare you reduce Mrs Lorimer to tears in front of her class by your insolence? Every boy in this school knows the rules of courtesy and obedience. And you are a third-year now, Johnson. How many more times must I—" Then, seeing Florence standing at the threshold, he stopped abruptly in mid-sentence and turned pale, much to Kath's horror. But Florence smiled across at him and nodded as if to reassure them both. Philip regained his composure and turned back to the boy.

"I'm sorry, Johnson. I suspected bad news. But I return to my point. You cannot keep returning to my study for one misdemeanour after another. It must stop. This may be your very last chance before I send for your parents. Now, *go!*"

As Johnson fled muttering his apologies under his breath, Philip sat with a bump and looked up at Florence and his good secretary with something akin to hope. "Florence, what's happened? Is she awake? Tell me quickly."

"Oh, sir, it's going to be alright. She opened her eyes and looked around as if she didn't know where she was and then it all came rushing back. Father knelt down beside her in utmost relief then ran to the farm to tell the others. I knew by one look from her that I must get to you too, and here I am. But I really can't stop. It'll be difficult restraining her now but she's very weak. We'll have to let her rest till she gets her strength back."

Kath uttered one cry of thankfulness at this, and Philip pulled himself up out of his chair and took both of Florence's outstretched hands in his. "Thank you for coming, my dear. It is so good of you to include us in your good news. I'm afraid boys like Johnson have been getting the worst of my temper over the last two weeks. This awful time has cleaned out my usual equanimity like a predatory bird sucking out a stolen egg. But enough of my ramblings. I am utterly thankful and am not making any sense. You must go straight back. Don't let your father get back before you. It would upset him *and* your mother."

Giving Kath a quick hug of farewell, Florence was on her way.

Shadworth had had its full share of this contagion, but the funeral of Maggie Holt was its final act. Attending there beside Elsie Granger was a very thin and weakened Emma. Her inner strength had at last come to her rescue alongside the knowledge deep inside her that there was a widowed father and a little boy who needed her, a family which relied on her, and a man who would also be bereft without her.

Chapter 37

Normality returned as spring once more arrived in Shadworth in all its effulgence. If Philip expected the weather to match the mood of them all as in the poetry he loved, it was not to be. There was no "pathetic fallacy". There were no storm clouds and pouring rain to drench the trees and soak the fields in dour empathy with the emotions of those in Shadworth who were suffering. The spring sunshine shone out and awoke the buds on the almond trees into delicate pink flowers, the catkins fluttered merrily on their branches, and lovely grey pussy willow brought charm to the hedgerows. Down at Tempest's farm, the lambs were being born and new life had its way.

Little George Holt was enchanted by these delights and was welcomed at the farm by adoring well-wishers just as he always was when he visited the head's school. He was sturdier now and seemed to have grown out of the baby asthma which had dogged him for so long. He would still ask for his mummy, but his bereft father had controlled his own grief for his little boy's sake. His grandfather taught him well the lore of nature, so he learned how to plant and succour growing buds and how to watch out for tadpoles transforming into frogs. Best of all, he was allowed to creep into his grandparents' bed each night with his toy rabbit and snuggle back to sleep against Emma's breast.

He loved to sit on Uncle Philip's knee when Philip was not teaching or administering his school. Philip enjoyed his visits hugely as something of a godsend to him, taking his mind off all his sorrows.

Meanwhile, despite the terrible loss of Maggie whom she had loved like her own daughter and whose departure from them lay like a weight on all their hearts, Emma felt the vigour coming back into her own body as she recovered from the dreadful fever that had taken her over for so many days. As soon as she felt strong enough, she began the task of preparing for Florence and Ned's wedding day. It was set for the school Easter holidays, April 12. She was relieved of catering for it by Ron's wife, Ned's mother, herself a most capable hostess, as everyone knew. The Methodist minister was to preside at Shadworth Wesleyan Chapel at noon that day and then they would all get Turton's new charabanc, hired by Emma, to take them to the farm for the party.

Florence's dress was sewn from a length of broderie anglaise which Emma had obtained from the drapers in Cranston. She had embroidered daisies all across the bodice and had found a piece of net she had saved to serve as a beautiful veil. Florence hardly knew herself when she looked at the finished product in her mother's long mirror. But she still had a question to ask her mother which had been on her mind since Maggie's death and since her hurried ride to the school. She had promised herself she would ask it:

"Mother, do you know that Mr Manners loves you? Do you, Mother?"

She was horrified to see her mother sit suddenly on her bed and put her head in her hands.

"It's alright, Mother. Please don't cry. But I wish I could understand how this can be. Do *you* love *him*? I know you would never hurt Father, and neither would he, but how could you let such a thing happen? Do you not know how much this would hurt Father if he found out? How can you bear to carry that knowledge and pretend it doesn't affect us all?"

Emma turned to Florence with a quiet dignity. "We will not speak of this again, Florence. You must believe me when I tell you I would never hurt your father. But there is no better or more honourable man than Mr Manners, and were I free, I would run to him."

Florence gasped at the nugget of truth in this admission but resolved to keep it only to herself. "Mother, I shall not breathe a word of this to a soul, but I beseech you not to harm my father or your family who love and trust you."

"Of course I shall not. Now, Florence, that is quite enough."

April 12, the wedding day, dawned. The warming spring sun shone for Florence and Ned that day, and beside Ned stood his friend, James Thomson, whom he had asked to be his best man and whose recovery was all but complete. There was no bridesmaid, as the one who should have been there had left them all those sad weeks ago. But there was a little excited page boy who carried the ring to Ned on a large cushion and then demanded to be picked up by the bride. Thus, George Holt shared in the ceremony that day. Even Harry had to smile at that even though it held felt almost too painful. He remained in a dark place of the soul, missing Maggie almost intolerably, but he determined to remain strong for his child's sake.

Philip, Alan, Beatrice, Kath, and Edna all sat together, and Alan put his hand on Philip's knee as Emma entered the church, for he felt him tremble next to him. She was still painfully thin, dressed in a plain brown dress, and had exchanged her station uniform cap for a feathered concoction she had made herself. This made Philip smile as he thought of how he really preferred her *ridiculous* station cap. He was grateful that day for his friend's understanding support.

The meal and the dance were all that could be desired. Ron Tempest glowed with pride at his son, and the Thomsons' relief at the sight of James in the midst of it all was palpable. Emma could not bear to let Philip simply watch from the sidelines and took his hand and led him into a gentle dance whilst Jack was partnering Edna. He hardly dared look at her as they danced for he knew he would give himself away, so he contented himself by grasping her tightly round the waist and touching the tip of her ear with his lips. She sighed a long, sorrowful breath at that touch and, albeit carelessly, allowed her head to rest for a moment on his chest.

George made up for a great deal, however, for he threw himself into all the dancing, made his grandma dance with him, and jumped onto Uncle Philip's knee for cuddles at regular intervals. Florence observed it all from her vantage point and was reassured that all was as safe as it could be.

What no one knew, however, was that the stress of it all had made Philip's leg ache more than usual, and he knew very well that the old problem was returning. He said nothing to anyone but was relieved once he got home to be able to finally lie on his bed. Monday, he would need to contact Leonard Thomson at the surgery for some advice.

When Sunday dawned, however, he found he could hardly bear the painful heat in his knee, and he was horrified to see his leg swollen out of all normal proportion. Yet his concerns about the terms of peace in Europe, now being made public, had been playing on his mind, and he was determined to put a clear Quaker perspective into writing and get it to Frank Jacques as soon as he could. He sat at his typewriter, trying to ignore the pain, and penned a letter to his old acquaintance. He was aware that the arrangements for the signing of the final peace treaty of the war were underway. And indeed, in his heart, he knew that nothing he could say would make any difference to the outcome.

April 13, 1919

Dear Frank,

You will recall our last meeting in July last year as the final throes of the war were underway. Your visit to my school for the speech day was much appreciated as you know.

You have sought my views previously as a head teacher and a Quaker, so I trust you will forgive my outspokenness in sharing with you my deep concern regarding the treaty soon to be signed in Versailles.

My anxiety about it is huge, for I fear that the emphasis will all be on heavy reparations from Germany and on removal of territory that once belonged to Germany. This so-called Covenant of the League of Nations seems doomed from the start if Germany is not a member of it.

It cannot be effective if they have no input and will only stir bitter resentment amongst nationalists.

Frank, for heaven's sake, try to ensure that a modicum of mercy enters into the agreements. Revenge may be sweet to some, but it may only succeed in building up future resentments.

As I write, I am nervously aware that this may make no scrap of difference but be assured my prayers will all be for a peace that will not nurture the seeds of further conflict.

Your good friend,
Philip Manners,
Headmaster,
Shadworth Quaker School.

Philip sat back in his chair, satisfied that he had expressed his real concern for the negotiations soon to be concluded. But by this time, his leg was agonisingly painful. It was not only swollen but violently hot and red, and he could feel himself beginning to shiver though he was not at all cold. There was no one to tell at that moment. He would send for Kath to get the doctor as soon as Monday dawned and, meanwhile, he must retire urgently to his bed.

God, if only I could get Emma here. She would sort me out.

Emma, of course, had no idea of this and had been preoccupied with the events of the wedding and catering back at Holt House for all the extra guests, including Will's Laura who had come for the occasion. Emma was so pleased to see the growing love these two had for each other.

She gave a gasp of horror when she found Alan Lorimer at her door knowing instantly that something must have happened to Philip. He had come to tell her and Jack the news that there was an emergency at the school. Philip had been rushed into hospital after Kath Hanson had found him in a fever at his house. The good doctor had not minced his words. Philip's life was in danger if they did not act quickly, and he had asked Alan to let the Holts know. Philip's friend knew exactly what remained unsaid and had accordingly come to see if Emma could accompany him.

"Kath Hanson is almost hysterical. She went to find him because she knew there was a letter he wanted her to type urgently. But she found him unconscious by the door. Could you come with us to the hospital? The doctor is afraid septicaemia will set in, and they need to act quickly. Emma, Jack, will you come?"

Jack watched silently as Emma pulled on her coat, frantically fastening the buttons. He made no comment as she muttered, "I have to go, Jack. You do see that, don't you? Will you come too?"

He shook his head as Alan looked at him questioningly. Jack didn't say anything at first, just merely looked at Emma, smiling sadly. He too shared the concern for Philip, but he could not help but see that Emma's feelings went well beyond this and knew that it was futile to resist the force of events. "Of course you must go. I'll stay here with the family. Give him our best, Emma."

Leonard Thomson was waiting for them at the school gates, and he joined Emma in Alan's new Austin. Beatrice and Kath watched them set off for Cranston, and Beatrice took charge of a distraught Kath.

"Alan told me the situation, Kath. What a tangle it is."

"He would never be dishonourable, Beatrice. They would never hurt Jack but they have been in love for years. I've observed it for a long time. Oh, for pity's sake, pray he can recover from this. If the leg has gone septic, there is no medicine that can stop its spread. Oh God, I can't stand to even think about it."

Beatrice led her back to Philip's study where they both sat immobile and lost in thought.

Chapter 38

At his bedside, Emma kept watch with Alan Lorimer. Leonard Thomson was in intimate discussion with the hospital consultant while Philip was unconscious, far, far away in another world. Nevertheless, Emma laid her hand on his as it lay flat on the sheet and spoke quietly to him as if, perhaps, her presence would register with him. She had repressed all despair, merely focused on praying for his life. She knew emotion could come later.

At last, the consultant approached with Leonard and his own colleague, the orthopaedic surgeon who had been rushed in from the military hospital close by where the wounds of the troops were managed.

"I gather you are his closest friends and his wife is no longer with him? I'm not asking your permission for this but would be glad of your approval. The risk of septicaemia is imminent if we do not amputate the leg. He must have been coping with cellulitis in it for far too long. I'm afraid we cannot afford to wait any longer.

We must stop any flow of infection into his blood-stream, and the only way is to remove the leg." Even as the surgeon spoke, he was nodding to the nurses to prepare Philip for surgery.

Emma gave a little cry but battened it down hastily. Alan took her by the arm and between him and Leonard they ushered her away into a small and empty waiting room.

An empty waiting room was all we used to desire, she thought, *And now look at me. Dear God, spare my darling.*

"There is nothing more we can do but wait, Emma," said the doctor kindly. "I know you want to be here but, Emma, you have a duty to Holt House and its inhabitants, and Philip will know nothing until he wakes up from the operation. That won't be till tomorrow at the very least because I'm sure they'll sedate him heavily. Let Alan take you home now."

"Must I really go, Doctor? I would so much like to stay here."

"Emma, get your perspective back. You are needed elsewhere and really can do no more for Philip until it's all over. Come on, Emma. You know I'm right."

She allowed Alan to lead her to the car with just a backward glance at the ward door, then sat in abject silence as they drove back to Shadworth. In the silence, she felt she was quietly tearing herself up inside. Her loyalties were divided as they had never been before, torn with an adamantine force that impelled her back to stay with him and let everything else be lost; but also torn at thoughts of her family and their reliance on the mother who had always "held the world up" for them all. And her secret was out. There was no pretending that her reaction today was anything less than a devotion that was entirely illegitimate; a passion for a man who was not her husband.

Will, Laura, and Jack were waiting anxiously for her return. Harry, Florence, and Ned had taken the little boy back with them to the farm. And she knew that George loved Florence's cuddles almost as much as hers. But she grieved that the two just married had to shoulder this particular responsibility at this time, a time which should have been entirely theirs.

She could see that Jack was controlling his emotion, but she knew that he was doubly upset inside. Alongside his natural fear for his friend's life, he was deeply troubled by the way she had acted. Hadn't she brazenly exposed to the world the depth of her feelings for Philip? How would that make him feel? He stood by silently whilst Laura shook Alan Lorimer's hand, and Will led her inside.

"How is the head?" asked Laura.

Alan shrugged. "We won't know till they have done the operation. He's got to lose his leg and we have to pray he survives the severity of what they have to do. It's a dangerous operation. I suppose I shall be in charge at the school until such time as we can reassess what is to happen. But I heard you are an English specialist and a teacher. Is that true?"

"I am." Laura smiled. "Though I have a contract to fulfil at my school in the south. I could be free to help you out as soon as I am clear of that."

"You may be needed more urgently than you could have dreamed," said Alan with a weary shake of his head. "Philip is himself an English specialist, and his classes are going to be without him for quite a while."

Inside, Jack had pulled Emma down onto the sofa beside him and was questioning her as Will looked on. She apologised over and over to him for being away for such a long time but begged him to try to understand that she knew Philip would be glad of her company.

"And you see, Jack, that Dr Thomson thought it for the best. That's why he sent for me. He knew I would be able to bring some comfort to Philip. Jack, you have to trust me. I do indeed love the man but you must never doubt how strong my love is for you. And, Jack, he could be dying at this very minute."

Will gasped at this outpouring in shock at her words and at his father's reaction. Jack's brow had darkened. She had spoken the words that had been unspoken for a long time. Jack felt utterly overwhelmed almost to the point of violence with the weight of what she had at last articulated. But he stood up and desperately turned towards Will.

Will was alert to his father and spoke soothingly to him.

"She was only being her natural loving self to go as requested, Father. She's back with us now and of course we all care for Mr Manners. You do so yourself. We should be praying for him to survive this, not quarrelling about where our loyalties lie. Let's all sleep on this, then see what the morning brings," said Will, unable to believe what he'd just heard his own mother say but also wanting to defuse the situation.

A weekend that had begun with such joy and ended in such fear and sadness came to its close. Jack allowed the wise words of his son to calm him, and though he and Emma slept fitfully that night, they stayed close to each other in the old double bed.

In the operating theatre, Philip's inflamed leg was removed from above the knee and he was put under heavy sedation for forty-eight hours. The surgeon sewed up the wound with professional expertise for he was a much-experienced practitioner after the many amputations he had been forced to perform over the war years. Alan Lorimer and Leonard Thomson remained nearby so that they could be beside him when the full implication of the operation began to dawn. Beatrice stayed with Kath Hanson that night for she knew that Kath was in distress. Emma knew she must stay away and play her well-practised part at home for them all, not least for Jack. But she was in a perpetual state of torment awaiting news, desperate for him to recover safely.

How can I bear yet another torture after George and then Maggie? Now my beloved Philip, she thought silently to herself.

When morning came, they still had to wait another day for Philip to surface from the sedation. On Thursday, April 17, the two practising doctors woke him. Alan stood with them, hugely relieved to see him breathing normally, all signs of fever gone. He was very weak after such a long period of unconsciousness and had no idea of what had happened. He had lost all sense of time passing and was expecting to get up and go to his study for the day.

"Alan, Leonard, what am I doing here? Am I in hospital?"

The two men grew solemn as they watched him come to his senses, listening to the words of the surgeon whose task it had been to remove his leg. He explained very gently what he had had to do and then patiently allowed Philip time to recognise that he was bandaged hugely above his knee.

"I know I was feeling ill but can't remember anything after that." He went very pale as it dawned on him, that awful truth he must now bear for the rest of his life.

"My God, Alan, what will happen to my school? How on earth am I to manage?"

Alan was swift in reassuring him. "I can act as head while you recover and learn to walk with crutches, Philip. Think of all those injured soldiers who have learned to walk again. You will not be beaten by this. But it will take time, my friend. One day at a time now."

Philip shut his eyes and gave out a terrible, heart-wrenching groan that almost finished Alan and the good doctor, whose energies had already been sapped as they'd watched by his bedside. A nurse scurried in at that and suggested it was time to leave him to rest. She gave him another shot of sedative, and he sank back into slumber.

"Doctor Thomson, do you think it would be acceptable to bring Emma Holt back to him now?" Alan asked. "I'm sure that would help him as he faces this."

The doctor nodded thoughtfully but suggested that Jack and Kath should return with her. He felt Jack coming too would cover the etiquette of the situation more safely. His heart was bleeding for this man whose life was to be changed so drastically, and it was not the first time he had wished for a magic wand rather than his doctor's bag.

Accordingly, Alan drove back to Shadworth and invited Emma and Jack to return with him to the hospital. Emma shook with relief at the news of Philip's survival without daring to think what it meant. She felt as if she was going to choke and kept taking deep, violent breaths. Her hands were trembling so much that she could hardly open the car door, but Jack held on to her tightly and kindly, once more swallowing his own emotions to stay steady. She was very glad to see Kath as Alan stopped at the school to explain the situation and invite her to join them. Emma took a tight hold of Kath's hand.

"Kath, thank God he is alive. That's all that really matters. But how will he be able to stand losing his leg like this? Kath, what will he do?"

Ever competent, ever calm, Kath squeezed her hand tighter and put a finger to her lips. She knew patience had a healing virtue and patience was what they would all need now.

Philip had been moved into a private ward, and Leonard was at his bedside as they all arrived. He was sitting beside Philip as he slept but stood to shake Jack's hand, then he took both of Emma's hands in his and smiled reassuringly at her.

"He's come through the worst and he's fighting hard. All will be well. The surgeon's action has stopped any chance of septicaemia. We shouldn't really wake him, as sleep is the best healer. Come, Emma, take my place by his side. Kath, it's good that you are here too. He's always lost without you."

Alan and Jack stood together at the bottom of the bed as Emma once again laid her hand over Philip's.

Alan, as tactfully as he knew how, suggested he and Jack go and find a cup of tea, and Jack nodded in agreement, much to Alan's relief. Emma knew Kath would understand what she felt as she was free now to bend down and kiss him gently on the forehead.

"My darling, don't be afraid. We can win this one. Let's get you well again."

Then his eyes opened, and his face lit up at sight of her. "Emma, oh, Emma, I'm so glad you're here. But, Emma, I'm so tired and they've taken my wretched leg. What is to become of me? How can we win when all my resolve to make a difference in this world is reduced to nothing?" He closed his eyes again in utter weariness.

"Sleep, my dear. Sleep is what's best for you. Be patient. One day at a time," she whispered. "Kath is here too, and we both want you to rest and get well."

Kath drew closer to him. "Mr Manners, you must not fret. Alan Lorimer is a perfect standby and will fulfil all your tasks as head until you are well enough to come back to us. And, would you believe, Will Holt's new sweetheart is an English teacher. If we can persuade her to stay with us in Shadworth, she can fill in for at least some of your classes. Isn't that fortuitous? I promise you we will manage. And you mustn't worry your head with it all."

There was the sound of the two men returning, Leonard Thomson with them.

"We are the bearers of tea, my friend," came Alan Lorimer's voice.

"Enough talking, all of you, let him rest," said Leonard. "Philip, can I sit you up to give you this drink?"

"Let me," said Emma and put her arm round his shoulder just enough to let him sip the tea. He barely drank at all before his head fell back exhaustedly on the pillow. She looked up at the doctor who shook his head at her to warn her not to push him any further.

"I do believe we must leave you in peace now, Philip. There is nothing you need concern yourself with but to get well. We shall leave you now in the good graces of these splendid nurses and the consultant who has done such a fine job. He will be watching over you as the wound begins to heal."

Once again, Philip groaned at the reality of what had just been voiced and closed his eyes.

Emma went across to where a grim-faced Jack stood watching silently. She put her head on his shoulder with a pleading look. "Jack, may I stay with him? Would you let me?" she asked. "I'm not deserting you, only playing my part for the best."

It was a very gruff response from Jack but he nodded in agreement, and Alan promised to get her home to Holt House as soon as she was ready. Alan felt keenly that much was being asked of this tough, weathered gardener at that moment, and he admired his willingness to accept what was indeed a sacrifice. Leonard, observing, merely nodded sadly at this more than generous gesture made solely for Emma.

Kath took Jack's arm as they left the ward and smiled back reassuringly at Emma as she once again put her hand over the hand of the now sleeping Philip. Emma simply sat by him, caressing his forehead with her lips, and he slept peacefully knowing deep within himself that she was there.

Jack was almost numb with all the mix of emotions he was feeling as he arrived home without her, but he knew that he had made this particular sacrifice out of a kind of grace he had been given when he perhaps least expected it. Yet he couldn't help but feel a deep, human resentment at the necessity for it. Will and Laura received him back at home, but he quickly went out into his garden and stood looking at the chickens in a dour mood. Will found him there deep in thought.

"Come in, Father. Laura's cooked us a meal, and you'll hurt her feelings if you don't try and eat something."

"Eh, lad, I'm not very hungry, truth be told. I like your young woman though. I expect I'd better try." Jack allowed Will to take hold of his elbow and lead him into the kitchen.

In that kitchen that so much bore the hallmark of its regular mistress and was so obviously without her presence, Laura served him the meal she had cooked for them all. She felt very keenly for Jack at that moment, and she touched his shoulder as she served him as if to say how sorry she was.

"Father," said Will, "You mustn't mind Mother staying. She'll be home to you soon. She's only being her own loving self."

"Aye, Will. But sometimes she forgets who to love."

Will swallowed this truth down with a glance at Laura. He knew her love for Ralph would never die whatever she was beginning to feel for him. And maybe, just maybe, it was the same.

Many days now followed in much the same pattern: time at home and time by Philip's side at the hospital. Little George, his daddy, and Aunt Florence were completely happy to stay at the farm. George came to visit his Uncle Philip on one of these days, and the little boy asked to sit on his bed. Emma shuddered in case he jolted him, but it was worth it to see the old smile returning to Philip's face.

In some strange way, they were happy days, almost idyllic in the opportunity given to Emma and Philip to be very close to each other but tinged with a huge disappointment in Philip's heart. He gradually became used to the stump so thickly bandaged where his leg had once been, used to sitting up in the hospital chair, used to the oddness of feeling unbalanced in a new and strange way. But there was a bitterness inside him that would not go away.

The thought that his love for Emma had brought her to be tied in love to a cripple, as he now viewed himself, was like an extra wound he had to bear. And his thoughts about it were grim indeed. He could not ignore the fact that Emma was spending so much of her time with him when her allegiance should always have been first for Jack and the family that relied on her so much. He felt that this time with her was a glorious indulgence that he could hardly bear to relinquish, but his conscience was troubling him mercilessly about it. If he had been well, he would never have allowed himself this luxury. But in his weakened state, bearing so much pain as the wound healed, he did not fight it.

However, several weeks later, the day inevitably came when Leonard Thomson announced to them and to all those gathered visiting that the time had come for Philip to be moved to convalescence and rehabilitation.

"We want him to learn to use a wheelchair and even begin to use crutches. Then we can have him back to his accustomed place in the school study," said his old friend.

"But where will you send him?" asked Emma anxiously.

"There is a place for him at St. Oswald's Convalescent Home in Scarborough, a place I happen to know is the absolute best for care and rehabilitation. It may seem a bit of a way away, Philip, but trust me. You can recover there."

Over the next few days, Emma and Philip talked frankly with each other. He felt very afraid of the distance that would be put between them, and he knew his recovery was going to take a long time. Yet he also felt it would be better in the end for Jack who had so ungrudgingly allowed her to stay at the hospital for such long periods of time. He cared deeply for his old friend and this drove his purpose, cruel as it would be. He knew he would have his books with him to catch up with all his precious reading. That must be his consolation now. And maybe it would at last be better for Emma to let him go so that she could return to normality and her life as it had always been.

Without me, thought Philip in his worst but cogent moments. *She does not need a cripple to burden her.*

As the day drew near for his departure for Scarborough, he knew he had to voice this thought to Emma before he left, though he knew it would cause her untold pain.

"So, Emma, how can I refuse the good doctor? We both trust Leonard Thomson absolutely."

"My darling Philip, I do trust him, but I can't bear to part with you."

"Come, Emma. We've always professed to be strong and faithful in the face of everything. But now is the moment, Emma. You are Jack's wife, and we are not free to be together. Neither can you be tied to a cripple. It's too much. I must face this alone now, and Scarborough gives us the opportunity to separate cleanly.

"Maybe this has come at the right time to save Jack from the awful knowledge that you have given your heart to another man. That man, my darling, is telling you we have to stop now. You should not visit me in Scarborough. Our love will never change or die but somehow it must be laid aside for the sake of all the others who need you, my dearest. Think of our little George and of Harry whose hearts must also be breaking for Maggie. You and you alone can lift all this out of tragedy and keep us faithful to what we profess as followers of Jesus Christ."

It was painful to articulate these thoughts to his beloved Emma, for he knew that in speaking them he would be about to break her heart. And it almost choked him to speak the words that meant such self-denial.

As he spoke, she cried out in acute distress for him to stop. "No, no, no, Philip." Tears convulsed her until, at last, wearied with crying, she laid her head on his breast. He simply stroked her hair with unutterable sadness.

She could not believe what she was hearing. How could he relinquish all the treasures of love they shared and make her leave him? She shuddered at the very thought of how much she would miss him and at the thought of him alone dealing with the amputation and all the consequences which inevitably followed. She would have to take up the threads of her ordinary routine and show a brave face to the world once more.

But, God help me, she thought. *I don't think I can.*

"Come, Emma, my love," he said. "I've heard you sing that hymn that goes:

'Be our strength in hours of weakness,

In our wanderings be our guide;

through endeavour, failure, danger, Father, be thou at our side.'

Emma, we need to put our trust in God now, more than ever. It is a test of our faith. And God knows it is very hard. But we must be strong now." There were tears in his eyes as he spoke.

"Don't say it, Philip. You must not cry, my darling," she begged. "I promise I'll try, but I can't promise all you are asking. It's just too much. I've got to be able to write to you at least."

It was at that desperate moment that Alan and Beatrice arrived to take her home and say their goodbyes. Leonard Thomson had been swift in the arranging, and the ambulance was booked to go to Scarborough the next day. Kath had helped Alan to pack his belongings—among them were his Bible, his poetry books, his precious *Quaker Faith and Practice*, and his volume of Shakespeare.

"You know I'll need a lot of paper and my fountain pen, Alan," he smiled. "I have many letters to write to thank all those who have sent me their good wishes over the past weeks, and also to my students. They are all working harder than I've ever known as though to make up for what's happened. And, Alan, I think I need to able to write to this woman here. Look after her, will you?"

Beatrice put her arm round Emma as she ushered her away. Emma was thankful that he had at least let her know in his own way that she could be assured of his love for her and that he would write to her. He was not cutting himself off from her completely, and she knew that meant she could write to him. Otherwise, she felt she would have broken down completely.

He lay back on his pillows, alone at last, and prayed for grace; grace to bear it all and come to terms with it. But in actual truth, he felt as if he had signed his own death warrant.

Chapter 39

The convalescent home of St. Oswald's was set on the cliffs above Scarborough, overlooking the South Bay. Philip was welcomed there by a kindly matron who had known Leonard Thomson whilst training years earlier. She was ready to make everything as easy as she could for a man who came so highly respected by her old friend.

Philip's room looked out over the bay, and its beauty was a healing balm to his soul. The weather was immaculate in those early days for it was high summer now after all the passage of time in Cranston. The sea shimmered silver and the gulls cawed incessantly as they rode on the eddies of wind which pushed the cotton wool clouds around the turquoise sky.

The gardens at St. Oswald's had many pathways on which to push a wheelchair, and he gradually accustomed himself to being ferried round by the nurses and chatting to them about their lives. They had never quite been used to such a patient who took such an interest in them, and they were all his devoted followers before very long.

Best of all, he enjoyed the journey along the promenade down from the home, reaching the harbour with its bobbing fishing boats and its stalls of winkles and cockles, crabs, and shrimps. Holidaymakers enjoying the beach beside the harbour and children playing in the sand with their tin buckets and spades gave him a lot of pleasure though it also gave him a stab of nostalgia for little George.

All this while he was being cajoled by the professional physiotherapists who visited him daily to encourage the strengthening of his limbs and prevent the muscles weakening. They encouraged him to try the crutches and the balancing act that it required, and he worked hard at it. He was determined to return to his post at the school as soon as he could.

It was a long, painful, and exhausting business that took all his energy to sustain and all his courage to keep up a brave front. On many a night, he fell sound asleep at only eight o'clock but woke in the night frequently and then allowed his desperate loneliness without Emma to engulf him again. He turned again and again to his Bible which was more well-thumbed than it had ever been. In the letter to the Hebrews, he found the best consolation against his suffering. There he read of Christ's identification with the pain of the world, and for him, it spoke so much more meaning-fully than it ever had in the days of his better health.

"*For we do not have a high priest who is unable to sympathise with our weaknesses, but one who in every respect has been tempted as we are, yet without sin. Let us then with confidence draw near to the throne of grace, that we may receive mercy and find grace to help in time of need.*"

He was shocked one day by a visit from a group of the school governors all the way from Cranston who wanted to ascertain whether a return to the headship would ever be possible. He assured them he was mak-ing good progress, nevertheless praising Alan Lorimer to the highest heavens as one who was a perfect re-placement for him. They all roundly agreed with this but promised to keep his place open for him for when-ever he felt ready to return.

His fountain pen was always in use, and he wrote many letters including one to Frank Jacques who had responded to his latest one with details of the proceed-ings in Versailles, none of which gave him a great deal of optimism. So, he prayed for the needs of the world as well as his more pressing intercessions.

The absence of Emma was almost intolerable for him, and in his volume of Yeats' poems, he found a poem that expressed the very essence of how he felt about her. Yeats had a passionate love for Maud Gonne—a fiery, outspoken Irish Republican who would never concede love for him in return. Yeats wrote about her in terms that Philip felt could have been his own for Emma. Emma was no Maud Gonne, albeit indomitable in her own way, but in his own passionate heart, Philip knew he, in the loss of Emma, personally equalled anything Yeats could have felt:

"One that is ever kind said yesterday:
Your well-beloved's hair has threads of grey,
And little shadows come about her eyes;
Time can but make it easier to be wise
Though now it seems impossible, and so
All that you need is patience.

- - - - - - - - - - - - - - - - - - - -

Heart! O heart! if she'd but turn her head,
You'd know the folly of being comforted."

So, there was little or no comfort except in his books, and he went through many days where he found he could hardly eat for the sickness of his loss. His resolve to give her up was agony. *It is a kind of homesickness for her*, he thought. Through these long days, the nurses, who were all his slaves by now, tried desperately to cheer him and get him to eat, but he simply couldn't face their offerings.

There were even some days when the frustration of making such slow progress with his crutches, which cost him so much effort and pain to manage, caused his temper to fray to the point of throwing them to the ground in anger. These fits of temper, which so appalled him afterwards, put him back to bed for days, recovering from the falls that ensued. His nurses were desperately anxious as they watched him struggle like this and became even more determined to do everything in their power to help him get used to the crutches. A letter from Harriet, forwarded on by Kath to him, brought him little cheer during these months. It informed him of her newly found happiness with Godfrey Langdon, but with a curt final paragraph:

I was sorry to hear you had lost your leg. I hope you manage to carry on at your beloved school despite it. There's always wheelchairs, I suppose. I wish you well with it. Godfrey sends his best wishes.
Harriet.

Emma maintained a steady and resigned atmosphere of comfort and homeliness at home in Shadworth as the many long weeks went by, turning gradually into months. Jack relaxed again in a quiet confidence that things were not going to fall apart, whatever she felt for Philip Manners, and they all thrived accordingly, especially George who was very much the apple of everyone's eye.

Harry had now settled into a steadier life in the cottage he and Maggie had made home, and there he was beginning to find life had its compensations. He had got himself a small job helping the local cobbler up in High Shadworth, and this gave him back something of his will to live. He took immense pleasure in his little son though he had to rely on his mother's help whilst at work and whenever there was a real need. He also knew she would always understand if he needed to escape his grief and his sense of loneliness with a couple of pints at The White Swan. He and his father kept each other company there on many a night whilst Emma babysat the little one. Jack himself benefited from these times and took much pleasure in his youngest son's company. He had visited Leonard Thomson to report some chest pains he had been having though he had never breathed a word to Emma. Leonard had reassured him but warned him not to work too hard at the heavy gardening tasks.

"Let my James carry the heaviest tasks, Jack. He thinks the world of you and will do anything you need. Take aspirin if you feel it coming on and rest."

Emma always ran to meet the postman when she saw him at the gate, looking for a letter from Philip like a soul famished for want of water. But he only wrote on rare occasions because he had determined to hold fast to his decision not to raise expectations or stir up feelings that must be subdued. In this, however, he was mistaken because in sending these letters, her equanimity was preserved. In them, she could see all his fortitude in the face of what he was enduring and all his love which pervaded every sentence. They did not damage her family for they enabled her to stay strong for all its members. Yet she could hardly bear to visit Kath and Alan Lorimer in Philip's old study though they always welcomed her with open arms. The sight of his desk where he worked and where his face used to light up when she visited with little George was almost too much. It reminded her of her huge loss and that was when the passing months seemed intolerable. She read and reread every letter, when at last one came, smiling at his way of finding comfort in his beloved poetry. He was an English teacher to the very depths of his soul and Emma was herself comforted by that thought.

St. Oswald's Convalescent Home,
October 19, 1919

My darling Emma,

I write today to tell you what a pleasure it has been to be pushed down to the harbour here in Scarborough. I believe it must be around half-term time for there were quite a number of families out enjoying the autumn sunshine.

I was able to watch the fishermen unloading their lobster pots and see the pleasure boats taking the holidaymakers out for a sea trip. The young ones were excited and laughing with pleasure and I thought of little

George and of you, sweetheart. I do hope you are keeping up your spirits as I am. These trips do my heart good.

But do not think, my love, I am merely resting here. I am working hard at the exercises set for me by the physiotherapists who pound me daily. I have managed to walk a little with the crutches. Quite a feat, I can tell you.

Darling, I am reading Milton at present and find a help in one of his sonnets. He too was handicapped but by blindness, and the sonnet in question has a very encouraging last few line:

"God doth not need
Either man's work or his own gifts. Who best
Bear his mild yoke, they serve him best. His state
Is kingly. Thousands at his bidding speed
And post o'er land and ocean without rest:
They also serve who only stand and wait."

So, you see, Emma, I am not alone in feeling redundant. Others have felt like this too, but here is an answer to that pessimism. I can surely serve too by trusting.

You know you are constantly in my heart though we cannot be together. So, we must carry on bravely as I know you do.

Philip

Emma had to go away and hide from the family as she read this particular letter full as it was of quiet determination and still that sense of forfeiture of all that he had hoped. She wept many a tear but managed to sustain her affection and love for everyone as she coped with the many demands on her time. Her letters were much briefer but just as efficacious.

Holt House
October 21, 1919

My beloved Philip,

Your letter reached me as an oasis of love which I enjoyed all by myself upstairs.

I'm so proud of you for working so hard with all the experts who are doing you good, I trust, and, meanwhile, I am working hard at holding the world up as usual.

All are well and school is in safe hands with Alan, Beatrice, and now Laura, Will's sweetheart. Kath Hanson misses you terribly, but she bosses all the others with a firm hand, as she always has, until they fall in line. Jack, with James' help, is furnishing the gardens with glorious colour, and James is really recovered now, thank goodness.

Scarborough sounds truly charming. You know how much I would like to be there by your side. This is sometimes almost beyond bearing but I know I have to endure it. I too can quote poetry at you. I like best John Donne and found in your beautiful birthday present to me a poem that says it all:

'Think that we
Are but turn'd aside to sleep;

392 ~ JANE ALLISON

They who one another keep
Alive, ne'er parted be.'
I'm closing for now, sending all my love as ever.
Emma

Philip had to smile on receiving this particular letter with the quotation from Donne that had struck him so forcibly when he was teaching his sixth-formers.

My dear Emma, our minds work as one, he thought to himself and sat back in his chair, letting that love sink into his tired soul.

Leonard Thomson came in late autumn to talk with the medical staff in the home. Philip was delighted to see him though he did not enquire too closely about all the ones he most wanted to hear about. The doctor's questions were designed to get a clear idea of how soon Philip could return home. The convalescence was a very slow affair, given the huge operation he had undergone and the massive wound that had healed well but was still a point of great fragility.

How was his friend doing? Had they managed to teach him to use the crutches effectively and safely so that he could return home and take up his old position? Would the wheelchair be a permanent necessity? All these questions were discussed at length between him and the specialists in Scarborough. Philip told him that the leg still pained him even though it was no longer there. This often happened with such cases where the amputated part had a kind of invisible existence. This was normal, the specialists told Leonard, and were quite definite that all signs of septicaemia were completely cleared. His recovery was continuing positively.

Thus, they concluded, to Leonard Thomson's delight, that the convalescence had established him well as a competent wheelchair user but also one who could effectively manage with crutches. If he had perhaps a live-in housekeeper at home, he could return to Shadworth before much more time elapsed.

But Philip was kept in ignorance of these discussions for the time being, as his friend wanted him to enjoy the fullest benefit from his time in Scarborough. Moreover, the good doctor found himself unable to think of anyone who could adequately take on the housekeeping role. Philip would need to be more independent still. And so, Leonard planned for the stay to go through the Christmas period and into the New Year, 1920. He arranged everything with St. Oswald's to his own satisfaction for he could see Philip's health improving vastly and knew he was profiting from the care.

Leonard talked it all through with Alan Lorimer on return. Alan was enjoying his part as head, and the school was on a very safe footing under his leadership, but he was ready to relinquish that as soon as Philip was able to take up the mantle again. What none of them wanted, however, was for Philip to wear himself out again by hurrying back to it. They all knew how difficult it would be to cope with the handicap. So, the longer rest at the home would settle the question.

That Christmas 1919 was almost unendurable for Philip, however. The thought of the family in Shadworth, of little George's fifth birthday, and Christmas at Holt House happening in the old and comfortable way it always did but with his chair empty, was cruel in the extreme. And he knew Emma would feel it just as surely yet he could offer her nothing but the emptiness of his absence.

Oh God, there is no comfort.

Throughout it, Emma maintained her ruthless efficiency in all things, making a wonderful fifth birthday cake in the shape of a turreted castle at George's request, a cake that exceeded anything Hagenbachs could ever create. The Christmas bird stuffed with her own sage and onion mixture was pronounced her best ever by all the company. Yet inside her heart, she had a most terrible vacuum that consumed her and kept her wakeful in the dark hours of the night as she allowed herself to think of Philip alone in Scarborough. Her only consolation was to see Jack's enormous pleasure in his family as they all gathered around the table.

That has to be worth something and I should be grateful, she thought.

The year turned and 1920 dawned with cold, grey skies over Scarborough and Shadworth.

Pathetic fallacy indeed, thought Philip as he laboured with the crutches and found himself unable to sleep in the icy January nights.

In early spring 1920, something happened that stunned everyone in its shocking enormity. James came running into Kath's office and thence to Alan's study, gasping from running and stammering out the words.

"It's Jack. It's Mr Holt. He's lying out on the garden path. I can't wake him."

Alan and Kath ran down with him to find Jack Holt—their strong and trusted gardener—lifeless. Kath took one look and rushed for help while Alan and James both tried desperately to give him back his breath. They had learned the methods of artificial resuscitation the hard way out in France. He had fallen awkwardly in the middle of digging a space for a rose-bush and his spade lay by his side.

James' father arrived and checked with doctor's expertise Jack's prone form. Yet in his heart he knew it was hopeless. Jack had sloughed off this life's encumbrances in a massive heart attack. He would have suffered only momentarily, and now he had gone to that place he had always believed he would discover one day. He was peaceful in death. The tribulations of life had hung loose on him though he had often felt their

396 - JANE ALLISON

sting. This recognition did not make it any easier for Leonard who respected and loved his old friend. He was devastated in this moment.

"His family... we must break this news to them all as gently as we can. As if they have not had enough sorrow to bear these last few months," said Leonard. As he spoke, he thought of Philip Manners for so long struggling with his feelings for Jack's wife. But he dismissed the thought as a betrayal and prepared to instigate the procedures for another death so hot on the heels of Maggie's passing. So, it was left to Alan Lorimer and Kath, who had the task of driving down past the fingerpost to break the news.

Chapter 40

Each of the family members received this unspeak-able news from Alan all in different ways. Emma opened the door to them and sat abruptly upon seeing Kath's face. She felt a maelstrom of emotions for she had feared first for Philip and now was faced with quite another horror.

"My God, my God. It can't be! Jack has never been ill in his life. How can this be true?" This awful news hit Emma as an earthquake might rock a building. The whole steady foundation of her life had relied on the solid fact of Jack and his love for her, a bond secured over all the years and unchanged despite her love for Philip.

Kath, who had thought to be an aid in distress, sud-denly found herself unable to control her weeping. Her tears fell and would not stop, no matter how hard she tried.

Will was upstairs and heard Emma scream. He rushed down and, taking one look at Alan Lorimer's face, realised that the unbearable had happened. How could any of his family go on without his beloved dad? Will had looked death in the face many times but this particular death was like no other. He sat next to his mother and put his arm around her. She had turned a sickly white, and both onlookers thought she was about to faint. But no. She merely leaned her head against Will. No tears would come though she felt again that terrible sensation of choking.

For a few seconds, Will relived that nightmarish moment when he had watched Ralph die in front of his eyes and then he rubbed his eyes and saw instead an image of his beloved father whose constancy to them all had never failed. His hands trembled. Silence fell on the room. Alan stood by, unable to find words of comfort. He was numb at the sight of their grief.

Finally Will got to his feet, and set off for Tempest's farm, leaving his mother in the loving hands of Kath. There he hugged his sister and simply looked across at his younger brother who was playing with George. That one look said all that was needed. Harry felt opening up in his heart a yawning abyss where nothing of any worth could survive. The wilderness he had experienced already at Maggie's death loomed frighteningly larger and he began to tremble. Seeing it, Florence clutched his hands, looking across at Ned to fortify her. She felt a terrible need for her father's reassuring presence but the knowledge that he had left them and would not ever return was unspeakable.

Mary Tempest took charge and called in her husband to take the little one out to see the piglets just born. She would keep George safe while they grieved. Then they all held out their arms to each other and were swept into an embrace together. It was truly unbelievable—something totally unexpected and shocking. They had always known their father to be maintaining a steady backdrop and support to all their mother's many endeavours, all her work for the community, all her efforts for the school. They could not quite imagine how it could be that he would no longer be the foundation stone at the heart of his family.

"Let's go home," said Harry quietly. "Mother will need us." As one, they stood up, held hands, and walked back to Holt House.

Those following dreadful days passed as in a ghastly dream as the funeral arrangements were made and everyone learned to accept their huge loss. Emma was terribly torn in her spirit. She couldn't imagine a world where Jack was absent. She had maintained their loving partnership through all the turmoil of the war years and its aftermath. She knew she had kept the faith though she loved another man like life itself. But Jack had known he was safe in the home she had made for him and in which she had borne his children. And she was truly bereft. She found herself looking round for him or telling him something in the old way, then pulling herself up with a start and a sad shake of her head.

Florence especially was alert to some of the feelings she knew must be running through her mother's mind. Alan and Beatrice had sent a telegram to St. Oswald's Home to tell Philip what had happened, and they too were conscious that many more emotions were going to be in play once he received the news.

As it was, he was dumbfounded. A guilt he could not resist haunted him. He felt his integrity had not always been intact and that he had let his very good and resolute friend down at the end by allowing Emma to stay so close to him at the worst of his illness. *My Quaker conscience has not always kept me honourable*, he thought with a bitter sigh.

He sat in his wheelchair by the windows of his room and looked out over the South Bay, drinking in its beauty as a kind of balm for his grief, and he prayed for forgiveness. His appetite had never returned properly since his parting from Emma, but when he got the news of Jack's untimely death from Alan Lorimer's telegram, he refused food completely all day. Even little Evelina, his favourite and sweetest little nurse, could not persuade him to eat the delicacies the kitchen cooked up to tempt him. He merely sat silently. He hardly dared think of Emma, nor of the implications of this death, closing his mind to the sneaking thought that crept in unannounced.

Now she is free.

He was glad he was a long way away in Scarborough then. He must allow her to grieve and do all that was inviolate for Jack and her family.

And indeed, she did. Solemnly and tearlessly, she followed his coffin into chapel that had been so recently ringing with the happiness of Florence's wedding. She wore her best black dress and carried a sheaf of white lilies. Inwardly, she felt as if she walked in some kind of echo chamber—her ears dulled, cut off from the sights and sounds of the massive congregation that had gathered to honour this man whom she had lived with for so long. Yet she carried in her heart a comfort that was quite astonishing, for Will had found in Jack's garden shed, Jack's own domain, a note addressed to them all beside a large wooden ramp he had carved out of an old piece of wood. The note simply read: *"For the time when Philip Manners may need to enter our house in his wheelchair."* Emma, having been shown it by Will, felt a benediction from Jack which spoke his gracious forgiveness of her.

Leonard Thomson was well aware that it was doing no harm to Philip to remain in Scarborough for he was a long way from being able to manage everything back at the school. So, Leonard allowed time to pass and matters to take their own natural course. Neither

Philip nor Emma wrote to each other during this space, and both understood without need for words that this was the right way to be true to Jack and themselves. Philip sent a card addressed to the Holt family, expressing all his love and deepest sympathy for the loss of a man who was his dear friend and whom everyone respected. Emma was silent as Will opened this missive, aware of the writer's great sensitivity in dealing with it in this way, though she longed to snatch it from Will to claim it. She restrained herself, clenching her fists, taking deep gulping breaths to calm herself though her heart was beating rapidly.

At last, she found herself able to talk to Will, Florence, and Harry about how it might be if she were to begin a new life with Philip. Jack's ramp had helped them to comprehend what she was talking about, and Will and Florence both found themselves able to give her their loving approbation.

Perhaps it was hardest for Harry to accept for in those weeks after Maggie's death, he and Jack had grown closer than they had ever been. And what if his mother should forfeit her care for George and exchange it to care for this handicapped headmaster? He challenged her furiously one day after Will had tried to explain the situation to him.

"Have you been unfaithful to my father? How could you entertain thoughts of any other man when you had one as good as my dad? I cannot believe such a thing of you. It is unworthy."

This struck Emma to the heart, and she wept bitterly at his words, assuring him that she had never failed his father and that Jack had always known that she would never leave him. "You must believe me, Harry. Your father cared for Mr Manners too. They were friends, and Jack trusted him and trusted me. Can you not see the evidence of your own eyes? The ramp he made, without a word to me, is his way of telling us all that he has understood and forgiven me. I know he felt absolutely at peace in the love I had for him. And, Harry, in these last few months, we have grown closer than ever. Please believe me."

As she pleaded with him, Harry made no attempt to respond, turning on his heel and striding off into the garden where he took up Jack's spade and began digging furiously. So, it was left to Florence to pacify him. She found him in the garden and there remonstrated with him for accusing their mother, reminding him that Emma had never once deserted Jack, and that Emma, Jack, and Philip too had always been nothing but loving to little George. In the face of his rage at his mother's apparent unfaithfulness, Harry had to take time before he could really accept Florence's patient comfort. She assured him that all could be resolved safely and that she herself had absolute confidence in the man who was so dear to her mother.

"Whatever happens, Harry, George will be beloved by all and given the very best chance of a joyful and wise upbringing in the hands of a secure and caring family," said Florence. "And, Harry, I promise you that includes the new member whom you will learn to love as I have."

The day came when Philip summoned Alan Lorimer to visit him. Alan knew exactly why he was needed.

"Two things, Alan," said Philip in the old headmasterly way he had, "And perhaps you'll let me voice them both before you answer. I am going to resign finally from my position as head. You can live up to all my expectations, and I won't be far away, I hope. Perhaps I can be your wise old advisor, if you'll have me.

"Second, and this is much more important to me than anything else. Will you push me into Scarborough town? There is a jeweller there who has a beautiful supply of rings, and I would quite like to buy one, if you think that would be appropriate. I shall have to guess the size of her finger, but we can cope with that. She has very delicate little fingers, and I think I can find the right one. You must reassure me that I am right in this project, for the last thing I want is to tie her to a cripple if you think she would rather be free."

Alan stepped back and looked at him. "You do talk a lot of nonsense, Philip. Well, I have just two things to say to you. I'm not sure you should be so hasty as to resign, but do so only if you really feel you would be better without the stresses of the position. If I have my way, we shall get you back to your old desk where you belong. So, let's wait and see how you feel. For the time being, you can certainly take your sixth form Oxbridge candidates at the very least. And do so only until such time as you feel you can take up your old position again, for you are certainly not finished in your role as head with all that means for our school. And you cannot give up helping me to maintain all the Quaker values which you hold so dear.

"The second thing, and this is indeed important. The lady in question would, I suspect, die for you. And of course I'll take you into town. Let's go."

Having bought the ring, chosen with a great deal of love and delight, all that remained was for Alan to summon Emma to tell her that she was at last required to visit Scarborough. She gasped at the prospect though he kept secret what Philip had in mind.

"Beatrice and I will take you at the weekend if you are willing?" he enquired. "You'll see a man who is now very adept at managing the chair though not so good with the crutches. He looks a little older, thinner, and greyer after all he's been through, but you will gladden his heart. And, Emma, it is time. You have been absolutely fair to Jack's memory, and you can begin to live again."

Emma could not speak for a kind of joy that was beginning to blossom inside her. She nodded in response to Alan's loving look, then walked into Jack's home garden and strolled along its pathways thoughtfully. The chickens clucked around her, looking for food, and she had to smile. Jack did not feel far away. His spirit would always abide in this place, she knew. She spotted the garden shed where he had spent so many hours and remembered the ramp he had made. She smiled again and whispered quietly, "Thank you, Jack. Thank you, my lovely man."

The date was set. They made the journey to Scarborough in Alan's car. But once they reached St. Oswald's Convalescent Home, Alan and Beatrice retired to the gardens beyond Philip's open window. They knew they were not needed at this reunion.

Philip and Emma were both aching to see each other at long, long last. Philip was sitting, looking out of the window at the now very familiar view of the bay with his back turned as she tiptoed into his room. She crept up behind him and put her arms around his neck, kissing his cheek tenderly.

"Emma, my darling. Emma, are you really here?" was all he could say through real tears of joy. And her tears now fell too after weeks of dryness as she turned his chair to face her and knelt beside him. He contented himself with caressing her hair, pulling out all the grips with which she had put it up so that it fell in a shower over his leg and over the bandaged stump. Then he pulled her up to sit perched on the side of his chair and kissed her face and her lips till they were both drenched in tears.

"Are we going to drown in our tears, my darling? I think it must be relief," he managed to say. They both then laughed as they sat there together in a kind of glorious liberty. Outside in the garden, Alan and Beatrice heard the sound and looked across at each other, smiling.

"I haven't heard Philip laugh for a very long time," said Alan. Beatrice leaned on his shoulder and wiped away a quiet tear.

Inside, once their laughter subsided, Philip spoke more gently. "Come, Emma, can we lie down a while, sweetheart? Can you manage to help me onto the bed? I am so sorry I am so crippled."

"Philip never, never say that again. My darling, I am so glad to be here at last." Helping him from the wheelchair onto the bed, she lay next to him. He reached into his pocket and retrieved the ring he and Alan had bought in the anticipation of this moment and then spoke very solemnly. "Emma Holt, will you do me the courtesy of marrying me so that I can at last make an honest woman of you? And will you marry me soon? I can't wait much longer to ravish you as I've wanted to for so long."

"Philip, you know the answer before I speak it. It is such a joy to be able at last to give you my "yes", my dearest." And she beamed at him in relief. Neither of them had expected this moment could ever come, but now they allowed it its full rein.

He smiled as he repeated what had been his words in the bedroom in York: "Too many buttons, Emma, too many buttons." He gently undid them one by one and then buried his head in her breasts and kissed her again. She sighed in pure delight, murmuring passionate words of endearment.

His relief that at last they could be together was euphoric. He could hardly believe that this was to be their crowning joy after all the vicissitudes they had endured. This would never deny the respect and love they each had for those others who had shared their long and painful journey, most particularly for Jack Holt. Philip's early marriage to Harriet receded into a memory that would never leave him but which, he knew, he had tried never to betray. And this moment and its promise was a fulfilment richly deserved.

When Alan returned to his room with Beatrice, he simply said, "Alan, Beatrice, meet my future wife."

They married in the school Meeting House after Philip's return to Shadworth had been approved by Leonard Thomson. It was a very quiet affair with only their closest and dearest there to observe. George, already adept at carrying a ring on a cushion, played his part delightedly, then swung himself up to sit on Philip's lap. This helped towards relieving Harry Holt's anxieties enormously. They erected what indeed seemed like a wedding present from Jack at the doorway to Holt House, enabling them to push the wheelchair through to what would be their marital home.

If the villagers and the school staff found this astonishing, they quickly got used to the new circumstances and rejoiced that their old headmaster was still able to teach, at Alan Lorimer's request, in anticipation of returning to his old role. In joyful union with Emma, he continued to be the wise and well-honoured man he had always been, whilst his new wife remained the same, industrious woman they all loved at the heart of village life.

Emma often walked in what had always been Jack's garden remembering the loving years she had spent with him. Surrounded by the beauty of the garden, she knew Jack had planted every part of it. Sometimes she spoke aloud.

"Always know this, my dear Jack. I never failed in my love for you and I never will. You will always be a part of me even as I share my life with Philip. I know he understands that and is glad. Thank you, Jack, thank you."

Printed in Great Britain
by Amazon